Praise for Lorelei James' *Dirty Deeds*

5 Hearts "Ms. James has a winner in *Dirty Deeds!*" ~ *Brenda Talley, The Romance Studio*

4 Angels "Sex, love and romance are just the tip of this book…" ~ *Lena C., Fallen Angel Reviews*

4 Cups "…a story that will keep you up until the wee hours…This book left me wanting to read more by this author." ~ *Sherry, Coffee Time Romance*

"…a refreshing romance that you can just sit back and enjoy." ~ *Susan, Two Lips Reviews*

Dirty Deeds

Lorelei James

A SAMHAIN PUBLISHING, LTD. publication.

Samhain Publishing, Ltd.
2932 Ross Clark Circle, #384
Dothan, AL 36301
www.samhainpublishing.com

Dirty Deeds
Copyright © 2006 by Lorelei James
Print ISBN: 1-59998-297-8
Digital ISBN: 1-59998-073-8

Editing by Angie James
Cover by Scott Carpenter

First Samhain Publishing, Ltd. electronic publication: August 2006
First Samhain Publishing, Ltd. print publication: December 2006

Dedication

Thanks to everyone at Samhain Publishing. And to Cat, who gave me a good, hard shove when I needed it. You rock, girlfriend.

Chapter One

"The closest I've ever been to nirvana was during an orgasm."

Tate Cross rolled her eyes. Where did Val come up with this stuff?

Undaunted, her friend Val shifted her pregnant belly. She broke the chocolate bar in half, sucking at the apricot filling oozing over her finger. "But this…" a satisfied moan escaped, "…is running a close second."

"I wasn't talking about nirvana the *place*; I was talking about Nirvana the *band*." Tate slid the CD case across the dining room table and switched off the boom box, doubting Val would appreciate the subtle nuances of Cobain and company's "Heart-Shaped Box".

"Sorry. I never understood that whole grunge thing."

Tate narrowed her eyes. "But if we were talking about sweaty, grungy cowboys in tight jeans, whinin' 'bout lovin' the wrong woman, drivin' off in dusty pickups to the local bar for a shot of pain-easin' whiskey, you'd pay attention."

"Country music always gets me hot."

"No wonder you've been pregnant four times."

A sly, dreamy look drifted over Val's face. "This one was conceived when Rich brought home that Stetson and we played—"

"Baby roulette? Apparently Richard's six-gun was fully loaded that night." With a grin, Tate gestured to Val's stomach. "Seems that elusive slice of sexual heaven has a high price."

"Being pregnant isn't bad." Val lovingly rubbed her hand over her swollen abdomen. "And a great sex life is not elusive."

"Maybe not for you. You have the perfect man." Tate tamped down on a rare surge of jealousy. She doubted Val's perpetual rosy glow was entirely pregnancy related, the lucky duck.

"So sue me."

Tate cocked a blonde brow. "Your lawyer husband laughs at your lawsuit jokes?"

"Of course." Val tipped her glass of milk against Tate's in a mock toast. "My fabulous sense of humor is the reason he married me."

Tate choked back a giggle; milk nearly squirted out her nose. How mature. Here she was trying to have a sophisticated conversation about sex and not act like the goggle-eyed ingénue Val remembered her to be.

Val smiled. "I'll admit our compatibility inside the bedroom played a key role. Love at first sight. It can happen."

"Not to me." Tate snatched the candy from Val's plate. Swapping sexual quips was one thing, forking over the last piece of chocolate fell into an entirely different realm. Mmm. She savored the sinful flavor; it was indeed close to orgasmic. Not that she had anything to judge it by lately.

"This is the first lunch we've had without my kiddos since you've come back to South Dakota and we're discussing *my* sex life? I should be spellbound by your wild sexual adventures in Mile-High Stadium. Or cavorting naked on the beach in Cozumel."

"Get real." Tate snorted. "There's nothing to discuss."

A cascade of auburn ringlets brushed Val's heart-shaped face when she shook her head. "Then I'm sorry for you."

"Me too." Tate traced the ruffled edge of the crocheted placemat. "I have no life at all, besides getting this house ready to sell. I haven't done the deed for—" Mentally, she counted back and shuddered. "At my sexual peak. What a joke. I'm supposed to be worried about my partner pleasing *me* instead of whether I've got enough AA batteries."

Silence. Tate slid Val a sideways glance. Talk about bold statements.

Without missing a beat, Val said, "No judgment, but I couldn't live without that intimacy. Connecting with Rich on an elemental level whenever, wherever we want." A satisfied sigh gusted forth. "Except now we're forced to be discreet."

Didn't Val's beach ball condition belie that statement? Tactfully, Tate didn't point it out. "I'm the epitome of discreet."

"You and Chris Taylor weren't very discreet, if I recall."

"That's the *only* time," Tate grumbled. "No one believed 'Miss Goody-Two-Shoes' boinked the school bad boy that night at the lake anyway."

"How did you pull it off?" Val mused. "I mean, didn't you find it awkward to roll a cold, wet Speedo over a stiffy?"

"Hah! Didn't it just figure my first experience with a penis outside *Playgirl* magazine and his dick was more like a clammy, fat worm than the 'throbbing rod of manhood' I'd expected."

She drifted back to the summer of her senior year she'd spent with Aunt Beatrice. It'd been easy convincing studly Chris to change her virginal status. But the quick tryst on his Harley hadn't included passion, and Chris had been clueless on demonstrating carnal secrets. That flagging sense of disappointment still dogged her. Would she ever discover the powerful sexual connection her friends raved about? When?

"Forget Chris and his unimpressive rod. Although it makes sense why he's fat, bald and married to his motorcycle shop." Val paused and offered, "I could set you up with someone, if you're interested."

"Who?" Tate snapped back to attention. "Is he nice?"

"Of *course* he's nice." Val sniffed.

"Then nothing doing."

"What?"

"Nothing doing. I'm done with nice. This little chat has just reinforced my decision. The next affair I start will be purely that. An affair. No strings, no promises. Just sex. *Lots* of hot sex."

Val daintily wiped off the milk mustache before expelling a surprisingly unladylike burp. "Excuse me. Run that by me one more time?"

"You heard me. Sex. I want sex. The steamier, the nastier, the better. I've never been impulsive. Never dated a guy just because he could give me mind-blowing orgasms." Tate shoved an agitated hand through her short, spiky blonde hair. "I want the heady out-of-control passion I've never experienced before I lose what little nerve I've got left."

Val's jaw nearly hit the parquet floor.

There. She'd actually shocked the unflappable Val.

"But honey, don't you want a man—"

"No. I don't want the same kind of man I've been dating for the last ten years. I don't care if he's suitable as a lifelong mate. Or if he'd make a great father. Or whether my parents would approve. I want a man that can find my G-spot in two seconds flat."

"Who-ee Tatum Cross!" Val fanned herself.

"Oh, don't play innocent with me, after you admitted to the 'my-husband-has-a-Stetson-and-I-ride-him-like-a-pony' scenario."

"I'm not. I just don't want you to get hurt."

"I'm not naïve." Well, not as much as she used to be. She longed for the chance to act outrageous, to unleash the sexual tigress lurking beyond her kittenish exterior. Aching to prove—if only to herself—that a purely physical relationship didn't have to end in dreams of picket fences, cocker spaniels and mini-vans.

"Men do this all the time without emotional repercussions. Find me a guy who has nothing on his mind besides awesome sex, and cutting loose his libido because that's all I'm in the market for."

"Not even one date?" Val asked skeptically.

"Nope. No relationships."

"Good." Val's resounding smack on the antique trestle table knocked an ornate silver candlestick into the leftover chicken salad. "Then I've got an even better guy in mind for you. A purely sexual relationship is right up his alley." Val's eyes met hers, sporting a devious twinkle. "I think you'd get along with my—"

The ancient doorbell pealed.

"Hold that thought," Tate said, sliding from the chair and crossing to the foyer. She froze, catching sight of the deputy sheriff's brown uniform through the heavy screen.

"Are you Tatum Beatrice Cross?"

Horrid scenarios drifted through her mind. Her heart thudded, her palms went sweaty even as her mouth went dry. "Yes."

"Legal document."

She opened the door.

"Sign here." The baby-faced deputy removed his hat, waiting while Tate scribbled her name.

She trudged back to the dining room, reading the letter.

"What is it?" Val lumbered to her feet.

"A legal notice from the City Beautification Committee. Seems since I've inherited Aunt Bea's property, it's been rezoned from residential to residential/commercial. Now I'm subject to a whole new set of regulations." Tate glanced up, unable to hide her despair. "How can they do this? I barely have enough money to make the repairs on the inside."

"Let me see that." Val scrutinized the letter, then waddled across the room, picked up the phone and punched in a number.

Sunny Val's uncharacteristic irritation jolted Tate from her dejection. "What are you doing?"

"Calling Rich. I can't decipher this legalese, but he can."

❖ ❖ ❖

Two days later, Tate and Val glumly faced each other again between the masses of cardboard boxes heaped on Tate's dining room table.

Val slid a manila envelope across the dusty surface. "Rich said if you have any questions to call him."

"I appreciate you bringing this over in person. I know you're busy with the kids and all—"

"Hey, you're my best pal. It's the least I could do."

Tate eyed the envelope, hating the power wielded by one innocuous piece of paper. She bent the metal clips back, and pulled out the official cream-colored letterhead of *Thiebold and Duncan Attorneys at Law*. Her hopes plummeted as she scanned the document.

"So? What does it say?"

Tate pinned Val with a shrewd look. "Rich didn't tell you?"

"Of course he didn't tell me," she chided. "Attorney/client privilege and all that. Come on, spill."

She searched the document again praying the words had morphed into a different answer. No such luck. "Basically, it says I'm screwed. I have to comply with the rules set in place by the Beautification Committee within sixty days or I will be subject to fines. I am legally bound to meet the requirements before I can transfer ownership of the property."

Val sighed. "I'm so sorry. I'm sure Rich—"

"Did everything he could. He filed an extension. Thankfully the sixty days won't go into effect until after I've hired a contractor."

"What are you going to do?"

"No clue. I'm struggling right now to pay the electrician." Tate scowled at the paint cans and buckets of plaster taunting her from every corner. "As it is, most of this is just surface work."

"If I might offer a suggestion." Val bent to retrieve her purse but Val's extended stomach stopped her progress halfway. After a loud *uhhff,* Tate rescued Val, tossing the enormous bag on the table.

"What are you carrying in that thing? A Soviet submarine?"

"Just wait 'til you have kids, smarty," Val muttered.

Tate gathered the papers, shuffling through them one last time. *Hey, wait a minute.* She'd dealt with enough lawyers since her aunt's death to know they never neglected to remind clients of pending charges. "There's no bill in here," Tate said tersely.

It was comical, the way Val averted her monkey-eyed gaze to the cuckoo clock above the oak buffet. "Would you look at the time? I've got to run."

In her advanced state of pregnancy, Val's escape attempt was pitifully slow. Tate snatched Val's purse from the table and held it hostage. "Nice try. But if I remember correctly, due to your lousy acting skills, you were relegated to the concession stand at theater camp. 'Fess up. Is Rich taking on pro-bono cases now?"

"No." Val crossly brushed a curl from her eye. "But we agreed this problem wasn't that much work for him, and we—"

"Agreed to take pity on me? I am not a charity case."

"For heaven's sake, I didn't think you were. We aren't trying to offend you; we're trying to help. People ask Rich for free legal advice all the time. This is no different."

"It is different because it's *me*," Tate reiterated stubbornly. "I don't owe anybody anything. That's why I didn't take out a loan to update Aunt Beatrice's house when I inherited all the problems. Or borrow money from my we-know-what's-best-for-you parents."

Val was quiet for several moments. Too quiet. "Fine. Since you're short on funds, we could do a trade, like they used to do in the Old West. Services for services sort of thing."

Tate tightened her death grip on Val's Coach purse. A trade? What could Val and Richard need? A nanny? Although she dreamed of having children someday, practicing parenting skills on the rambunctious Westfield brood scared her spitless. "Like what?"

"Stay with the kids after I have the baby. Just until Richard comes home."

"What about Grace?" As a counselor at the Girl's Club, their mutual friend, Grace Fitzgerald, was better equipped to deal with a hoard of rowdy kids.

"She's got enough on her plate. Besides, you can handle them."

Alone? For eight hours with four kids under the age of eight? Tate scratched a phantom spot on her elbow; the very idea made her break out in hives. "Umm…isn't your mom coming?"

"After the baby is born." Val gnawed at her lower lip and confessed, "Frankly, I could start labor anytime. I'm afraid if this labor goes like the last one, I'll be racing to the hospital. It'd be a huge relief to know I've got someone on call."

Tate sighed. Val's anxiety was more pressing than her own petty worries about not being a "Mary Poppins" type. She extended her hand, grateful Val only had one child in diapers. "Deal."

Val's immediate wily grin was in direct conflict with the Madonna-like way her hands clasped over her belly.

"What are you not telling me?" Tate demanded. "The kids have rabies or something?"

"Pooh." Val waved her hand. "You are so paranoid. This whole trading thing. Pretty good idea, right? Mutually beneficial?"

"Yeah. So?" Tate shoved her hands in her camo short pockets and waited for the other baby shoe to drop.

"*So*," Val preened. "While Rich worked on your legal issues, I might have figured out a way to get your required beautification updates done at a reduced cost."

Free legal advice and now this? Ka-ching. The slot machines in Deadwood had nothing on her; she'd hit the friend lottery with Val. A warm wave of hope tugged on the edges of her doubts. "Really? How?"

Val passed over a crumpled business card. "You don't know my brother Nathan since he was in the Army those summers you were here, but he lives here now and installs utilities."

Her fuzzy warm feeling cooled a bit. "Utilities?"

"It's a fancy way of saying he digs ditches and creates sewage systems. However, he does the occasional landscaping job. He did all the outside work on our new house."

Tate looked up. Val gazed at her so earnestly she knew she'd made a serious error in judgment. Come to think of it, Val *had* brought up her brother's name, in nearly reverent tones, many, many times. "If he's that good I'm sure *I* can't afford him." She discreetly passed the card back.

But Val blithely tucked the card into Tate's shirt pocket. "He is good with his hands. Unfortunately you couldn't tell by the schematics he's trying to pass off as drawings. Chicken scratches make more sense. Poor man can't draw worth a darn."

But she could.

An idea caught fire. How hard could it be to teach him the rudimentary points of drawing plants and trees? Or give him a tutorial on any of the landscaping computer programs? "You think he'd be up for a partial trade? Art lessons for landscaping work? Or something?"

"Knowing him the 'or something' would be the most appealing." A catlike curl lifted Val's lips. "But I'll warn you, don't fall for him because Nathan isn't into relationships."

Val's every phrase and innuendo clicked into place like the missing piece of a jigsaw puzzle. Tate's heart thumped double time. "Valerie Westfield. Is your brother the 'no-strings attached' guy you planned to fix me up with?"

Val's eyes shone, her curls bounced, she looked like a woman who'd been gifted with a get-out-of-labor free card. "Yep."

"Why?"

"Because he's the perfect solution to your problem."

"To my orgasm shortage?"

"That too, but first and foremost he is an awesome landscaper. Talk to him. See what you can work out. What have you got to lose?"

Nothing. Tate had never been one to look a gift horse in the mouth, even when this situation with Val's brother smacked of strange coincidence. Yet, here was her chance to unleash the wild woman lodged inside.

"Offer him art lessons, huh?" she mused, tapping the business card on her chin. "Think I can persuade him to throw in a few sex lessons as well?"

❧ ❧ ❧

"She asked if I'd *what?*" Nathan LeBeau gaped at his sister.

"You heard me."

He shook his head. "I thought I heard you offer my—" Nathan glanced at his crotch then back up to Val's amused eyes. "Exchanging dirt work for down and dirty sexual favors?"

"No. Trading art lessons for your landscaping expertise." A sneaky smile spread across Val's face. "If you decided to throw in sexual favors, well, that's just a bonus."

Nathan angled the beer bottle at her in mild reproof. "Ah hell, Val. Is this another one of your hormonal pregnancy things?"

Val mumbled something suspiciously prayer-like.

"Amazing grace, my ass. Miraculous as it may seem to you, I can procure my own dates and she *will not* be a friend of yours."

"Why not?"

He shoved aside his niggling fear that no woman would ever want him for the man he was inside, not what showed outside. Lightly, he said, "You want the reasons alphabetically or numerically?"

"Always with the smart comments, no wonder you haven't gotten laid in months. Just hear me out—"

"Nope. Get yourself another chump, or should I say *hump*, and leave me out of it."

He stood abruptly. No way was he getting sucked into another one of his sister's crazy schemes. No matter how crazy he was about her. No matter she was eight months pregnant and apparently delusional.

Shit. This whole thing smacked of Val's penchant for matchmaking. Except she'd stepped up her campaign to pair him off by boasting of his "stud" services to her friend. If it didn't involve him personally, he'd be rolling on the ground busting a gut.

Yet, it bothered him that Val didn't think he was capable of a more meaningful relationship. Maybe he shouldn't try so hard to convince his friends and family he was the love 'em and leave 'em type.

"I'm going home," Nathan said, irked at the dust swirls falling from his work clothes to Val's pristine carpet. He set the empty beer bottle on the counter and marveled at the atypical quiet in his sister's house. Without her kids interrupting, yelling, throwing toys everywhere, the place was downright eerie. Strange, that he preferred chaos to quiet. He had too much silence in his life as it was. "When will Rich be home with the monsters?"

"Not for another hour." Val's expression soured and she groaned, smoothing her palms over her lower abdomen.

"What?" He demanded, "Val? What's wrong?"

She moaned again, bit her lip and closed her eyes.

Terrific capper to a bad day. He settled her on the couch, placing a Scooby-Doo pillow behind the small of her back. "Are you having contractions?" Hell, for all he knew, after kid number four maybe there were no contractions and the sucker just dropped to the ground unaided.

"I don't know."

His gaze sharpened. Val was a pro at this pregnancy stuff. Wouldn't she know if she was in labor? And why hadn't she started those weird breathing exercises yet? He kneeled on his haunches in front of her and murmured, "You okay?"

"Maybe you should stick around just in case..." Val opened her eyes, only to quickly glance away from his penetrating gaze.

Too quickly. He'd seen that *"who me?"* bright-eyed look on baby sister's face a million times. Before he knew it he'd be knee-deep in another of her harebrained plots to ruin his life. "Nice try," he said, "but you are so transparent."

"What?"

"You know *what*. False labor is pretty low, even for you. Don't bother crying, either," he warned. "It won't work."

"I'm not going to bawl, you big bully. Don't be such a jerk."

Man, he did not need her name-calling, on top of her friend's insulting "trade-sex-for-yard-work" proposal. He'd endured enough insults from his last girlfriend—for lack of a better term—to last a lifetime. "If you're not gonna plop this one out right now, I'm leaving."

Contrite, Val grabbed his hand, delaying his exit. "Sorry."

He kissed her forehead. Her manipulative nature aside, he couldn't stay mad at her for long. "Don't worry about it."

"But I do worry. That's why when this came up, I thought of you."

"Nice that I bring to mind hard-up-for-sex thoughts."

"Hah! We both know that's not true, since all of your past relationships have *only* been about sex."

Val had a point. An emotional connection usually proved pointless. Few women looked beyond his dirt-covered clothes, his unimpressive job, his long hair and even longer hours. Kathy, the last chick he'd dated had informed him he wouldn't recognize romance if it bit him on the butt.

Duh. He dug ditches, for godssake. Romance rarely entered the world of dirt. He knew there must be a way to sweep a woman off her feet or make the earth move without the benefit of heavy equipment; he just hadn't found the right combination yet.

How would Val react if he admitted that, for once in his life, he'd prefer a good old-fashioned romance to a frantic, meaningless tumble between the sheets? He considered it for two seconds before he realized she'd laugh her ass off...and hang that unmanly need over his head for eternity.

No wonder he was still single.

Val's plea interrupted his thoughts. "Can you just hear me out? Give me a chance to explain the details?"

He groaned. "Are we *still* talking about your desperate friend?"

"She's not desperate, at least not in the way you're imagining." She frowned. "I can't believe you are giving up on all women."

"I am not giving up on *all* women. I'm just not bedding one in exchange for bedding plants! Jesus, Val! This is insane. Even for you." Nathan flicked his braid back over his shoulder, glaring at his sister, champion of the underdog. Dog. His face went stern. "This friend of yours. She's ugly, isn't she?"

"No!"

"Fat?"

Val's auburn curls shook violently. Her hazel eyes stormed and she seemed too angry to speak.

He should be so lucky. "So what? She's stupid? Manic? Poor?"

She gave him that steely-eyed look she'd perfected at age five. "I'll give you two reasons to consider it: A) your artistic skills suck and Tate can help you; B) Tate's house is on the corner of Jackson and Main. Maybe you've passed it? Since it's on the busiest intersection in town? If you take on this project," she spread her arms, miming an invisible billboard, "you could put up a big sign; *Landscaping Design by LeBeau* and jump start your business plans."

"I thought you had funny business in mind for me." Val's immediate scowl made him grin. "Besides, I've driven by that house numerous times. This pal of yours would need to be Picasso *and* a nympho to pay for the sheer amount of dirt work it needs."

"Fine. Your life. Your missed opportunity."

One opportunity in particular nearly blindsided him. An opportunity he'd missed last year. That house would be perfect for the Maxwell Landscaping Competition. Damn. He'd given up on entering this year and consequently had put it out of his mind.

Humiliation still tightened his throat when he recalled the bold, red REJECTED stamped across his application from last year, courtesy of the City Beautification Committee. He'd believed Val's landscaping job and his extensive construction experience had more than qualified for the prestigious contest. Wrong. Seemed he didn't meet the city's criteria as a professional without the "Certified Landscaping Designer" title behind his name.

Nathan had rectified that situation. His research paid off when he stumbled upon a new branch of design: xeriscaping, a type of landscaping which utilizes indigenous plants and trees native to a specific geographical area to conserve natural resources. He'd enrolled in an online course, did three weeks of hands-on training down south and graduated.

Hadn't helped his drawing skills one whit, but as the only landscaper in town able to add xeriscaping to his resume, he figured after a profitable summer installing sewers, he'd hang out his landscaping shingle in the autumn when the utility business slowed down.

This opportunity was too good to pass up, even if he was busy as hell. Utility work paid extremely well. But pretty as his septic systems seemed to him, they did not qualify for awards or generate lucrative city contracts.

Not only would revenge be sweet if he won the competition, he'd prove his ideas about expanding his father's business beyond sewage construction weren't a pipe dream. And he'd land the city contact for the new fire substation, a near guarantee of additional landscaping work. It did seem like his golden chance.

"You okay?" Val murmured behind him. "You're awful quiet."

Nathan shook his head. Jesus. He *was* hard up if he was seriously considering this woman's off-the-wall proposal. "Just thinking." He faced her, imparting a winsome smile. "Look, I'm not sure—" When her eyes shimmered, his heart sunk to the tips of his steel-toed boots.

Shit. Val was doing that puppy dog eye thing—a last resort because it always worked. He scrubbed his hand over his stubbly jaw and groaned defeat. Round one: meddlesome sister.

"Nice going. You win, even though you fight dirty. Why didn't you line up my nieces and nephews on the couch and have *them* cry?"

She smiled, a bit smugly, in his opinion. "That was phase two if phase one didn't work. So you'll talk to her?"

"Yeah, I'll talk to her."

"Good. I'll introduce you at our barbecue tomorrow night. Oh by the way. It's a western theme this year."

He'd suffered though her themed parties before, but there was something innately wrong with an Indian dressing up like a cowboy.

When Val didn't gleefully elaborate on what outlandish costume she planned on foisting on her poor husband, Rich, Nathan knew she'd withheld other vital information from him too. Especially with the rapt manner in which she studied the tiled floor, as if she could actually see her pink toenails beneath her extended belly.

He tipped her face up to meet his gaze. "Tell me what you're hiding, little sis, or the deal is off."

"Fine." Petulant, Val raised her chin higher. "Tate's return to South Dakota is temporary. Once the landscaping is done and the house she inherited is saleable, she'll head back to Denver and her job as a graphic artist." She frowned. "This 'no-strings' fling thing is a new kick. Tate is so sweet. For all her bold talk, I don't think she's had much experience with casual sex."

Val's admission hung in the air for several awkward seconds.

Nathan felt choked by the sudden silence. And the sudden possibilities.

Sweet? Sweet usually meant shy, right? Wouldn't a shy woman— especially one with limited sexual escapades—eagerly welcome his ideas for exploring his romantic side and keep her legs primly crossed? Even if this Tate confirmed his incompetence in the romance department, she wasn't sticking around. She wouldn't be a constant reminder he wasn't cut out for the kind of life Val possessed that caused his sharp pangs of envy.

How could he lose? If he kept the particulars about their intimate relationship—or lack thereof—from nosy Val, soak up Tate's artistic expertise

21

to bolster his pathetic drawing skills, and keep both of them from discovering his application in the Maxwell Landscaping Competition...

It put a whole different spin on the situation.

He grinned. "What time and what should I wear?"

Chapter Two

The street in front of Val and Richard Westfield's house was jammed with SUVs. As Tate approached the slate walkway, she studied the landscaping surrounding the glass and rough-hewn lumber house with a fresh eye.

The trees, shrubs, and clumps of ornamental grass didn't detract from the beauty of the impressive structure. The subtly curving patches of green grass bordered by tiny river rock blended with the hard angles of the architecture and gave an appearance of constant movement. This wasn't the style of landscaping that screamed ostentatious. It was brilliantly understated.

Damn. Val's brother *was* good. Just how good in other areas remained to be seen.

Several other guests sidled past her dressed in full western regalia. Tate backtracked to a concrete bench tucked under several Black Hills Spruce trees. She tried to convince herself she was merely pausing to gather her jumbled thoughts, not playing chicken.

Hah! Who was she kidding? She was such a big chicken she should be clucking. When she'd first half-joked to Val about the trading art lessons for sex lessons to entice her brother into helping her solve her landscaping ordinance woes, Tate had treated it as a lark. An erotic fantasy; burly construction guy performs backbreaking labor in the promise of getting the mistress of the house on *her* back. Seems Val had taken her, I'm-looking-for-a-man-purely-for-orgasms, conversation to heart *and* had contacted her older brother as a potential partner.

She'd never met Nathan LeBeau. He'd already moved out of the house during the summers she'd spent in Spearfish. Naturally, Val had fervently filled her in on Nathan's pertinent details; attractive, never been married, owned his own business, loved kids and dogs. No big surprise Tate's automatic defenses kicked in: that described half the men in America—single and psychos alike.

What if he was revolting? Come on, if the man was single, attractive, over thirty and *not* gay, what was wrong with him? More importantly, if he resembled a toad, how could she admit to Val that she wasn't enthralled with her beloved brother?

Worse yet, what if *he* wasn't enamored with *her*? She knew she wasn't the type of woman who inspired steamy male fantasies. Despite her girl-next-door appearance, in the classic "Mary Ann versus Ginger" debate, she'd likely wind up tied with Gilligan.

Tate shut her eyes, tempted to trot back home and forget this insane idea. God knew she had plenty of remodeling chores to keep her mind off her nonexistent sex life.

A deep voice startled her. "Are you lost?"

"No." Her stomach jumped at the man's intrusion, but she kept her eyes closed. Maybe he'd get the hint and leave. "Just hiding in the guise of communing with nature."

He chuckled. The rich, masculine sound arced through the humid air, landing softly on her skin like a lover's contented sigh. "I don't blame you. Pretty overwhelming party. I'd say there's close to a hundred people back there."

"So you were searching for a hiding place, too?"

"Guilty, I'm afraid."

Tate winced. No doubt this was one of Richard Westfield's lawyer colleagues. "Well, sorry. This particular hiding spot is taken."

Fabric chafed against the bench seat. A warm, hard shoulder brushed hers as he sat down; the immediate contact initiated an unexpected shiver.

"Looks plenty big to me," he said, sidling closer yet so she felt heat from his body. "I'll just sit here and enjoy the scenery and the solitude, if you don't mind."

"Suit yourself."

Apparently the man didn't take offense to the absence of small talk. Silence stretched. The occasional loud burst of laughter or the pungent scent of barbeque smoke wafted over them reminding Tate she couldn't hide forever. She sighed heavily.

"It's too nice a night for such a profound sigh." The man paused and Tate heard the chink of a bottle against the stone bench. "Are you sure you're all right?"

"No. Actually, I'm…" She opened her eyes and blinked at the hunk sharing her space. *Definitely not fine now.* Mama. When had the Indian Warrior statue from Val's backyard sprouted legs and sprung to life? The bulging muscles under his polo shirt appeared to be made of marble. She tore her gaze away, up to his chiseled face and caught sight of the most beguiling set of lips she'd ever seen.

He smiled. "You were saying?"

"Never mind," she said breathlessly.

"Come on. Sometimes it's easier to tell things to a perfect stranger."

"Interesting that you'd think you're perfect." No doubt he was close to perfection. The long black braid trailing down his back added a roguish touch, bringing her pirate fantasies front and center. God, was there a chance he'd cart her off and ravage her?

"Good one," he chuckled. "A *complete* stranger. That a better word choice?"

"I guess." His intense gaze never wavered. Definitely a lawyer with that stare-down technique. She ignored the temptation to confess her attraction to him. But if he pulled out an eye patch, she'd lose all decorum and ravage him.

He playfully nudged her knee with his own. "So tell me."

The rasp of his crisp leg hair brushing against her smooth thigh felt intimate. Erotic. "Seriously?"

"Seriously. I'm imagining any words tumbling from your rosy lips," his intent stare lingered sexily on her mouth, "will leave me spellbound, wanting more."

She bit back a purely feminine sigh. "Are you a professional charmer?"

"Interesting that you'd think I was charming. So tell me." His sultry voice slid through the evening air like dark, luxurious silk.

Tate clamped her hands down on the bench until concrete bit into her palms. Yep. Really happening.

"That wasn't a trick question," he drawled.

"I know." She inhaled, drawing in his clean, soapy scent. Lord he smelled divine. "Here goes. You ready?"

He gripped the bench with mock fierceness. "Ready."

On second thought, she'd never be ready for the havoc this hunk wreaked on her senses. His smile alone made her knees quake. One sweep of those caramel-colored eyes and she felt tingles in places she'd long forgotten actually tingled. "Ever been on a blind date?"

"Not for a long time. Have you?"

"Not really. That's why…" Blast it! Why did her cheeks redden at the most inopportune times?

"Ah. That's why you are out here hiding." His heated gaze skimmed her breasts before zeroing in on her shoulder. Those large fingers flicked a pine needle from her shirt, and he carefully smoothed the puckered material back in place. "So where is your date?"

She watched the gentle movement, silently willing those deft fingers to stay put. "I don't have one. Mostly I was using that as an analogy."

He signaled for her to continue.

Tate's tongue had gone bone dry from his close contact. And weren't all his muscles sucking up every bit of available oxygen? She managed to swallow once before she pointed at the bottle resting on his muscled knee. "Since I'm sharing my bench, you have to share your beer. No cooties, I promise."

He smiled, wiped off the top and passed the bottle without comment, again letting his eyes loiter on her mouth.

Damn if her lips didn't tremble.

"If I had a shred of self-respect, I'd high-tail it home before I follow through with my crazy plan."

His dark, expectant gaze wandered over her body, intimate as a caress. "What does self-respect have to do with a blind date?"

Tate shrugged, offering a rueful smile. "You wouldn't believe me if I told you."

"Trust me. I've had some strange goings on myself this week."

"Must be the phase of the moon." She tilted her head to catch a glimpse of the silver orb through the treetops. Her cheek brushed the skin-warmed cotton fabric stretching across his broad shoulder. She plucked the bottle from his hand. "Now, aren't you sorry you asked?"

"Only sorry you're drinking all my beer," he murmured. "Don't you believe some unexpected things can be..." His glance read *pure sin* when it dallied on her mouth. "Promising?"

Tate moistened her lips slowly, pleased when a sound resembling a groan gusted from his. "Not in this case."

Her attempt at legal humor evoked a low, sexy chuckle that suggested he was imagining illicit acts performed outdoors in fading daylight.

"Your turn." His purely male presence enveloped her like a sensual fog as his large palm covered hers. Lifting the bottle, he leisurely outlined her lips with the wet rim. "Open for me," he said huskily, tipping the amber liquid past her parted lips. The yeasty taste rolled over her tongue. His rough thumb wiped an escaped drop of beer from the corner of her mouth, and he slowly brought his thumb back to his mouth and licked it.

Tate's amazement that the glass hadn't returned to its molten stage from his hot touch was second only to her blazing desire to launch herself straight onto his lap and generate some serious sparks.

"Are you real?" His hungry eyes roved over her face. "Or just a wood sprite sent here to tempt me?"

"I'm real," she whispered.

"Prove it," he challenged, canting his lips over hers, a mere breath away.

Her heart leapt. Her mouth watered. Her skin broke out in gooseflesh as she softened her lips and held her breath.

His eyes burned hotly as he oh-so-slowly lowered his sinful mouth toward hers.

Crashing footfalls through the underbrush broke the spell.

Tate jumped back and almost toppled off the bench.

"There you are! We've been looking everywhere." Six-year old Tanner Westfield wiped the sweat from his brow as he stepped to the bench. His twin, Tyler, followed behind him. Arms covered in scratches, leaves tumbled from his auburn hair.

Why had Val sent her kids out as a search party?

"You're in big, big trouble." Four-year old Chelsea Westfield shoved her way in between her brothers. Despite her tattered cowgirl ensemble, she stood directly in front of the man, blonde ringlets shaking around her dirt-smudged face. "Mommy wants to talk to you. And she's pretty mad."

The man lifted a dark brow. His amused glance swept the disheveled children. "Yeah? She gotten a good look at you guys lately? Just where were you searching for me? The shelterbelt?"

Tyler and Tanner looked guiltily over at the long line of trees and bushes sheltering the house. But Chelsea crossed her arms over her chest and grunted. "So? We climbed a few trees for a better view. Now Mommy's gonna be mad at *us* too." She poked him in the chest with her little index finger. "If we don't get ice cream tonight Uncle Nathan, it'll be all your fault."

Every muscle in Tate's body seized up. *Uncle Nathan?* She slapped a hand on her flaming cheek. "You—you're Val's—*brother?*"

The man's instant, glorious smile said it all.

Lord, she'd been flirting. No, she'd practically thrown herself at his big feet. Hmm. Was there truth to the rumors about using the size of man's feet to gauge the size of his...?

Tate gave herself a mental slap. What was she thinking? More importantly, what was *he* thinking? Mortified, she grabbed the beer and drained it.

"You okay?" he taunted, dangerously close to her ear.

"Y-yes." She scrambled to recover her wits. Breathe Tate. Think. Thank the stars Nathan LeBeau wasn't a toad, but a drop-dead gorgeous he-man posed even more problems. He was way out of her league. How could she handle him, especially when her wanton behavior suggested she could? She offered him a tentative smile.

Which he matched with a wicked, wicked grin. He lifted her hand to his sinful mouth and used those mesmerizing lips to nibble kisses on her knuckles. Hot, sweet, kisses that didn't seem to end.

The parts of Tate's body that didn't go all hot and tight, turned into a wet quivering mass.

Why did she suddenly feel legal repercussions with the city of Spearfish, South Dakota were the least of her worries when it came to dealing with Nathan LeBeau?

ະ ະ ະ

Nathan glanced over at Tate. This darling blonde pixie with bewitching blue eyes, curves the envy of a Formula One driver and luscious lips made for month-long kisses was *the* Tate Cross?

It had paid off, bribing his niece and nephews into pointing out the elusive Tate. When she'd bolted, he seized this time alone to present his softer, charming, romantic side.

He dropped another gallant kiss on her knuckle. Fascinating hands; small and unadorned. He was sorely tempted to taste those tiny fingertips. He reminded himself to play it cool. "Well, well. I'm very pleased to finally make your acquaintance, Tate."

The blush pinking her cheeks deepened and she seemed to have lost the ability to speak. It'd been a long time since Nathan had left a woman tongue-tied.

Speaking of tied...how would this nymph look tied to his headboard while he ravished her nine-ways-til-Sunday? With just his tongue? He imagined her naked, writhing. Her peach skin flushed. Her juicy mouth parted in ecstasy as he licked a path from those outstanding breasts down her soft belly...

She pulled her hand away. "You all right?"

"I believe we have some business matters to discuss." He winked at her over Tanner's head.

A darker shade of rose swept down her neck to her cleavage.

He glanced down her compact shapely body. Wow. Sweet indeed.

Tanner and Tyler interrupted his thoughts by attempting to yank him to his feet. "Come *on*. Mommy wants you now."

"Hold your horses, partners. You run along or you'll blow what little chance you've got left for ice cream." Within seconds, they'd vanished and Nathan chuckled.

He met Tate's direct gaze. A spark, hot like a comet, moved through the air between them.

"Mission accomplished. Although, you do realize Val will be swarming in here, probably with a pair of binoculars, five seconds after they inform her we were spotted together."

"We both know she won't be doing a belly crawl recon in her condition. Does that worry you?"

"No. I've got to be honest, Nathan. I'm glad we stumbled across each other this way."

"Why?" The sexy, breathless way she'd uttered his name startled him.

Tate's fingers plucked at the hem of her shorts, revealing another inch of creamy skin. "This is all so bizarre I don't know where to start." She stared straight ahead, past the low-hanging pine branches to the crowded street beyond.

"At the beginning." He was distracted by glimpses of her white teeth as she gnawed the pink lipstick from her plump bottom lip. He had a serious hard-on for her wanton mouth. He couldn't keep his eyes off it.

She sighed, kicking the dirt with the heel of her Birkenstock. "I'm being court-ordered to meet the city requirements. Unfortunately my finances are shaky right now. But we both know that isn't the only reason I wanted to talk to you."

Her answer seemed rehearsed, although her embarrassment about the "trade" appeared real. "Go on," he said.

"Val knew about my lack of...male companionship before I came back to settle my aunt's estate. I also told her I'm not looking for anything permanent, just the physical side of a relationship."

"Why?"

"Why?" Her pale blonde brows lifted. "Don't you believe me?"

"No." Seeing her soft expression turn hard, he clarified, "But only out of habit. Most women won't consider dating a man who isn't prospective husband material." Or they were content to play hide the sausage behind closed doors, hoping like hell their friends wouldn't find out they'd been slumming, banging a guy with red skin.

"Exactly. I'm tired of dating a man for his long term potential. I want to have fun, be impulsive and not worry about whether or not we'll be picking out china patterns next year."

"In other words, you want to act like—"

"—like a man," she finished without looking at him. "Sex without strings and nothing else. Just like the type of relationships Val says you're used to. I thought we'd meet, you'd get a chuckle from my scandalous proposal and hopefully do the work—the yard work that is—at a substantial discount." She

31

glanced up warily. "Is that why you're here? To politely hand me a ten percent off coupon?"

"No."

Tate's blue eyes clouded. "Explain to me why you'd be willing to work so hard and consider tossing in recreational sex when you don't even know me?"

It was on the tip of his tongue to tell her about the Maxwell Landscaping Competition, but he refrained. Tate would tell Val, who in turn would blab to their parents, who would think he was thumbing his nose at the utility business his father had entrusted to him a few years ago. No. It'd be best to wait and see how this scenario played out before coming clean with the lovely Ms. Cross. Her skepticism was warranted. A little improvisation to ease her fears was necessary.

Without meeting her eyes, he confessed, "Val doesn't know this, but my last girlfriend said I was lousy in bed. First time I'd gotten a complaint to my face. Still, it makes a man gun-shy about trying to get intimate again. Problem is, I've been so busy working I haven't had time to find a woman who's willing to prove those accusations wrong. That's why when you suggested this…"

She blurted, "Of course I'd be willing to help in any way I can. You know…to recoup your manhood."

Everything inside him cringed at his deception. Even his balls seemed to shrivel up. In a diversionary tactic, Nathan reached for her fingers, repeatedly pleating the cuff of her shorts. "Can I ask you something else?"

"Sure."

"Were you really out here hiding from a meeting with me?"

"Yes." Her gaze swept his features but she didn't release his hand. "I was nervous."

"Why?"

"Besides the crazy purpose of proposing art lessons for landscaping? With wild and crazy sex thrown in as an added incentive? Even if you are my friend's brother, you have to admit it sounds desperate and sleazy."

He caressed her knuckles in a manner meant to reassure her. Tate's satiny skin beneath his rough hands shot another hot wave of awareness through him. "Whatever we choose to do, or not to do in private as consenting adults is not sleazy, Tate. Whatever our agreement is no one's business but ours."

"Glad you see it that way." She laughed quietly, turning her delicate hand to thread their fingers together. "I've never done anything like this. And you aren't what I expected. Not at all."

"Am I better or worse?" That same niggling fear arose. Would her cute freckled nose wrinkle with distaste when she saw him in his usual dirt-caked work clothes? Or wasn't she expecting the darker reddish color of his skin and the long hair?

"In most ways better. In some ways worse."

Before Tate could elaborate on that statement, the dinner bell in the backyard clanged. She leapt to her feet like someone had tossed a firecracker underneath the bench.

As usual, his sister had the worst timing. He stood and noticed again Tate was a little whip of a thing, barely reaching his shoulder. It made him extremely curious about how they'd line up horizontally. Or vertically. Or any way at all.

"Nathan?" Tate looked up and searched his face. "You didn't really answer my question."

"Which was?"

"After meeting me, are you still interested in my proposal?"

The stubborn tilt of her elfin chin contradicted her simple question. This woman had stirred something in him from the moment he'd sat down. What besides lust? His true romantic, tender side? Hell if he knew, but figuring it out filled him with an excitement he hadn't felt in ages.

He kissed her fingertips, thankful she kept short nails instead of the crimson claws so many women preferred. "After meeting you face-to-face my interest in the proposal has increased tenfold."

Her immediate blush charmed him.

"I'll come over, look at the project and we'll talk more." At her protest he briefly placed a gentle finger over her plush lips, wishing he'd had the foresight to use his mouth. "Trust me. We'll figure it out. Tomorrow. At two?"

"Fine, but I want to point out that you are as persistent as your sister."

I want to point out you are as sweet as Val claimed you were.

He grinned, letting his thumb graze the moist flesh of her bottom lip until her breasts rose and fell. "Runs in the family."

"Do we really have to go inside?" She gestured to her clothes; khaki shorts and tie-dyed tank top. "Seems Val didn't tell me this was a themed party. I'm not exactly dressed in the appropriate western attire."

"And Denver is famous for being a cow town underneath the towering skyscrapers. You mean you don't own an outfit with sequins and fringe? Where's your Stetson? And your tassels? What kind of cowgirl are you?"

"The kind who prefers to show her sequins and fringe in private. Can't keep a hat on if you ride 'em as hard as I do." She leaned forward and whispered, "There are plenty more interesting places to put tassels than on clothes, don't you agree?"

Nathan's tongue stuck to the roof of his mouth. Another part of his anatomy reared up with excessive interest.

"Besides, I don't much feel like socializing."

"With me?" His pulse leapt a warning. Tate wasn't embarrassed to be seen with him was she? Although he hadn't followed Val's suggestion to dress up in ostrich skin boots, chaps, spurs, and wearing a bolo tie in place of a shirt, he thought he'd cleaned up pretty good.

"No, with anybody." Apparently ill at ease, she turned away.

Nathan snatched her hand and spun her back around. In the twilight, her wide eyes reflected periwinkle blue. Man. He had this overwhelming need to kiss the corners to see what hue they turned from desire. "If you want to leave, I'll make your excuses to Val." He lifted her palm to his mouth for a taste, pleased when her breath hitched. "Because I feel the same. I don't want her gawking at us, wondering if we've—"

"Signed the contract?" Tate finished, amusement lacing her tone. "If you've dipped your pen in my proverbial well?"

He grinned, nipping the tempting, tender skin beneath her thumb until she gasped. "Took the words right out of my mouth."

"Val didn't mention you were in—"

"—Indian?" he finished brusquely. It figured his sister hadn't told Tate his heritage. "I was adopted. I'm a full-blooded Lakota where as Val has lighter skin tones because she's only—"

She placed a finger over his mouth. "I was going to say incorrigible, not Indian. You think I care about the color of your skin?" Her touch lingered on his freshly shaven face. "I'm jealous, actually. It's the most beautiful shade of red-gold. I'd love to paint you sometime to see if I can get the tone right." Her thumb feathered over his jaw up to his cheekbone, teasing across his half-parted lips.

The cautious contact sent a stirring straight to his loins.

"Neither did she mention you were so tempting, Nathan LeBeau. Or," her gaze roamed over him, a look that bordered on curious hunger, "so big. Damn. You are one big man. Everywhere?"

Her combination of bold actions and innocent wonder piqued his interest. Hell, it piqued his desire. Nathan gave her another sly smile. "Everywhere."

"Yikes." She brushed a soft open-mouthed kiss on the pulse point above the vee of his shirt collar.

He nearly stumbled over his feet at the guileless, erotic gesture. He reached for her, but she slipped through his grasp like quicksilver.

"Yep, definitely incorrigible," she whispered and disappeared.

Nathan stared after her. The gently bouncing pine boughs were the only indication she hadn't been an apparition.

Chapter Three

Tate placed sugar-dusted squares of lemon shortbread on the plate and shut the cupboard with a swing of her elbow. She nervously mopped the sides of the iced tea glasses sweating on Aunt Bea's prized teak tray. Then she dabbed sweat from her brow. Scowled at the stupid bird chirping from the cuckoo clock.

2:30. Nathan LeBeau was late.

Paranoia set in. What if he didn't show up? She'd be out of luck in more ways than one. Once she set the goodies on the apothecary table in the parlor, she pulled back the Priscilla curtain and scanned the front yard again.

Her breath snagged in her throat when masculine, sexy Nathan ambled into view.

Although she was thankful he hadn't backed out, she also admitted a man like him, well, *scared* her.

When he bent over to examine where the curb met a weed patch, exposing his tight backside, dry mouth was no longer a problem. The drool that mixed with her sharp intake of breath made a strange gurgling sound. Oh yeah. Nice buns. Correction: fabulous buns. He stood and the black braid swung jauntily over his wide shoulder, giving her an unobstructed view of a black tank-top stretched over his pecs. Whoo-ee. Absolute killer chest.

Anticipation prickled her skin, leaving behind a fine sheen of perspiration. Tate slowly stroked the sweat trickling between her breasts. She wondered why *he* wasn't sweltering. In this heat, covering that fine, fine body in pesky clothes seemed a waste of fabric.

She fanned herself, imagining her zealous hands easing off his shirt. No, *tearing* off his shirt. Running eager fingers down his long, muscular arms. Or using her teeth to lift the flimsy tank top to expose his lean stomach…

He turned and seemed to look right at her.

Tate dropped the curtain back into place and stepped from sight. Yeah, that'd be great. Attacking the man in her front yard. That was a sure way to scare him off. When he paused to jot on a clipboard, she deemed her hormones under control and stepped outside.

The sun beat down as clouds of chalky dust kicked around her ankles. Nathan smiled, but remained intent on inspecting both sides of the street, running a stick with a wheel on the end parallel to the curb. After adding to his notes, he used a red bandana to mop the sweat beaded on his forehead. "Give me another minute, okay? I want to check something in back."

"Why don't you come through the house? I've made some cookies and iced tea." Tate could've smacked herself in the head. *Cookies and iced tea?* What had she been thinking? *And then we can adjourn to the backyard for a rousing game of croquet.* Sheesh. Nathan LeBeau was probably used to women who offered themselves as refreshment, not geeky girls with questionable seduction skills.

In the small backyard, he studied the white paint peeling from the slats of the eight-foot high wooden fence.

"I know that fence needs some work," she said.

He faced her, seeming surprised she'd stayed. "Nothing a power washing and a coat of paint won't cure. Let's talk specifics."

Once inside Nathan seemed to relax. Strange, his enormous frame didn't look silly perched on her aunt's prissy brocade sofa. "This is a great house." His gaze swept the newly painted walls against the mahogany woodwork and the antiques, books, knickknacks and artwork scattered about.

"Thanks." She dabbed powdered sugar from her fingertips and reached for her glass, accidentally bumping his knee. "An inheritance from my Aunt Beatrice."

"Is that why you're back in Spearfish?"

"Yeah. Took some time off to settle her estate," Tate said. Surprising how easily that half-truth slipped out. "It needed updating and I went a little gung-ho at first until…my poor checkbook balance screamed stop."

His eyes reflected understanding. "Remodeling can get expensive in a hurry."

"Tell me about it." She gestured to his clipboard propped on the scarred coffee table. "Once everything has passed inspection I'll put it on the market and head back to Denver."

"Seems a shame to do all this work and not get to enjoy it." Nathan studied her curiously as he drained his tea. "Val told me you're a hotshot graphic artist with a pretty high-powered job. You must miss it if you're so eager to return."

Better not confess she might not even have a job in another few weeks. "I don't miss the hours. Luckily we didn't have any huge projects looming, so this mini-sabbatical was perfectly timed."

He frowned at the ice cubes in his empty glass. "Does seem odd that a company would let you take such an extended leave."

Not odd. Unheard of. Pretty shrewd question, however. "It's unpaid, falling under the 'family emergency category', hence my precarious financial situation."

"Can't your family help out?"

Her mouth tightened. Perceptive man, but again, she didn't want to detail that horror either. "They've offered. I've refused." Forcing a smile, she held out the silver platter. "More shortbread?"

He waved the plate away. "Val knows all this?"

"What? That I single-handedly want to kill Bob Vila?"

"Funny, but not what I meant. She knows that you aren't getting financial support from your family."

"Yes." *Change the subject before he delves too deeply.* "I'm stubbornly self-supporting, so I've come up with some pretty funky ideas to solve my cash flow problems. Grace Fitzgerald is paying me to teach art at the Girls Club.

And now this trade with you will serve a couple of my needs." Tate cringed and dropped her gaze to the Oriental rug. God. Talk about a crude implication.

Awkward silence.

Nathan said softly, "Tate, look at me."

Her gaze met his, expecting pity. But something dangerous and unbelievably sexy lurked there. "Look, Nathan, I don't blame you if you've changed your mind—"

His mouth, soft, warm and insistent, was on hers before she finished the sentence.

He set her glass on the table without breaking the kiss. Hauled her onto his lap as if she weighed nothing. His large hands circled her hips as he gently coaxed her lips to soften, to respond to his sweet heat.

Tate yielded to him without hesitation.

Their breath mingled while warm, tender flesh brushed across warm, tender flesh. A nibble. A lick. A soft sigh.

When Nathan's tongue darted toward hers, Tate canted her head and opened fully for his kiss. Her heart thudded madly as he swamped her senses with the delicious, erotic ways he used his tongue. He explored patiently, not trying to reach her tonsils on the first go-round. Her blood pulsed.

Six months wouldn't be enough time to delve into the mysteries of his succulent mouth, let alone six measly weeks. The scent of aroused male surrounded her; heat from his remarkably firm body burned her from the inside out. Her dizzy moan of delight turned into a surprised gasp when he broke the kiss.

"I've wanted to kiss you since last night." He nipped her bottom lip between his sharp teeth. Slid his strong hands around her hips to squeeze her rear. "Damn if you don't taste as good as I imagined."

"Then why did you stop?"

He lifted her back into her corner of the couch. "Because we need to talk about the project and set up some ground rules."

"Ground rules?" Why were they discussing business when her lips positively tingled and she'd finally experienced her first real taste of passion?

"About the deal. The business end is easy. You'll pay for the raw materials; I'll provide the labor and act as mediator with the Beautification Committee. Since I'm booked for the rest of the summer, my work here will be limited to weekends. That okay?"

"Fine." She toyed with his long silky braid before wrapping the thick plait around her palm. Heartened by his quick intake of breath, she tugged him closer by his captive hair and crushed their mouths together.

It didn't take him long to take complete control.

Nathan scorched her lips in a manner that left Tate gasping. Good God he scrambled her brain. Made her sweat in places she hadn't realized she had glands. Her body was damp and needy…from a kiss.

"I'll be surprised if I get *any* work done with you around, sweet stuff." Her bottom lip trembled under the soothing stroke of his thumb. "You are a disruption to my already weak train of thought."

Tate smiled before climbing back onto his lap. When he let loose a lusty groan, her smile grew, as did her confidence.

"Why did I think you were *shy*?"

"I usually am."

He blinked in confusion.

"It's true," she argued. "You don't know a thing about me."

Nathan had the grace to balk at that. "Meaning?"

"I'm not a freckle-faced little blonde waif, helpless, cute as a bug and all those nauseating descriptions."

His gaze darkened. His rough fingers smoothed the silky skin of her nape until she nearly purred. "I don't see you that way at all."

"Really?"

"Really. So what else do you want out of this deal?"

Tate curled the tips of her fingers over the jagged planes of his cheekbones. His rugged face looked hard, but his hazel eyes were soft, like melted toffee. "I'll get real specific about what else I want if you promise not to laugh."

His sizeable hand stroked a swath of warmth over her spine that bespoke of sexual heat, not comfort. "Nothing you could say would make me laugh."

"Okay, here goes." She buried her face in the warm curve of his neck, inhaling a unique mix of sweat, soap and an underlying hint of the outdoors. "In addition to expanding your professional boundaries, what could be better than you and me exploring our sexual boundaries?"

"Sweet Jesus."

Her hope bloomed when he didn't protest further, but tightened his hold. "What do *you* want?"

Nathan sure took his sweet time in answering. "I want that too, eventually, but I'd rather get to know you first."

Why wasn't he delighting in the idea of their naked damp bodies rolling around on sweat-drenched satin sheets? Or in the dirt? Or anyplace at all?

She couldn't stop the dismayed, "Why?"

"Can we talk about those particulars later? We need to address another thing first: Val."

"What about Val?"

"Because you're her friend and she's my sister I do *not* want her to know the intimate details between us."

Tate's hopes deflated. Hells bells. Who was she supposed to rave to about her great new sex life *now*? Unfair, when she dangled on the precipice of experiencing sexual bliss. "But—"

"No buts. This is a non-negotiable point."

She blew out an exasperated sigh. "Anything else?"

Nathan fingered the dent in her chin and softly brushed his warm lips over it. "I should schedule those art lessons, but the only thing I can think of right now is how badly I want to eat you up."

And he tried. Moist flicks of tongue wended down the column of her throat, followed by the graze of teeth. Tate's breath caught. Her thighs clenched. Her hopes soared. "Would you like to go upstairs and see my etchings?" she murmured.

He rested his forehead against her chest in mock defeat. "One more comment like that and I'll haul your cute ass straight to bed. To hell with taking it slow."

Her body threatened to liquefy at the gruffness of his tone and his hot breath teasing her nipples. But she knew this was her big chance to lay everything out up front without any misunderstandings. "Uh-uh. I don't want to take things slow. Nor do I want our first time to be in a bed."

Beneath her, he went rigid. "*What?*"

"Not in a bed or in missionary position. Something inventive." She licked the inside whorl of his ear and flouted her newfound bravado, "Something erotic and entirely unexpected."

"*Winyan*, you're going to be the death of me."

"What's *winyan* mean?" she asked, hoping it was Lakota for goddess.

"Woman."

"Mmm. Big guy like you can handle this *winyan* just fine. Now kiss me."

Locking their gazes, Nathan captured her mouth in a wet kiss that sucked all lucid thoughts from her head. He touched her, floating his hands up her stomach, caressing her ribcage, cupping her breasts with his wide palms.

The ripples of pleasure made a mockery of anything she'd felt before. Her nipples grew taut under the steady rhythm of his stroking thumbs. She melted into him while his mouth continued to destroy her. Dizzy and aching, she tipped her pelvis forward, wishing all barriers between them were gone and they were skin to skin. Man to woman.

His cell phone trilled.

"Sorry," he mumbled against her mouth.

She attempted to convince him to ignore it by reattaching their lips, but Nathan scooted her back into the corner of the couch.

With a muffled curse, he flipped open the phone. "LeBeau... Yeah... When? It was fine an hour ago. No, don't touch it. I'll be there in ten." He stood. "Sorry."

Tate sighed with regret, extending her tongue over her lips for another heady taste of him. When she glanced up he was watching her with unabashed hunger. "Something serious?"

"Got a piece of machinery acting up and Steve can't figure out what's wrong with it."

"Can you fix it?"

He shrugged. "Probably. Don't know how long it'll take."

There went her plans for a little afternoon delight. "You're leaving?"

"Yeah. Then I've got to check on another job in Deadwood. I won't get back into town until later tonight." He scratched his chin, adding as an afterthought, "Which also means I can't even think about starting on your project until next weekend. Provided you can help me finish the preliminary sketches before then." He reached over to straighten the mess he'd made of her shirt. His rough-skinned knuckles arced over the bare flesh on the inside of her arm, lightly teasing the swell of her breast.

Her mind nearly shut down at the sensuality of his simple touch. She laid her hand over his, threading their fingers together before rising to her feet.

Nathan peered at her intently. "Have plans for later?"

"No."

"Would you like to..." He shifted, his gaze glued to the striped rug beneath his booted feet. "I dunno, can I come by later and take you..."

Take you. God, yes. The prospect of hot sex lit her insides like a neon sign. Visions of him taking her every conceivable way. Against the pillars on the porch. On the hood of his monster-sized pick-up. Hanging upside down from a tree in the backyard—

"Tate?"

Somehow she climbed down from the branch of that particular fantasy and shifted her focus back to him. "Mmm?"

"What do you say? Wanna go out for ice cream?"

"Ice cream?" she repeated inanely. Not exactly the decadent treat she had in mind, which indicated how far she'd gone out of her mind with lust. She never turned down ice cream. Next to the potential of licking Nathan LeBeau, the sugary confection definitely plunged to last place.

"Yeah, ice cream," he said, his brown eyes twinkling. "I love swirling my tongue around those incredibly sweet, creamy mounds. Lapping up every inch until I've had my fill." His scorching gaze descended to her cleavage, dawdled, then took the long way back up to meet her eyes. "What do you say?"

Tate licked her lips. "What time?"

❦ ❦ ❦

"Oh God, that was sooo good." Tate stretched languidly, arching her arms above her head with utter abandon.

"Can you handle some more?" Nathan inched closer to drag one blunt fingertip down her cheek.

"No." She shivered when his breath tickled her collarbone. "Two is plenty for one night, don't you think?"

"I don't know. I liked watching you enjoy it with unrestrained gusto." His hot mouth brushed her ear. "It was sexy as hell."

Tate purred, "Is it that obvious?"

"That you love ice cream?" He used the callused pad of his thumb to clean a chocolate smudge from her chin. "In some places more than others."

"So what now?"

"Want to go for a walk?" He held out his hand and pulled her to her feet. "It's a nice night."

It was perfect; warm, balmy summer air with the faint twinkle of stars. The only things missing from the romantic moonlit evening was the sweet scent of jasmine and a strolling violinist.

And a super-size box of condoms.

Lord. What was happening to her? She'd *never never never* in her adult life had crazy, strictly sexual thoughts like this. Unless…her older friends had warned her sex drive would change dramatically when she hit the big three-oh, but that was more than five months away.

"Tate?" He tilted her face up to meet his quizzical gaze. "Would you rather go home?"

"Sorry. The sugar high must've affected my brain." She placed her hand in his, pressing her face against his sleek bicep. Fantasized about running her tongue between his thick fingers up to his massive shoulder. *Take a deep breath and get your mental mouth off his body.*

They strolled companionably through the deserted park. The dichotomy surprised her. The level of comfort they'd attained in such a short time and yet a casual brush of his skin across hers made her burn. Made her ache to know the intense side of Nathan that showed no comfort whatsoever.

No time like the present to find out.

Tate's clever yawn had the effect she'd intended; he took her home immediately.

Beneath the arbor at the front gate, she asked, "Want to come in for a nightcap?" *Or to see my nightgown?*

"I can't. I've got an early day." When her disappointment showed, he promptly backtracked. "Although I can't start any dirt work until the weekend, we still can see each other."

"Anxious to get started on those art lessons?"

"Soon." He rested his shoulder on the porch pillar. "Would you like to go out tomorrow night?"

"Is this some of that 'getting to know you' stuff you were talking about earlier?" Tate asked suspiciously.

"Yep."

"O-k-ay." This wasn't going the direction she'd hoped, but she was adaptable. "Where, when and what time?"

Nathan grinned. "Impatient little thing, aren't you? Tell you what. I'll swing by the night after next. It'll be a surprise."

"Will you at least give me a hint?"

"Sure." He kissed her chastely on the forehead before his lips nibbled a seductive path to her ear. "I guarantee after I'm done with you, your head will be spinning. Until then," he whispered, "sweet dreams."

As Tate watched him disappear into the darkness she knew there wouldn't be one sweet thing about her dreams tonight.

Chapter Four

Tate watched as her friend Grace Fitzgerald shoved aside the chips and salsa to make room on the table for her briefcase. Grace popped the locks and rummaged around until she unearthed the spiral notebook.

"Aren't you having a margarita?" Tate asked.

"No." Grace shut the briefcase and set it on the floor.

"Why not? Because this is an official meeting?"

"Partially. But the main reason is because I'm tired. I need something to perk me up, not make me slide under the table. Sorry I had to push this meeting back three hours."

Tate sighed and put the menu behind the condiments, glancing around the mostly empty Mexican restaurant. "I understand. But I'd like to point out between Val being pregnant and you officially my boss, I've got no drinking buddies while I'm here."

Grace withheld a laugh. "Leave it to you, Tate, to get right to the point. I promise I'll knock back some shots of Cuervo with you before you head back to Denver, okay?"

"I'm holding you to that."

The waitress brought two glasses of iced tea and took their order.

Tate slapped a sketch book next to the silverware. "Okay. I've come up with a couple of variations on curriculums depending on the age groups. Remind me again how many classes I'll be teaching?"

Grace squeezed lemon into her iced tea. "Five per week which roughly translates to one class a day."

"That's not too bad."

"The problem is I've got girls ranging in age from four to fourteen."

Tate reached for a chip and dipped it in the salsa. "I'm guessing the teens are at the 'this is so lame' stage."

"Yep. Don't you remember that summer we met at camp when we were teenagers? Now that I think back on how much grief we gave the arts and crafts teacher…I literally cringe. Probably gave her a complex."

Tate laughed and brushed salt from her fingers. "You and Val were the older bad girls, cutting out pictures of half-naked guys from *Cosmo* for the decoupage project. My stuff was innocent and sickeningly sweet."

"We had to do something outrageous because we couldn't compete with your artistic skills."

Tate still blushed whenever someone singled her out for praise.

Grace smiled. "I think Val and I would've gotten kicked out if you hadn't bullied the teacher with the 'freedom of creative expression' argument. I'm surprised *you* didn't become a lawyer."

Tate's gaze turned thoughtful as she stared at the velvet painting above the table depicting haciendas painted in vivid tones of orange and pink. "Funny. I'd totally forgotten about that. I guess I have stood up to authority before, but I still run from confrontations most the time."

Tate didn't bring up the problems she'd suffered through with her job in Denver. Being in limbo about the status of her career made Tate crazy if she dwelled on it. She was determined to put her limited time in Spearfish to good use.

"Since I'm the authority figure this time around I hope we can talk about any problems you're having before it turns into a confrontation."

"I'll defer to you. You're the boss."

"And on that note… Show me what you've got."

"Here goes." Tate flipped open the sketch book. "For the younger girls I thought I'd start out creating abstract work with crayons. Mixing it up with colored paper and 3D objects. You know, multi-media type things. Then we'd move on to simple subjects like apples and flowers so they get a feel for realism."

"Sounds good. What's up for the next age group?"

Tate nervously twirled a section of hair by her ear. "Umm. Ceramic painting using tiles and plates and mugs. Then if that goes well and if we have time, I might try to teach them how to make clay pots." Tate glanced up uneasily when Grace didn't immediately react. "Do you think they'd like that?"

"Anything that involves getting dirty and flinging paint is always a big hit." Grace placed her hand over Tate's restless fingers drumming on the table. "I'm not like your last boss. I'm not going to shoot any of your ideas down just because I can. Remember I'm your friend first. And I'm thrilled you agreed to do this at all."

Relief sang through Tate's system. "Good. I'm afraid pitching ideas isn't my strong suit."

"You're doing fine. So whatcha got planned for the terrible teens?"

"No decoupage." Tate grinned. "The main problem is everything is black and white to girls at this age. If they don't think they're good at art, they don't want to try. Especially anything new. So instead of having them all work on the same project, I thought I'd divide them into groups. Those who want to work on improving their skills with charcoal or acrylics or watercolors. And those who'd rather create something that involves less…"

"Talent?"

Tate winced. "I hate even thinking along those lines, but yeah. Making paper mache masks. Maybe even painting on tiles like the middle age girls."

Grace didn't say anything. Normally she didn't have a problem voicing her opinion, so Tate knew something was up. Finally Tate said, "What?"

"Okay. The mask thing sounds a little juvenile. The first thing that popped into my head were pipe cleaners, buttons and glued on feathers. I'm not sure group 'B' would be into that. Especially if the other girls are commanding most of your attention for 'real' art."

"I see your point."

"I like the tile idea though. Any chance you can expand on that?"

"Probably. Let me think about it for a sec."

Mariachi music blared from the speaker above them.

Grace sipped her tea and waited patiently.

Tate snapped her fingers. "I know. How about mosaics instead of tiles? There are some pretty cool things like beads and glass we could incorporate into the designs." She frowned. "However I didn't consider that type of project and don't have a detailed lesson plan."

"No problem. You've got time to work something up. Come to the office in the next couple of days when you've got it figured out."

"Whew. Had me worried there for a second, boss."

"You're paranoid. I'm a pussycat." Grace uncapped a pen and opened her notebook. "But since I'm also such a type 'A' personality I'll need a weekly breakdown. Mostly so I don't forget what's on the agenda, but also I'll need to order the supplies ahead of time."

They'd just finished diagramming the schedule when their food arrived. Tate noticed Grace scowling at the tortilla strips and sliced tomatoes atop her iceberg lettuce and staring longingly at Tate's fried chimichanga, covered in guacamole and sour cream.

"You can have some if you'd like," Tate offered.

"Thanks. Problem is I'll get indigestion if I take even one bite. Then I'll toss and turn all night."

"Bet Luke loves that. What's he doing tonight?"

Grace glanced at her watch. "Probably cursing my name. Neither of us has been home much this week."

"Is everything okay?"

Grace's smile was completely fake. "Fine."

Tate gave her a dubious look.

Without missing a beat Grace unrolled her silverware from her napkin and poured dressing on her salad. "So. How did the meeting with Nathan LeBeau go?"

For the next twenty minutes Tate filled the void in the discussion with mindless chatter. The little bit of salad Grace had managed to eat looked as if it might come up any second. Something was bothering Grace, but Grace wasn't ready to share. Tate let it slide and feigned exhaustion so Grace didn't have to keep up the pretense of enjoying her meal and the conversation.

At the front door Grace and Tate made plans to hook up at The Girl's Club to finalize the curriculum.

Despite the fact Tate barely reached Grace's chin, Tate wrapped Grace in a bear hug and said, "I know you don't want to talk about it. But if you change your mind, call me. Day or night."

"Thanks."

Tate drove home in her little VW Bug. She left the radio off and rolled down the window in her car, hoping the sweet night air would calm her concern for her friend. The streets were quiet. Seemed everyone was tucked in bed. No wonder. It was almost eleven o'clock.

Not a single light shone inside her house. She trudged up the sidewalk and inserted her key in the lock. Quietly opened and closed the door. The place was quiet as a grave. A shiver broke free.

Even if Grace and Luke were having marital difficulties, at least Grace didn't have to face an empty house. All the time. Sometimes the loneliness of single life hit Tate like a sledgehammer. Like now.

She sighed, knowing sleep would be elusive. After popping a bag of microwave popcorn, she opened her sketchbook and got to work.

Chapter Five

Tate gaped through the bug-splattered truck to the neon lights flashing across the midway. "A carnival? You brought me to a carnival?"

Nathan shifted in his seat. Was he idiotic to think city girl Tate would get a kick out of this slice of rural living? Did she prefer trendy art openings and smoky jazz clubs? "It was just an idea. If you don't want to go—"

"Are you kidding?" She wheeled around and gave him a sexy grin. "This is great. I haven't been to a fair since high school." Something caught her attention. She gasped and tugged insistently on his sleeve. "Omigod! There's a double Ferris wheel!"

Tate bounded out of the truck and practically dragged him to the ticket booth. When she dug in the pockets of her jean shorts for cash, Nathan gently, but firmly moved her aside. He slid two twenties through the half-circle hole in the bottom of the plastic partition.

"I can pay my own way," she said.

"I know." He folded the ride tickets before tucking them into his shirt pocket. "But this was my idea, so it's my treat."

She seemed ready to debate the issue. When he held out his hand to forestall another argument, she grabbed it, and brought his knuckles to her lips for a swift, surprising kiss. "Then thank you. Speaking of treats...what should we eat first?"

Her impulsive affection made his heart skip. How sad he had precious little spontaneity in his life. "I thought you were hot to try the rides?"

"Yeah, but after we check out the vendor stands. I'm starved."

Nathan frowned. "But won't you get sick if you eat first?"

"Isn't that the point? Ooh, look." She yanked him toward a small camper. "Indian tacos." She stopped, clapped a hand over her mouth and faced him with a horrified look. "I'm so sorry. I didn't think. Did that offend you?"

"No."

Relief crossed her face. "Good. Let's split one, then we'll have room for corndogs."

He found himself swept up in her enthusiasm and added a beer to their order. They sat side-by-side on sticky picnic table facing the fairgrounds and soaked up the fair's ambiance.

Scents and sounds carried through the warm night air: fried foods and candied apples mixed with the smells of livestock and exhaust fumes from the rides. Exhilarated shrieks blended with the booming voices of the carnival barkers. The whoosh of machinery competed with the rock music blaring from the loudspeakers. Through it all, babies cried from strollers, couples laughed—old and young alike—as the crowd shuffled through the discarded food wrappers and flyers on the way to the rodeo arena.

With a pang of self-awareness, Nathan realized it *had* been a long time since he'd actively pursued fun. As he relaxed, sipping the beer, he stole a glance at Tate. Her wide-eyed gaze darted everywhere.

Although her tousled short blonde hair and cheeks pinked with excitement cried wholesome, Nathan had a sneaking suspicion a wild woman lurked beneath that innocent persona. He was equally afraid she had every intention of showing it to him up close and personal. Tonight. He squashed the rush of anticipation, strengthening his resolve to keep the evening light-hearted, with physical contact at a bare minimum. He mustn't forget his future hinged on this project, personally and professionally.

Tate finished her portion of the taco and rested her chin on her palm. "That was wonderful. So, what next?"

"Bumper cars?"

She took a drink of beer, licking the foam from her upper lip with a lingering sweep of her delicate pink tongue. "Nah. Let's walk around. See what screams 'ride me'."

Nathan clamped his teeth together against the urge to shout, Pick me! Pick me! When he glanced over and witnessed the cat-like curl to her mouth, he knew he was in big, big trouble.

And Tate enjoyed causing his libido trouble. She chose every ride that plastered them together: the *Scrambler, Tilt-a-Whirl,* and the *Octopus.* He couldn't fight the G-forces that smashed their bodies into one. Foolish of him to attribute the dizzy sensation to the crazy rides, not to the intimate manner in which Tate positioned her lithe body against him at every opportunity.

In his supreme state of distraction, he'd agreed to ride tandem down the enormous slide. With her tempting backside grinding firmly into his groin on the endless glide, he decided he'd suffered enough sweet torture.

"How about if we get that corndog now?" he suggested. Maybe fast food would take his mind off the slow throbbing in his crotch.

"Sure. You having one?" She stretched. The motion lifted her snug yellow shirt, giving Nathan a brief glimpse of her tanned, flat belly.

"No. But I could use a cold drink." Preferably something with ice he could hold between his thighs to cool him down a notch.

"Fine. You can watch me."

The mere idea of seeing Tate's full lips wrapped around the tip of a corndog, licking and sucking, set heat flaming in his groin again. Ice wasn't going to help him a bit. "On second thought, how about something sweet? Cotton candy?"

She looked at him as if he'd lost his mind. "I guess."

After procuring their food, they wandered through the midway. Tate pointed to various rides they'd yet to attempt. When they reached the tents where carnival barkers challenged them to the assorted games of skill, her chattering stopped entirely.

"Do these guys make you nervous?" Nathan watched several tattooed, multi-pierced young studs give the blonde teenage girls in front of them a lewd once over.

"No. It's just…"

"What?"

She stopped and sighed. "All right, here's the truth: I'm terrible at games. I can't tell you how many times I tried to win one of those stupid stuffed animals in high school only to go home empty-handed."

"Didn't any of your dates step up to the challenge and win something for you?"

Tate's head lowered until her expression was hidden behind the blue fluff of cotton candy.

He stepped closer. "Tate?"

"All right, all right." She tore off a chunk of cotton candy and chewed without making eye contact. "I'm sure it won't surprise you to know I never had a date whisk me to the carnival."

Somehow Nathan kept the shock from his face. How had such a sweet thing as Tate missed such an important rite of passage? Oh right. Teenage boys were complete idiots. Still, Tate's embarrassment about the long-ago situation lingered. He didn't care if his sympathy would be unappreciated. He gently lifted her chin to meet his gaze. "Then I'm glad to be your first."

Her breath caught.

"What do you say we win you one of those stupid stuffed animals?"

A smile lit up her face, captivating him even further. She pulled him down to her sticky mouth for an enthusiastic kiss. Her sweet tongue tangled with his until the desperate strokes gave way to slow seducing nibbles, followed by a sassy nip.

Staggered by the very public, very hot kiss, Nathan scrambled to recover his wits. He licked his lips, savoring the sugary confection along with Tate's underlying, unforgettable taste. He grinned. "I take that as a yes?"

Tate refused to let Nathan carry the gigantic stuffed dog he'd won for her. Sure, he'd spent far more that he would have had he just purchased the thing outright, but watching him swing that mallet… God, the man was something. Strong, sexy, surprisingly thoughtful. She clutched his bulging biceps tightly to assure herself she wasn't dreaming.

He not-so-subtly moved away.

Tate sighed. Yep, he was determined to keep physical contact at an absolute minimum. Why? The sexual current between them kept up a steady hum regardless if they weren't touching.

She was having more fun at the carnival than she expected. Yet she wondered why they were here, making out like a couple of moon-eyed teenagers without another choice. Why couldn't they fulfill his requirements of getting to know each other better at her house? Or his? In bed? Between screaming bouts of sticky sex there was plenty of room for revealing pillow talk, right? She sighed again.

"What? You tired of holding that damn dog yet?"

She stuck her tongue out at him.

He laughed. "Your tongue is an interesting shade of blue."

Tate batted her lashes. "Want to kiss me again and see if we can get yours the same color?"

His nostrils flared and his heated gaze lingered a beat too long on her lips. "Not right now."

"Spoilsport. I'll have to get my thrills some other way. Let's ride the double Ferris wheel." She spun and hustled toward the flashing lights without waiting for his response.

They waited in line without speaking. When their turn finally came, she released her prize into the attendant's care, whispering to him for several seconds. They climbed into the steel car. Once latched in, and circling through the air, Nathan surprised Tate by sliding his arm behind her and pulling her firmly against his shoulder.

"So, what were you and the ride operator discussing?"

"Nothing. I just told him to take good care of my prize." She bumped her hip closer and curled her hand over his on the safety bar. "Thanks again for tonight. I've had fun."

"No problem."

Tate lifted her face to the sultry night air as they spun higher to the next loop. After a couple of spins, then double spins, their wheel turned lazily until their car was perched on the very top.

Where they stayed.

Nathan leaned over the edge and looked down. "What the hell is going on down there?"

Tate kept her expression bland as she too leaned over and pretended to contemplate the problem.

"Dammit, we'd better not be stuck up here."

"You make it sound like being trapped up here with me is the worst thing that could happen."

He scowled. "No, the worst thing would be if one of those lamebrains didn't properly maintain their equipment. We could be stranded up here all night."

"Good thing I brought a condom then, huh? You know, to pass the time in case we *are* stuck?"

He faced her with his mouth hanging open.

"What?" she said innocently.

"You *did* plan this. That's what you and that carnie were talking about." He swore under his breath. The carriage rocked as he scooted to the other side of the car.

Okay, Nathan's reaction was not the "yippee-let's-rip-our-clothes-off-and-get-down-to-business" response she'd anticipated.

"I'm sorry," she said tightly. "I wanted to surprise you."

"Some surprise," he muttered. "How did you get the attendant to go along with this crazy idea?"

"Never mind."

A few minutes passed before he expelled an exasperated sigh. "Come on, Tate. Tell me."

"Nope." She let go of the metal safety bar and crossed her arms over her chest. She focused on the blinking lights below on the midway and the gentle breeze cooling the sting of humiliation from her cheeks.

"Talk to me."

She shook her head.

He slid close until his body crowded her into a corner, making the car sway. "I'm waiting."

"Gee, maybe you're right. Maybe we *should* use this time to get to know each other better."

She plastered on a Miss America smile. "Hi! My name is Tatum Beatrice Cross and I'm a Capricorn. My favorite food is Italian. My turn-ons include men willing to live on the wild side. Turn-offs are men who spoil everything with their prudish attitudes."

"Ha ha." He paused. "I'm *not* prudish."

"So you say." Tate faced him and challenged, "Isn't that what you wanted? To talk? Well here's your chance to share your deepest, darkest secrets."

"Fine. What do you want to know?"

Tate locked her defiant gaze to his. "Your favorite sexual position."

His teeth flashed. "Any in which *I'm* dominant."

Holy cow. Her heart jumped in her throat.

"Got nothing to say to that?"

She just glared at him.

A second later, Nathan lowered his mouth to hers and kissed the daylights and the temper right out of her. Butterflies in her stomach took wing and she felt herself spiraling higher even when the carnival ride stayed at a complete stop.

Nathan pulled his warm lips from hers. "Tell me why you staged this stunt."

Tate's fingers swept over her well-kissed mouth. "Because of that. Just once I wanted to make your head spin the way you make mine spin every time you kiss me."

He reached for her again and gave her one of those red-hot five alarm kisses that made her hair smoke and her knees weak as a rubber hose.

The Ferris wheel started to move. Neither of them noticed.

Once they were firmly on the ground, Nathan said, "Let's go."

The return trip to her house was swift and silent. Outside her darkened porch, she asked, "Do you want to come in?"

He tucked her prized animal under his arm. "Just for a minute."

Tate fumbled with her keys, keenly aware of how Nathan's ragged breath on the back of her neck sent shivers up her spine.

She turned on the lamp in the foyer and glanced at his reflection moving behind her in the hall mirror. His face looked beautifully masculine and strong, even bathed in soft amber light.

He set aside the stuffed dog.

His long fingers latched onto her hips. Aligning her back to his front, Nathan gradually trailed his wide palms over her every curve, gauging her reaction in the mirror.

Her breath hitched, lifting her breasts higher. Need settled low in her belly before breaking free to run riot through her blood. The rapid pulse beating at the base of her throat gave away her body's reaction. Fortunately, the hard male part of him digging into her lower back also gave away his.

Against her temple, he whispered, "You're driving me crazy. Those hot looks coming from such an angelic face. I ought to run, the way you make me feel."

Tate twisted into his arms. "So start feeling me." Standing on tiptoe, she touched her mouth to his.

The kiss spun them sideways, backward and utterly out of control. She wanted his big, rough hands on her bare skin. Wanted equal time to explore those intriguing masculine hollows. When Tate reached for the snap on his jeans, his hand braceleted her wrist. Just like that, he ended the kiss.

"Stop."

"Why?"

"I'll be damned if we'll make love tonight." His chest rose and fell as he tried to calm his breathing.

"Why not?"

"There has to be more."

In her passion-drunk state she must have missed something. She looked at him blankly. "More what? Nathan, what are you talking about?"

"Don't you think the anticipation between us needs to build? We should get to know each other first? Before we…"

Tate traced the interesting mix of fine dark hairs on his forearm almost absentmindedly. "You're serious?"

"Completely."

"I don't understand."

He brushed her fingers aside and his expression remained vulnerable, even when his words weren't. "Ever wanted something so bad you thought you'd explode if you didn't get it?"

"I don't see what that has to do with—"

"—and when you finally got your hands on it," he continued without pause, "it was better than your wildest dreams?"

Her mouth dried at his provocative tone.

"Tell me, Tate," he said huskily, bracing his hands on the wall behind her, his hot breath drifting across her skin. "Have you denied yourself that rush of pleasure until you're so hot you feel like you'll burn up inside?"

The shiver from his forceful question puckered her nipples beneath her blouse. The nubs hardened further under his immediate hungry inspection. Yet he made no move to look away.

"Who are you to say I don't have that burning feeling now?"

"You do?" He managed to raise his eyes back to hers.

"Yes." She ducked under his elbow and shoved her hands in her pockets. "There's some serious chemistry between us. Don't deny it."

"I don't."

"So what's the problem?"

"No problem." His jaw hardened as he gave her another curious once over. "But you'd rather have 'wham-bam-thank-you-ma'am'? Instead of romance?"

Romance? Where had that come from? Tate cocked her head. Obviously she *had* misunderstood. "What? Like tonight at the carnival? And last night with the ice cream and the walk in the park? Like flowers, poetry, slow dancing, champagne and candlelight dinners?"

"Yeah. Something like that."

An uneasy feeling settled in the pit of her stomach. "Nathan, I told you what I wanted. And I clearly remember romance wasn't on the list. I don't need it."

He studied her face until she believed she'd melt under the fierce scrutiny.

Finally he sighed. "Well that's too bad. Because I do." He backed up all the way to the door and hesitated at the threshold.

Tate sucked in an extra expectant breath. She held out hope he'd flash that devilish grin and say, "just kidding" before sweeping her straight up to her bedroom.

"Goodnight," he said quietly. "I'll be in touch."

The screen door shut, leaving a dumbfounded Tate staring after him.

Chapter Six

The next afternoon Tate waited at The Girl's Club for Grace.

Tired of cooling her jets in the conference room for thirty minutes, she poked her head out the doorway when she heard Grace's voice.

Grace sauntered down the hallway, as if she had all the time in the world, straightening inspirational posters, picking up stray fruit snack wrappers, chatting with Cynthia, a willowy grad student.

A pack of girls came around the corner at warp speed. Between the three of them they managed to tip over a ficus plant, resulting in broken crockery and clumps of dirt strewn across the carpet.

"Hey girls, be careful," Grace said.

Immediately, a tiny Native American girl, no more than five, threw her hands in front of her face, clearly expecting Grace to hit her for her part in the mess. Grace merely shooed them away with a gentle warning. The stark expression on Grace's face made Tate's heart break.

She knew Grace tried to reach as many of the girls as possible, but a few slipped through the cracks and Grace berated herself that she couldn't save every child under her care.

Grace finished giving Cynthia instructions and then warned the janitor, who'd come racing down the hall, about the broken pot and the dirt.

She looked up at Tate and smiled. "Don't you look like a ray of sunshine in that lemon yellow sundress?" Grace pointed at Tate's feet. "Cute. Love the matching flip-flops."

"Thanks, boss. Come and see my plans for making mosaics."

Grace groaned. "Don't call me 'boss'. It makes me feel old."

"No, calling you Mrs. Yellow Hawk would make you feel old."

Her smile faded as she closed the door.

"Bad joke. I'm sorry." When Grace didn't immediately respond, Tate said, "Grace? Oh man, what's wrong?"

"N-nothing." Before she could try to convince Tate everything was just sunshine-and-rainbows like she always did, Grace's voice caught on a sob and tears fell.

Tate's shoes smacked as she zipped across the room. She pushed Grace into a chair and perched herself diagonally from her sobbing friend. Their knees touched so Grace couldn't escape.

"I-I'm fine," Grace tried to dismiss Tate's concern.

Tate was having none of it. "Cut the bull. Don't tell me nothing is wrong because I don't think I've ever seen you cry."

Grace squeezed her eyes shut. "That's because I don't make a habit of it."

"And you don't make a habit of sharing your troubles with your friends either."

Grace's eyes opened. "What do you mean?"

"That you're perfectly willing to let me unload *my* frustrations on you anytime I want. I'm assuming Val does the same thing. Why don't you let us return the favor?" Her gaze sharpened. "Is it because we're not trained psychologists and you don't think we'll be able to help you?"

"No." Grace's hand shook as she wiped under her eye. "It's more like the 'physician, heal thyself' philosophy. I keep thinking I'll get a handle on it. Usually it works, but not this time."

Tate rummaged in her backpack-sized purse. She thrust a box of Kleenex at her.

Grace's eyes went wide at the jumbo-sized package.

"I saw that look. I started carrying them because Val's pregnancy hormones cause these erratic crying jags. When she gets started, Lord, she uses damn near the whole box."

Grace managed a feeble smile. "You must think we're both crybabies."

"Hardly." A beat passed. Tate demanded, "So are you going to tell me what's wrong?"

"You sure you want to hear this?"

Tate nodded.

"Luke and I are having some problems." She sighed heavily. "Major understatement. We're having huge problems."

"When did this start?"

"About six months ago." Grace chewed her thumbnail. "An old friend of his died. A female friend. Luke started acting distracted. He was gone a lot, but when he was home he was moody. We hardly spent any time together. Consequently our life—sex and otherwise—went from awesome to awful."

"Go on."

"Of course, I immediately jumped to the conclusion he was having an affair."

Tate's eyebrows lifted. "Is he?"

"No, thank God. The truth of what he was doing is almost worse." Grace let her gaze drift out the window. "I found out he'd applied for two new jobs. Both in Rosebud."

"Why didn't he tell you?"

She shrugged. "I don't know. If I hadn't found the letter confirming his appointment time, I don't know if he would have told me at all. He refuses to talk about it. Or tell me why he wants to make a career change. So I still don't know if the money is better or whether or not this would be permanent. Yet, he expects me just to drop everything I've worked for and go with him if he's offered the position."

"Do you think he's got a chance?"

"We already know he didn't get the first one. But he's on his second interview for the one at Rosebud Boy's Home. Truthfully, they'd be stupid not to hire him. A Sioux man who actually grew up on a reservation? Add in his master's degree in counseling..."

"Yeah, I can see why you're worried." Tate leaned back in her chair and looked outside the window along the cracked sidewalk, where rose bushes bloomed in a profusion of red and pink. "Is his job at the Boy's Club in jeopardy?"

"It will be if the board finds out he's been sending out his resumé."

"So you haven't talked to anyone about this because if word gets out..." Tate angled forward, knowing her eyes were filled with reproach. "Dammit, Grace. I can see why you were discreet, but you know you can count on me not to blab. I hate that you've been dealing with this alone. Why didn't you tell me the other night?"

Grace retreated to the sink for a drink. She clutched the waxy Dixie cup and looked at Tate. "The reason I didn't unload on you is because you've had more than enough things to worry about with your own job situation and now the city mandate. Have you heard from Nathan?"

"Are you kidding? He's avoiding me." Her mouth made a moue of distaste. "In fact, I get the distinct impression the man is scared of me."

Grace managed a hoarse chuckle. "Sorry. It's just you are the least threatening woman I know. Why on earth would he be scared of you?"

"Because I want to strip that hunky stud naked and have my wicked, wicked way with him until he screams for mercy."

"And that's a problem because?"

Tate lifted her shoulder in a half-shrug. "I don't know. Wouldn't most guys have jumped at the chance to jump on me? I know I'm not a statuesque redhead like you." She grinned. "But come on, I'm not exactly *The Hunch Back of Notre Dame* either. So, I wondered if maybe it's a Native American thing. Did Luke insist you two should get to know each other before you got naked together?"

"No. It's not an Indian thing."

"Then what do you think might be going on?"

Grace blushed. "Have you asked Val if he has, umm…a problem with erectile dysfunction?"

Tate snorted. "Leave it to a shrink to turn it into a flowery phrase. No, I've felt his *erection* on more than one occasion. I know he doesn't need a heavy-duty dose of Viagra. And I'm assuming the continual presence of a hard-on means he's somewhat attracted to me. As for the asking-Val-thing? I'm not allowed to talk to her about anything that's going on between Nathan and me. Not that there's much to tell."

"But you're telling me," Grace pointed out.

"Precisely. He only told me I couldn't talk to *Val.* He didn't mention anyone else." Tate smiled slyly. "So here I am, asking the expert for advice."

"Expert? Need I remind you we were just discussing my rocky marriage?" Grace lifted her cup for another drink.

"Sorry." Tate felt contrite for a second before her expression turned crafty. "But I'm not worried about getting into a relationship with him. I just want to get into his briefs."

Grace nearly spit out her water. She wiped her lips on the crumpled Kleenex in her hand, and Tate giggled. "I take it back. Nathan LeBeau has every right to be frightened of you."

"I'm serious."

"Me too."

"What was it like before you and Luke hit the skids? I mean, how much of your problems stemmed from his Native ancestry?"

"Some of our problems are directly related to his Sioux blood. Luke looks Lakota, so he's always dealt with insults, racism, and prejudice—even among his tribe members. The fact he married a white woman, a *wasicu*…well, I think his family performed a mourning ceremony after we eloped to Vegas." Grace fidgeted, clearly uncomfortable. "It's not easy, the glares we get from strangers for having different colors of skin. Spearfish is a long way from Pine Ridge—in miles and mindset."

Tate considered her words. "Nathan's been raised with a white mother and a half-Indian father. He doesn't seem to care much about his heritage."

"He should. In fact, Luke started a support group at the community center for Lakota men. They do everything from talk about problems in business and with family, to studying Lakota traditions and language. You should tell Nathan to come. I bet he'd love it."

"Probably. But he's so swamped with work that he's not making any time for me. Or sex. Especially sex."

"Is that really the most important thing to you in this deal with Nathan?"

"Absolutely. No regrets, no promises, just a case of condoms and a good imagination."

Grace looked like she didn't buy Tate's flip attitude. "Here's where the counselor imparts a word of caution. Despite your bravado, I don't think you are the type of woman who can just sign on for a totally sexual fling."

"But—"

"Trust me. I know these things. More specifically, I know you."

"Are you telling me not to have sex with him?"

"God no. I'm telling you to be careful. Don't fall for him, because he will break your heart."

Tate frowned. "Because he's Native American?"

"No. Because he's a man."

Grace scooted into the chair next to Tate, shuffling through the brightly colored papers on the table, ending the conversation. "Now, how about if you show me your ideas for the mosaics?"

Chapter Seven

Saturday morning, the Dixie Chicks blared from Nathan's flatbed truck as he pulled up to Tate's house. He jumped from the cab, whistling "Sin Wagon". After the loading ramps clanked to the ground, he hoisted himself onto the trailer. Once the tie-downs were tangle free, he unchocked the wheels and climbed into the Bobcat's ripped leather seat.

Thick black smoke poured from the stack as he started it up. Checking in the rearview mirror, Nathan eased the stick to reverse and the Bobcat jerked backwards. His ears automatically honed in on the loud *beep beep* echoing behind him. He grinned.

God, he loved the smell of diesel fuel in the morning.

He sped to the work area. He grabbed his notes, earplugs and hardhat before he hopped out. Once he'd made a few last-minute adjustments, he glanced at Tate's house.

No doubt she was awake now, with machinery grinding underneath her window at seven a.m. Was she bleary-eyed and cursing him for the interruption? Or were her eyes twinkling, wearing that hard-to-resist come-hither smile? What he wouldn't give to witness her waking mood of the day firsthand...after rolling bow-legged and exhausted from her bed.

He tried to focus on the enormity of the task ahead, but his mind kept wandering. What if he rang the bell and she answered the door in pink satin baby-doll pajamas? Her body soft, warm and rumpled from sleep? Or wrapped in a scarlet robe? Her wet hair slicked back, skin moist and sweet smelling? Her phantom scent beckoned him inside. He followed the mental path like a bloodhound, imagining her spread across the kitchen table as a veritable breakfast feast. A car backfired, jarring him from his vision with enough force that he dropped his clipboard.

Damn. Concentrating on dirt work, instead of conjuring sexy situations with his oh-so-dirty mind, was going to be sheer hell for this entire job. Especially knowing tempting Tate lay just a few feet away, willing to make fantasy a reality.

Her wholesome innocence coupled with a hot body…double damn. He could've gotten laid for the first time in months. *Months.* And he'd walked away? And being a true lout, he'd been too busy to call her this week.

Smooth. Add his comment about needing romance and Tate probably thought he was gay.

No use worrying about that situation now. He inserted his earplugs, donned his hardhat and climbed back into the Bobcat. The bucket on the front end clattered to the ground. For the next hour he concentrated on ripping out spotty patches of crab grass. Focusing on the smooth motion of the bucket as it scraped rocks and scattered piles of dirt into a single manageable mound.

After a while the repetition numbed his brain. Nathan's attention roamed to the application he'd dropped off for the Maxwell Landscaping competition. Luckily, he'd squeaked in under the deadline by two days and had a week before he had to submit his final design. The elderly woman in charge seemed skeptical about his qualifications, until he'd handed over the newly framed xeriscaping certification.

Unlike some of his construction colleagues, he hadn't spent the off-season loafing. Not that he'd confessed to anyone he'd been learning both the Latin and Lakota names for various vegetation. Easy to imagine the rash of shit he'd get from the guys for wanting to plant posies.

He gripped the stick hard. The ground resembled cement. No big surprise. For the last few years Spearfish had been in damn near drought conditions. Any landscaper that could guarantee heartier plants, less chance of winterkill and virtually maintenance free growth, would garner extreme interest. Not to mention piles of cash.

And that interest had the potential to change the focus of his business. Show his competitors he meant to establish himself as a serious landscaper. If all went as planned, the extra cash would enable him to hire someone to oversee the utility end. Freeing him to concentrate on building his reputation as a conservationist landscaper. If he had a trusted employee to share the load, he'd work fewer hours. After the excruciating week he'd put in, that was the most appealing prospect of this plan.

He scowled. Yeah right. He *was* pathetic if the prospect of additional work held more appeal than a naked Tate.

A twinge of guilt tightened his stomach. No matter how he justified the effects of the contest's outcome, the fact remained he was withholding vital information from her and the Beautification Committee.

But wasn't Tate leaving? She wouldn't care if the house she planned to *sell* won an award or not. The end result, improved curb appeal, guaranteed she'd receive top dollar from any buyer. Although footing the bill for expensive rare plants and natural stone without her approval was crazy. He believed she'd be so enthralled by the final arrangement she wouldn't remember to ask specifics.

But if the committee members discovered his nondisclosure...not only would he be disqualified, the solid reputation he'd maintained with his father's utility business might suffer. So, he wouldn't tell her anything except on a need-to-know basis. And right now, she didn't need to know anything except he planned on working his ass off to create an outdoor masterpiece. He snagged a rock and turned his concentration back to the ground where it belonged.

Nathan worked steadily all day. The afternoon turned brutally hot. Lifting and hand stacking the heavy chunks of flat concrete to create a layered retaining wall took its toll on him. He'd sleep like the dead tonight.

After refilling his water cooler, Nathan brushed the dust from his jeans. He blotted the mixture of sweat and dirt from his neck with a stained bandana and stretched out his tired legs under the shade of a large oak. A hot breeze rustled the leaves. Heaven. He closed his eyes to bask in the beauty of the day.

A better slice of heaven teased him as Tate's sweet scent drifted to him. He opened his eyes slowly, hoping it wasn't a figment of his overworked imagination.

"Hi." She stood underneath a low hanging branch. Her hands in the back pockets of a tiny pair of frayed cut-off Levi 501's. "How's it going?"

His mouth dried at the provocative sight of all that exposed skin. Nathan reached for his water bottle. "About like I expected."

"Got a better idea of how long this project is going to take?"

"You antsy?" He squirted a stream of water in his mouth. "After the first day?"

"No." Her gaze lingered thoughtfully on his lips. "Although I am antsy for some things." She pointed at his Bobcat. "That's a pretty cute little machine you've got."

Nathan groaned. "Tate, honey. Never, *ever* refer to a man's equipment as cute or little. It's like you're commenting on my-—"

"—manhood?" she supplied with a grin.

"Yes. Besides, that 'cute' machine is loaded with sixty horsepower and maneuvers like a dream. I even modified the cab roof myself, replacing the steel lattice with a roll-bar—"

Tate held up a hand. "More information than I need, thanks. I started painting the hallway and lost track of time so I thought I'd better check on you. Can you believe it's after four?"

He had a lot to do before the day ended. "Well I haven't been loafing under this tree all day."

She scanned the new cinnamon-colored retaining wall and then him, head to work boots. "I can tell. It looks great. Did you eat lunch?"

Her concern startled him. "I had a ham sandwich at noon. Why?"

Tate was frowning at her left forearm. Her short fingernails scraped intently at the splotches of purple paint.

When she still hadn't answered, he prompted, "Tate?"

"What?" Her uncertain gaze met his. "Sorry. Just thinking about us having dinner and…stuff."

By the redness dotting her cheekbones, Nathan knew the type of *stuff* she'd been contemplating. Heat shot straight to his groin. Her alternating boldness and shyness was becoming her most endearing trait. His gaze dropped and got an eyeful of her bountiful breasts. Damn if the creamy swells spilling from her halter-top didn't tempt him to bury his whole face between those firm globes. Suck the protruding tips greedily, slowly, to hear her whimper, feel the arch of her spine…

"Nathan?"

He snapped back to attention. Ah hell. He'd been so busy mentally licking her nipples that he'd missed the conversation. "Sorry. What did you say?"

"Do you have dinner plans?"

"Guess I hadn't really thought about it." He wadded the bandana and stuffed it into his back pocket.

"I could whip up something edible if you'd like to stick around."

"Sounds good." As he stood, his back and his legs screamed in protest. "I'm knocking off about seven."

Her mouth opened. "You're working *three* more hours? Don't you call twelve hours excessive?"

His spine stiffened automatically. Not another discussion about the amount of time he spent working. "No. Twelve hours is a normal day."

"So you always exert yourself this much?" she asked skeptically. "On *every* project?"

He could confess right now that this situation was special. Tell her about the contest and earn her support. Instead he bent down to retrieve his hard hat, and muttered, "Yep." It embarrassed him, the suspicion in her eyes and his answering shame that he had no life besides work. He was aware of the opinions most people held on Native American work ethics. He'd been called a *lazy Injun* more times than he cared to count. Every time it happened, it stung his pride and made him determined to prove himself an exception.

Tate softly called his name.

When he reluctantly met her gaze, she stepped forward and gifted him with a flirty kiss.

"Then I feel incredibly lucky you're working that hard for me." Petal soft lips brushed the shell of his ear, releasing an unexpected shiver. "I certainly hope I'm worth these long hours. I don't want my teaching skills to be a disappointment."

"Unlikely." Nathan was lost in the face of her sweetness. Didn't matter he'd spent the day covered in dust and the black fall-out from diesel fuel as he jerked her against his body. He gorged himself on her sweet mouth, tasting warm, willing woman. His stubbled cheek scratched the temptingly tender skin beneath her jaw. She smelled like ambrosia. He smelled like the sulfur pits of hell.

"Sorry. You probably don't want to get near me when I'm covered in dirt."

Tate wiped a shaky hand over her mouth and tipped her head back to look at him. "Why would I care about that?"

"Most women do." He studied her baffled expression.

"You keep forgetting I'm not most women. Dinner is at seven-thirty. If you want, you can shower here."

"You offering to wash my back?"

"No. I've got a loofah on a stick for those hard to reach places. But I wouldn't be opposed to scrubbing any other place you might need a little extra attention." Her eyebrows wiggled. "Or a lot of extra attention."

Nathan wiped the sweat beading on his forehead with the heel of his hand. "You are killing me, you know that?"

"I'm trying."

Three hours later, after reloading his equipment, Nathan dragged through the back porch door. He sagged against the doorframe, his energy level at rock bottom. He watched in quiet fascination as Tate rinsed a head of red lettuce at the deep enamel sink. Rock music surged from a boom box. The aroma of fresh herbs hung in the humid air. This domestic scene was rare, and all the more potent. What would it be like, what would it take, to have this setting waiting for him every night?

She smiled at him over her shoulder as if sensing his melancholy. "Hey. You look beat. Want a beer?"

"Sure." A cold bottle soothed his tired hands. His gaze zoomed in on her nicely rounded butt, dropped to the white strings of her cut-off shorts teasing slender thighs. Then wandered back up the curve of her back to the long sweep of her neck. Her nape exposed below her sexy haircut begged for the bite of his teeth. The heat of his mouth. The wet glide of his tongue. He'd usually dated women with long locks. How would it be to grasp that short hair and direct that pink mouth wherever he pleased?

"Stop staring at me," she said.

Chastised, he asked, "Does that offer of a shower still stand?"

"Sure. Use the guest bath upstairs." Tate gestured to his filthy clothes with the butcher knife clasped in her left hand. "I'll toss those in the washer. I found an extra pair of sweats and a T-shirt. Might be a little snug, but I set them on the counter just in case."

Her thoughtfulness was his undoing. He wanted a minute to hold her, taste her, absorb her. Her eyes widened as he pressed her against the counter. He nibbled the corners of her lips before slipping his tongue inside her mouth. The taste of her sent desire ripping through his blood. Nathan wanted to plunge into her body, touch her everywhere at once. Devour her secrets, feel her bucking and moaning beneath him. Somehow logic reasserted itself. By small degrees, he lifted his head. It was a halfhearted effort to remove his passion dampened lips from hers to end the kiss.

Her eyes fluttered open to reveal a dark, expectant look that whumped the air from his lungs.

"Why'd you stop?"

Because I'm an idiot. "I need a shower. Probably a *cold* shower would be in my best interest."

A tiny scowl crossed her face. "What about *my* best interest?"

He kissed her wrinkled nose. "That is your best interest because once I get my hands on you, we won't surface for hours." The warmth spreading over her cheekbones held particular interest and he nuzzled them until she whimpered. "Days, probably."

Whistling, he headed out of the kitchen through the swinging door.

ଝ ଝ ଝ

The old pipes rattled when the water kicked on. Tate wondered if she could breach Nathan's gentlemanly act if she crawled in the shower with him. Would he push her away when she lathered her hands with soap and thoroughly stroked every inch of his remarkable body?

Whoo-yah. She fanned herself with the dishtowel. He'd earned every one of those rippling muscles the hard way. Witnessing him hauling and stacking the concrete slabs with his bare hands. Muscles straining from all that backbreaking work, her mouth—and another part of her anatomy—had watered. That firm body was something. Yet when Nathan had been standing in her kitchen, looking lost and vulnerable, a funny tickle started in her stomach that owed nothing to lust. The urge to comfort him overwhelmed her. She wanted to just grab him and hold him tight until the shadows in his eyes disappeared. Although he had protested his ripe state, she'd been drawn to it.

Tate sighed. Thinking about Nathan's scent and physique wasn't helping her revved up libido.

She wandered into the dining room. Was this what Nathan had in mind? She eyed her Aunt Bea's crystal wineglasses, bone china and silver candlesticks. An intimate, romantic dinner for two?

Her vision of an intimate dinner was entirely different. She saw him stalking her, ripping her clothes to tatters as he arranged her nude, quivering body as a main course on the dining room table. Probably not going to happen, but one could dream.

The shower shut off and Tate hustled back into the kitchen to start the pasta. She opened the wine, turned the Alfredo sauce down to simmer, tossed the salad and sliced the French bread. Another thought struck her. The scene wasn't *too* domestic, was it? God forbid she gave him reason to bolt again.

Nathan snuck up behind her and kissed her bare shoulder. She closed her eyes to savor the rasp of his damp beard abrading her skin. Gooseflesh prickled her entire body.

He murmured, "Smells good."

"Thanks. It's nothing fancy," she said softly. Her heart tripped and her blood seemed to warm.

He turned her into his arms. A dangerous, dark fire lit his eyes. "I wasn't talking about the food, Tate." Dropping his mouth over hers, he coaxed her tongue to tangle and retreat with his. Wet. Warm. Hungry. He kissed her the single-minded way she'd longed for all day; like she was the appetizer and he was ravenous.

His hair flowed around them and she twisted her fingers through the silky strands. A man with long hair was a novelty. She imagined that satin curtain falling over her, caressing her neck, her breasts, their tangled bodies. Nathan slicked his tongue over her teeth, under her top lip, exploring every slick inch of her mouth. She trembled at the unfamiliar sensation, impulsively moving her hips closer to his.

The water boiled over on the stove, popping and hissing on the burner. Grudgingly, she released him. "Sounds like the pasta is done."

"Good. I'm starved. But first, where is your washer?"

"Around the corner on the porch." Tate grabbed the chili pepper potholders and dumped the contents of the pot into the colander in the sink. "Why don't you sit down and I'll bring everything out?"

Nathan hesitated in the doorway, large hands dwarfing the blue bottle of laundry detergent. "You don't have to service me."

She twisted toward him. "*What* did you say?"

"Just what you heard." He cleared his throat and offered her a sheepish grin as he set the soap on the floor. "But what I meant was, you don't have to *serve* me. I can help."

"Fine. Grab some salad dressing from the fridge and light the candles." Placing the pasta on the Fiesta-ware platter, she poured the thick, fragrant white sauce over the spinach noodles. "However, I do believe that was a Freudian slip."

"Probably." He held a jar of ranch dressing in one hand and Green Goddess in the other as they trooped into the dining room. "Can you blame me for being leery of you?"

Hah! She'd love it if he leered at her just once tonight. Yet she couldn't ignore the fact that Nathan-the-magnificent was scared of golly-gee-whiz-All-American-girl-next-door Tate? A thrill raced through her as she gripped the wine bottle. "Why?"

"Lots of reasons." His quick shrug fell short of nonchalant. "Mostly because you're a sophisticated city girl."

"Not really," she said. "Remember I spent summers in this small town you still call home."

He lit the wicks and settled in the ladder-back chair. "I'd forgotten that. Anyway, fear of disappointment runs both ways."

The wine glugged as she poured. She peeked at him through lowered lashes. "Are we talking about disappointing me with the landscaping project?"

"No."

"The sex lessons?" she asked hopefully.

Nathan reached for his wine. "Yes. I'm talking about the sex lessons."

She resisted the urge to shout "Hallelujah!" and launch herself straight on his lap. Too bad Aunt Bea's rickety chairs would collapse under her exuberance. She traced the rim of her wineglass with a single finger. "Hmm. Maybe we should get that awkward first time over so we can relax and set higher expectations for round two." With a wicked grin she added, "Got any after dinner plans?"

Chapter Eight

Nathan choked on his merlot. "Like tonight? After supper?"

Tate's eyes went wide. "You taking off right after we eat?"

"No. But because I got called away during our original discussion, we didn't get into specifics on…certain details of these 'lessons'."

He piled a gigantic helping of steaming pasta on his plate and three slices of buttered bread. She savored the smoky wine and watched the colors change from maroon to magenta in the facets of the crystal. "We didn't discuss frequency either."

"Frequency?" The silver fork loaded with noodles had stopped halfway to his mouth.

"How many times we're going to…have lessons."

He managed to start chewing, albeit very slowly. "Since I'm working here on Saturday," he paused to wipe his mouth on the linen napkin, "we should plan on spending that evening together. You know. To work on our lessons." Another bite of pasta, which he chased with a healthy swig of wine. "This is really good."

Tate frowned, ignoring the compliment. He only wanted to spend *one* night out of seven with her? If she was supposed to make time to get to know him and his wacky ideas for romance, when would they have time for art lessons? Or more importantly sex lessons? Especially when the crazy man worked himself into the ground and was unavailable during the week?

"You never scowl. What's wrong? Can't be the food since I didn't cook."

She twirled her pasta through the thick, creamy sauce, but she didn't glance up. Nor did the fork approach her mouth. "I thought we'd...never mind."

He sighed. She could almost hear him counting to ten. "How often did you have in mind?"

Everyday. At least once. "Definitely more than once a week."

Nathan's answering laugh was low and dangerous. "Can you see why I'm frightened of you?"

"Why? Because I speak my mind?"

"No, because you're trying to change mine." He squeezed her hand in that chivalrous, it'll-be-all-right manner. Tate wanted to stab him with her fork just to get some kind of passionate reaction out of him. Talk about depraved behavior.

"Come on, eat," he urged, putting an end to her violent thoughts. "Your dinner is getting cold. Can we talk more about this later?"

Hooray. More talking. She downed her wine and reached for a refill. Planted a fake smile on her face. "Sounds good."

The rest of the meal passed pleasantly. And if it hadn't been for the fact they weren't exploring the nuances of each other's naked bodies, Tate would have considered the evening a rousing success. Nathan LeBeau was a funny, well-rounded, interesting man.

So why was she far more interested in watching that well-rounded rear end of his pumping in and out of her?

"Earth to Tate. Why the dreamy expression?"

The desperate-for-action part of her wanted to confess the seamy direction her thoughts had taken just to shock the bemused look from his handsome face. She refrained and awarded herself a mental pat on the back. See? She could act completely unaffected. Even when her steamy ideas had almost started her brain smoking and set her hair on fire. "Finished?"

"Yes. Thank you." He shoved his empty plate aside and scooted his chair back against the wall when she stood and gathered plates. "Are we gonna do this right here?"

Tate froze. He had a change of heart? Were her fantasies finally about to come true? She scrutinized his face for an answer, but he was surprisingly calm for a man about to shed his clothes. "Umm. Don't you think we'd be more comfortable in the living room?"

Nathan ran his hand along the flat plane of the table and gave it a resounding smack. "Wouldn't you prefer a harder, more sturdy surface?"

Oh mama. What *did* the man plan on doing to her that he required such durability? The dirty dishes in her hands almost crashed to the floor. She stuttered, "S-sure. Whatever you think will work best."

He frowned and glanced through the paint-taped archway separating the dining and kitchen areas from the rest of the house. "Where do you normally do this?"

Tate deliberated on a breezy reply of "everywhere" or offering the sad truth that her sexual exploits had always begun and ended in a bedroom.

While she pondered her answer, he hefted a ratty cardboard box on the table. "Ah. Your art supplies are right here, you must do this in the dining room."

"You were talking about art lessons?"

"What did you think I was talking…"

She saw the moment the light bulb clicked.

Nathan gaped at her. "You thought I was gonna nail you right here on this wobbly table?" He shook his head. "Give me some credit, Tate, for planning our first time to be a helluva lot more romantic than that. Besides, we just finished eating!"

She snatched up the empty wineglasses. "I don't think the 'wait for an hour after you eat' rule for swimming applies to sex, Nathan."

"I wasn't talking about sex!"

"That's apparent." Cheeks burning, she inclined her chin toward the box sitting way too close to the candles. "Look, while I soak the dishes why don't you spread everything out on the table so we can get started?"

He gave her a dubious look. "Get started on what?"

"Making lo…" She couldn't resist teasing, "Lots of art, of course. You want coffee?" *Tea? Or me? Dammit, Tatum Cross, knock it off.*

"No thanks."

"Then dig out the graph paper and colored pencils and I'll be right back."

Tate tidied up the kitchen and strengthened her resolve to keep her thoughts focused on teaching Nathan the fundamentals of drawing. If he learned something maybe then he'd be inclined to teach her a thing or two.

She breezed back into the dining alcove and plopped beside him. "Now, I'm not gonna bore you with a bunch of artsy-fartsy techniques you won't need. Learning the still life form is sufficient for your purposes."

She ripped off two sheets of graph paper and set one in front of each of them. "Since you're used to working with angles when installing sewage systems, it'll be easier to think in linear terms." She grabbed a charcoal pencil and traced a line down the center of the page. When he mimicked her movement, she tapped his knuckle until he dropped his pencil. "Uh-uh. Watch first. Then you can get some hands on experience."

Hands on experience? Just what he didn't need, the mental picture of her capable hand gripping his thick cock instead of that skinny pencil. That'd be an experience he'd never forget.

"Are you paying attention?"

"No." Nathan bent closer to the perfect drawing she'd whipped off in the thirty seconds. "How did you do that so quickly? It looks just like a tree." He handed over his blank paper and urged, "Do it again. Slowly."

This time when she sketched, he focused only on how the stark simple line changed. How it took on a new shape just by linking smaller and fatter lines to it. Inspired, Nathan plucked up the pencil, slid the pad of graph paper under his elbow and copied her technique. He didn't watch or worry how his picture turned out.

Tate offered suggestions while she worked. Her tone was encouraging, never patronizing. It was almost…fun. When she finished her drawing, they both leaned back and looked at his.

Nathan felt a rush of humiliation. His picture was god-awful. His eight-year old nephews had creations on Val's refrigerator superior to this piece of crap. He threw his pencil down in defeat.

"Now don't get discouraged."

"Why not?"

"Because it takes patience. Besides, I'm thinking you'll be a natural. Aren't most Native Americans somewhat artistic?"

"Only the ones who've been to prison and can devote every waking hour to sketching and drawing."

She spun the pencil back to him, along with a white eraser on a stick. "You have some interesting break-away points, but we should be concentrating on a smaller scale. If you could keep these wild lines to a minimum you'll be an expert in no time."

That bit of praise lifted his spirits. "So I'm not completely hopeless?"

"After your first attempt?" She leaned over to blow out the candles. They were dripping red wax down the silver candlesticks and onto the lace doily. "Give me a break. And give yourself a break too. This isn't easy. Practice, practice, practice." She tossed the paper in front of him. "Try again. Except this time we won't freehand. We'll block it out using the squares on the graph paper as reference points."

They drew tree after tree. Then they worked on single bushes, clumps of bushes, hedges and shrubbery. Finally after what felt like the millionth attempt and dozens of pieces of crumpled paper later, he'd crafted one that wasn't half bad. When he passed it to Tate for her inspection, she beamed.

"See? You've made huge progress in just the last hour."

"All thanks to you. Anyone ever tell you you're a born teacher?"

If at all possible, her smile brightened further. "You really think so?"

"Absolutely." He tapped his pencil on the paper. Why didn't she talk about her job in Denver with the same zeal? "You head of the art department at your firm?"

Her face went blank. "No."

"Why not? You obviously have the skills."

"You're biased." With false enthusiasm, she lined up sharpened pencils in shades of black, gray and white. "Guess what's next?"

"What?"

"Rocks!"

"God no." The crick in his neck screamed when he'd straightened from the hunched over position. His poor backside had lost all feeling from sitting on the hard chair. No breeze had stirred the frilly curtains, making the already stifling atmosphere even more unbearable. How did people stand being stuck inside in one place all day, every day? He'd been at it scarcely an hour and he longed for a lungful of refreshing night air. He glanced at Tate to see how she'd fared.

She looked fresh as a daisy. Well, except where her hair stood on end from repeated, probably frustrated passes through it with her hands. And her bottom lip was temptingly plumped from pulling it between her teeth. Sighing, she extended her arms high, the middle flaps of the fringed halter-top separated, giving him a glimpse of her cleavage. "You have another suggestion?"

Hoo-boy, did he ever, but it didn't have a damn thing to do with rocks…unless getting his rocks off counted. He didn't dare let his thoughts follow that direction. Right now he had to convince Tate to finish the landscaping schematics. Tonight. His gaze shifted from the picture of cats playing poker on the far wall to the stained glass panel beside the front door. "I suppose I could get my clipboard from the truck and show you my preliminary ideas for your landscaping. Put all this newfound knowledge to the ultimate test."

Tate's elbows landed on the table and she studied him curiously. "You think you're ready for something so elaborate?

No. But you are.

Damn if beads of sweat didn't break out on the back of his neck and trickle down his spine. Had she sensed his ulterior motives? He shrugged, wondering if it looked as forced as it felt. "Truth is, I'd like to turn in the final landscaping design to the Beautification Committee before you start investing in plants, grass and rocks. Especially if they don't approve of the plans and demand a bunch of changes."

& & &

Although his explanation seemed reasonable, there was something slightly off about the way he'd phrased it. Tate was at a loss to put her finger on specifics. "I guess I could take a look."

Before she suggested they tackle the project another day and delve into the sex lessons, he'd bounded out of the house. He returned brandishing the clipboard. Plunked the plans in front of her tired eyes and waited expectantly.

One brief glance and she knew the plans needed way more than a quick look. She gave a silent groan at the childlike scribbles. Not that she dared vocalize her dismay. Nathan was mortified by his lack of artistic talent. But the Beautification Committee would never approve this dismal plan. Any delay in approval meant a delay in listing the house and returning to her life in Denver. She had no choice but to fix it right now.

In order to spare Nathan's feelings she'd have to divert his attention from the sad fact she was essentially starting from scratch.

After an hour he hadn't seemed to notice she'd erased every trace of his original drawings and replaced it with her own. The conversation hummed along, mostly about how he'd brainstormed plans for her landscaping. He asked and answered questions while she sketched like mad, implementing her skills to make his vision a reality. By the end of hour two, she worked in silence and he watched without comment. Finishing touches complete, she slid the clipboard to him for his perusal.

"Well? What do you think?"

"I think you are amazing," he said, his gaze glued to the almost 3-D explosions of color on the paper. "It's like you read my mind. This is exactly what I'd envisioned." Nathan looked up at her, his eyes wistful and pleased. He cupped her face and brushed his mouth across hers. "Thank you."

Startled by his show of affection, Tate leaned into his embrace. "I should be thanking you."

He chuckled against her cheek. "Oh yeah? My back would be singing your praises if we could veg on the couch for a while. These chairs belong in a torture chamber."

She'd forgotten he'd worked a twelve-hour day. "I agree. You want something to drink?"

"No." Batting away his hair, he vigorously rubbed the back of his neck as they strolled to the sofa.

"Why didn't you braid your hair earlier?"

"Honestly? My arms were too tired."

"Want me to braid it?"

"You wouldn't mind?"

Mind? She drooled over the prospect of wrapping that black silk around her hands. "Not at all."

Nathan placed his rough palms on either side of her face. He kissed her with a mix of passion and tenderness that made her lips tingle and her head buzz. "Where do you want me?"

In my bed. Naked. Above me. Or below me. Snap out of it.

God. Was she turning into a nympho? Okay, technically she couldn't be a nympho. One actually had to *engage* sex in order to be a nympho. Logical explanation for her behavior was Nathan emitted some strong pheromones when he was touching her. She hadn't exhibited these shameless sex-on-the-brain thoughts during their art lesson.

"Tate?"

"Oh right. Face the door." She squeezed in behind him as he perched on the edge of the couch. "Relax."

Her fingers untwined the smooth chestnut strands shot through with gold. The unique color must be from the hours he spent working in the sun. She'd kill for such perfect hair. No wonder he kept it long. When she noticed the tension rolling off him she began by massaging his scalp. Crown to nape, back and forth, left to right, from his cute ears to his strong jaw until he practically purred.

Eventually Nathan's muscular shoulders eased down. His head drooped toward his chest. She began to braid his hair. She took her time, enjoying the simple intimacy of touching him without restriction.

"Tate?" His voice was strangely soft and tentative. "About that first after dinner suggestion?"

"Yeah?"

"I'm considering it."

Everything in her body went tight. Feeling victorious, she kissed him. She let the tip of her tongue taste the fine surprisingly silky hairs on the back of his neck. "Forget I mentioned it. Not very spontaneous for me to plan it out like I did your landscaping design."

"Is that another thing you want? Spontaneity?"

Tate took another small nibble of his marble smooth skin. Inhaled his fresh manly tang with the underlying scent of her vanilla shampoo. "Now that I have this sneaking suspicion we're taking things slow, I'll admit I'd like to be surprised at that magic moment."

"Like crawling in your bedroom window at midnight kind of surprised?"

"No. Got something to put on the end of this rope?"

His triceps rippled when he passed over a fabric coated hair band.

She tugged his head back by the braid. "But I pretty much told you I'm up for anything. Soon, I hope."

He immediately tensed up.

Tate laughed. "But, hey. No pressure. Now that you've lost every bit of relaxation, why don't you lie down?"

"Come on, Tate, give me a break. A man can only take so much."

"Seriously. Your spine is so stiff I could crack concrete bricks on it. How about if you lie facedown and I'll massage your shoulders and back?"

His feet shuffled on the edge of the Oriental rug. "Why are you doing this?"

"Because I want to. No strings, Nathan, unless you want them. But you do have to take off your shirt." She doubted she'd con him into taking off his sweat pants so she didn't bother to suggest it.

Nathan winced when he lifted the too small Sturgis Rally T-shirt over his head. He barely fit. Lengthy arms and legs hung off both ends of the couch. His back was virtually as wide as the floral cushions.

Tate sighed at the glimpse of all that reddish-gold male flesh. She straddled his tight butt and flexed her fingers. It didn't seem like work. Digging into his taut muscles, following the curves and hollows of his sleek skin. His body was absolute perfection. Without conscious thought her insides contracted in response to his purely masculine form.

By the time she'd reached the tapered section of his lower back, she realized just how completely she'd relaxed him.

Nathan had fallen sound asleep.

She whipped his jeans, tank top and boxers in the dryer. Grabbed the romance novel from the library table and settled in the Barcalounger across from the couch. He didn't stir. He didn't snore either, which was a bonus.

Even the buzzing dryer didn't rouse him. With a resigned sigh, Tate placed his freshly laundered work clothes on the coffee table. She covered him with a faded wedding-ring quilt. Something sweet moved through her as she watched him doze so peacefully. Yet stomping like an elephant held a certain naughty appeal too.

When he awoke, would he come looking to surprise her?

She slept in the nude. Just in case.

Chapter Nine

The next morning when Tate woke up, Nathan was gone.

Teeth-clenching frustration set in that nearly undid years of orthodontics. Men. Why hadn't their whole worthless species vanished right along with the dinosaurs?

Still, it was scary to think her judgment was still skewed. Even after the disaster she'd left behind in Denver regarding Malcolm.

Malcolm. His name slithered through the recesses of her mind like the snake he was.

At the time she'd considered herself lucky to snag the attention of Sir Malcolm DuMond—the attractive, charismatic man on the firm's fast track. Working with him increased her chances of making senior designer. Especially when he'd all-but guaranteed her the promotion—if she kept the details of the new, plum assignment quiet.

Tate hadn't thought it an odd request. Jealousy ran rampant between artists and most of her colleagues were a secretive bunch. She shoved suspicions aside when Malcolm suggested they work from his private office—after hours, instead of her stuffy cubicle. She'd believed this was her shot at the big time and poured every ounce of creativity into layouts, giving up nights and weekends. A social life paled in comparison to visions of a corner office, her impressive job title etched on a brass plaque. The pride on her mother's face at the awards ceremony.

Two weeks into the project Tate had slept with Malcolm. Office romances were expressly forbidden. But they jumped headfirst into the affair. Consequences be damned. No one would suspect straight-as-an-arrow Tate Cross possessed the sex appeal to attract a player like Sir Malcolm.

Yet it had bothered her that Malcolm called all the shots—not only in the boardroom but in the bedroom.

Unfortunately the clandestine meetings didn't equate to great sex. When Tate summoned the guts to question Malcolm about his lackluster performance between his Ralph Lauren sheets, he'd assured her the "cuddling" portion of their liaisons appealed to him as much as the act.

An act she'd swallowed hook, line and sinker. The day before the final client meeting, Malcolm had abruptly pulled her from the big presentation. Then Tate discovered the truth; Malcolm claimed he'd single-handedly created the print campaign. Thereby being named head of the art department. Not only that, he'd recommended another graphic artist for the vacant senior designer position he'd left.

Betrayal stung on both a professional and a personal level. When she'd demanded an explanation, Malcolm found the *cajones* to admit the only reason he'd slept with her: she was the best artist in the company—with the smallest backbone. She was too nice, too innocent about the ways of the business world to jeopardize her future by seeking revenge. He'd warned her if she fought him, *she'd* be the one out of a job.

Tate shattered her meek persona when she confronted Malcolm at a staff meeting.

Proving he'd used her designs in the project was almost as vindicating as blabbing the details about their relationship. His denials fell on deaf ears. Management saw their intimate association as much a breach of company policy as Malcolm's purported ethics violations. They'd both been suspended pending investigation.

She dumped grounds into the coffeemaker and wondered if her career would recover. Especially after her labor rep had invoked the little-known clause in the company's family leave policy that allowed her to take two months off. Returning to South Dakota to handle her late aunt's estate seemed the ideal—albeit temporary solution. On the cusp of her third decade, logic dictated she take time to determine the course of her life, now that her entire professional future was in jeopardy.

As the rich aroma of coffee wafted toward her, she glanced at the patched cracks in the plastered ceiling. Now logic decreed she run as fast as her short legs could carry her. Not only was she over her head in basic home repairs, she had no clue what to do about Nathan.

The phone rang. Doubtful it was Mr. Romance calling to apologize, although part of her hoped.

"Hello?" she said brusquely on the fifth ring.

"Morning to you, too, sunshine," her brother, Ryan, drawled. "Did I wake you?"

"You wish," she sneered.

"Pretty crabby for first thing in the morning. Aren't you usually chipper as a bluebird or some damn thing? Singing folktales while you make a coffeecake from scratch?"

"Ha ha." She poured Froot Loops into a bowl. "Not even close."

"What are you doing?"

Wondering why I didn't get laid last night. Wouldn't that blow his Pollyanna perception of her straight to hell? "Having breakfast. What are you doing?"

"Sipping mai-tais. Watching babes in bikinis and sweating under the tropical sun. Oughta be paradise."

"But it's not." Tate filled her "Employee of the Month" cup with coffee and slurped. "You okay?"

"Yeah. Lonely. Missed talking to you last week. Get your city mandate straightened out?"

"Sort of."

Confessing that she'd agreed to trade art lessons for landscaping with sex lessons thrown in…not a good idea. She couldn't lie. Ryan knew her too well.

Plus, if the deal fell through with Nathan she needed Ryan's funding to hire a new contractor.

"Tate? Still there?"

"Yeah. I just remembered. I…found a freelancer and he's… " She said quickly, "He's willing to work with me."

"Really? That's great. How much is he charging?"

"Not any more than I can afford," she said, clapping a hand over her mouth to stifle a giggle.

"What are his qualifications?"

Tate dropped the portable phone on purpose, paused, then picked it up again. "Sorry. What were we talking about? Oh yeah. I do need to ask you something and I want an honest answer."

The soft strains of cabana music filled the silence as he shifted the receiver. "Shoot."

"Do you think I'm attractive?"

The line went silent. "Come again?"

Tate sighed. Her brother was being polite? The situation was dire indeed. "I realize I'm your sister, but you'd tell me if there was something majorly wrong with my physical appearance that would turn a man off, right?"

"Why?"

"Well I started dating this guy, but he keeps backing off. We mess around a little and he stops like he's appalled he's been caught going at it with the babysitter." She hoped that tidbit would fluster Ryan enough he wouldn't remember to ask any financial details about the landscaping contractor.

But Ryan's coughing fit on the other end of the phone sounded serious.

"You all right?"

"Fine," he choked.

"What do you think I should do? I know he's attracted to me but I need to convince him to act on those impulses."

"I'm going to need therapy after this conversation."

Tate gnawed her fingernail, waiting at his deliberate pause.

Finally he sighed. "Bottom line. You want action? Act like a guy. Think like a guy. Set out to seduce *him*."

"How?"

"How the hell should I know?"

"Because you *are* a guy? What would you do if you were striking out with the ladies and needed some inspiration?" Like that'd happen. Ryan was the brooding bad boy type. Women flocked to him like lambs led to the slaughter.

A menacing chuckle exploded in her ear. "*I'd* watch porn. Those flicks are a veritable candy store of inspiring seduction scenes."

Tate groaned. Ryan certainly had gotten into the spirit of the conversation. "Porn? That's your best advice?"

"Hey, you asked." He swore and the phone shifted away again. "Love to finish this chat, NOT, but my beeper went off. I'll touch base with you as soon as I can."

"Be careful."

"Always am." The line went dead.

Tate drummed her fingers on the table and considered Ryan's suggestion. What did she have to lose?

♚ ♚ ♚

Nathan rang the doorbell and stood on Tate's porch holding a fistful of daisies. Most likely she'd toss them in his face. Since he'd conked out on her couch and slunk away without a word.

Two days ago.

God, he'd been some kind of idiot. Her eager soft hands had been all over him he'd taken that as his cue to snooze?

He snuck a peek at this watch. Five-thirty. He'd knocked off early hoping to earn brownie points, grovel, whatever it took to make up for his boorish behavior.

When he rang the bell again and nothing happened, he turned the massive wrought iron handle and found the door unlocked. "Tate?" he called. "You home?"

Her cute little VW had been parked out front, yet the house had the silent feel he associated with empty. "Tate?"

No answer.

Nathan wandered to the kitchen. The backdoor stood wide open. A gentle cross breeze stirred the red and white checked curtains above the sink. He plastered a smile on his face and stepped out onto the hot concrete slab. His grin disappeared.

Holy shit.

Tate was lying nude on a plastic chaise lounge.

He blinked. Nope. Not nude, semi-nude. The shimmery flesh colored bikini left little to the imagination and Nathan's imagination had been woefully inadequate. Damn. Heat rolled through his body as his gaze moved: slim thighs, curvy hips, tanned stomach and delicate ribs. His hungry gaze ground to a complete halt at her cleavage.

Breathe man, remember to breathe.

Nathan LeBeau had found breast heaven. He inched forward, as if in a trance, drawn to her, his own personal mecca. The warm breeze delivered the scent of cocoa butter and the sweet citrusy aroma that was hers alone. A mumbled prayer tumbled from his lips as he drank in nirvana.

Tate's sunglasses were perched on the end of her nose. She sang along with the hard-rock music on the small boom box, tapping her pink-tipped toes to the beat. A beer bottle rested temporarily on the captivating dent below her navel.

Oh yeah. Things were definitely looking up. Tate was sipping his *favorite* brand of beer.

Nathan's grin came back full force. Hot damn.

Should he surprise her? Yell, *Hey honey, I'm home!* Calmly toss the flowers at her feet and plead forgiveness? Or ditch the normal approach altogether and see if that chaise was sturdy enough to hold their bouncing weight? When the song ended he cleared his throat.

Tate emitted a little scream. Her hand flew to her heart, bringing his attention to the way her nipples peaked under her skimpy suit.

His every good intention sailed right over her eight-foot high fence.

"Dammit, you scared me." She pushed the sunglasses on top of her head and squinted at him. "What on earth are you doing here?"

"Looking for you."

"Well you found me. Now go away. I'm hardly dressed for art lessons.".

He grinned, giving her a slow once over. "Tate, honey, finding you in that extremely sexy excuse of a swimsuit is not a social blunder."

Her pink tongue flashed at him. "Not funny. Don't you usually work until midnight or something?"

"Usually." He wished for his own shades to hide the avid gaze he'd locked on her lush breasts. Sweat trickled down her flat belly until it disappeared into her tiny bikini bottoms. Not knowing what else to do he clumsily thrust the daisies at her. "However, today I knocked off early."

"For me?" She stared at the flowers suspiciously. "Why?"

"To apologize for falling into a coma Saturday night."

When Tate crossed her arms over her chest, blocking his view, he nearly shouted, "No!"

"I was more surprised you'd vanished than that you'd passed out on my sofa after the long day you'd put in. Why didn't you wake me?"

Nathan resisted the urge to shuffle his feet. "Because I felt stupid and didn't know what to say."

She measured him. Satisfied with his answer, she signaled for him to hand over the daisies. "Apology accepted. First time I've had a guy fall asleep *before* we had sex. But flowers weren't necessary." She frowned. "I told you I don't expect—"

"It isn't about what you expect, it's about what I expect from myself. I was tired and that's a lousy excuse." He watched her bury her face in the blooms and inhale. "When I saw these in the clearing—"

"Whoa." Tate held the flowers straight-armed between them as if they'd turned into skunkweed. "You mean you *picked* flowers for me?"

"Uh, yeah." Now his feet did shuffle at her narrow-eyed gaze. This was where she'd make him grovel. "They reminded me of you. Innocent looking on the outside, but you'd never guess they were wild."

A beat passed. "That is so sweet," she murmured. She stood and kissed his chin. "Come on. I'll put these in water before they wilt. You seem a little wilted yourself. Want a beer?"

"Sure." When Tate turned toward the house, Nathan stumbled over the chaise and his own tongue. Her barely-there bikini was *no* bikini in the back. No triangular piece of fabric, just one section of string. Running right up her...

Sweet Jesus, Tate was wearing a thong.

He squeezed his eyes shut briefly and swallowed hard. How was he supposed to think of romance? Or landscaping schematics? Or anything else when all he wanted was to get his hands and his mouth all over her? Like right now. His jeans grew snug as the scent of hot woman permeated his pores. Her scantily clad image burned into his brain. He contemplated several illicit scenarios right there on the patio.

"Nathan? What's wrong? You look ready to pass out."

A low growl rumbled from his chest. "And you're surprised? You about gave me a heart attack when I noticed you wearing that."

"You act like you've never seen a thong before."

"I'll let you in on a little secret. Those things might be the norm in public in Denver, but they're pretty damn scarce around Spearfish, South Dakota."

Tate's wrinkled nose reflected her annoyance. "I don't care if you don't like it."

"Does it seem like I don't like it?" His hungry gaze rolled over her, making his pulse pound from throat to groin. "Do you have any idea how incredible you look? Very bad on my resolve to keep my hands off you."

"I don't want you to keep your hands off me." Her gaze dropped to his bulging fly and lingered, then cruised back up to meet his eyes. "From the looks of it, keeping your hands to yourself is the last thing you have in mind too." She flounced into the kitchen.

Nathan waited, hoping his tender, romantic side would surface. Because in about two seconds the aggressive, take-Tate-on-the-patio side would fight to be free.

Think of the job, man.

Big surprise it didn't work.

He tried conjuring romantic situations. Candlelight glowing across her petal-soft skin. Sultry music for slow dancing surrounding them. Sweet nothings he'd whisper in her perfect little ear. The innocent brush of her short hair across his smoothly shaven cheek. How exquisitely her feminine curves would melt into his hard body.

Hard. Yeah. Right now he had a hard-on that'd break concrete and he hadn't even touched her. What would happen when he did?

No time like the present to find out.

Inside the kitchen, erotic visions exploded; Tate bent over the table, anchoring his thrusts from behind. Tate perched on the washer, legs spread wide, while he dropped to his knees. Tate straddling him on a kitchen chair, his face worshipping her breasts. Hot need pounded at him from every corner of the room.

Even the cold beer on the butcher-block counter didn't cool off his frenzied thoughts. He wiped the sweat from his brow. He had to be strong, even in the face of his overwhelming lust. He could do this romance stuff. Dammit, he *had* to do it this way. His future depended on him retaining a cool head especially when the one in his pants burned red-hot.

He inhaled her scent and followed the mix of coconut oil and heated skin. She hadn't gone far.

In the doorway separating the living and dining areas, he watched her sort mail into the slots of a battered roll-top writing desk. Mmm. Mmm. Playing post office? He was game. Luckily she hadn't changed from her swimsuit nor had she in a fit of pique bothered covering up her near nakedness.

Good.

The muscles in his groin tightened as he stealthily moved closer. Seconds later he spun her to face him before he pressed her against the wall.

꿈 꿈 꿈

Tate blinked at the smoldering look in Nathan's eyes. "What?" His sheer size dwarfed her. Made her feel a little afraid and completely secure at the same time.

He held her gaze. Drank his beer. Bracing his left hand above her head, he lightly traced the ridged bottom of the cold bottle across her stomach from hipbone to hipbone. "You know what."

The muscles in her belly quivered, sending a rush of heat south. Nerves, nipples, throat tightened. "Save your breath if we're going to *talk* some more. I've heard enough."

"Me too. I finally got it."

She gasped when he zigzagged the icy bottle over her navel, rolling it over her ribcage so every bone felt the stinging cold. The slow glide up and down the valley of her breasts was pure torture. He outlined her nipples with the bottle tip, then brought it back to his mouth to run his wicked tongue around rim. Not once did those heavy-lidded eyes break contact. Her blood thickened. Her pulse raced. Tate moistened her dry lips. "Got what?"

He set the bottle on the floor. His mouth lowered, breathing cool air across her sun-warmed shoulder. "Got that you don't want to hear my ideas on romance or a lengthy lecture on xeriscaping. That you'd rather have this."

He kissed her. Hard. Crushing their mouths together, he angled her head, pulling her chin down with his thumb to open her mouth wholly to his assault. Hot, wet sweeps of his darting tongue. His taste sizzled. Teased. Then his greedy tongue found hers and soothed, thrust, suckled. Gentle palms framed her face. His fingers dug into her tingling scalp even as his mouth destroyed and branded her.

Tate couldn't catch her breath. His teeth seductively scraped her bottom lip. She inhaled and felt a butterfly brush of his warm lips against hers before Nathan dove in to expertly plumb the depths of her mouth again. This kiss was softer, but no less insistent. No less potent, the sensuous way their every breath mingled and fed the desire. Tangle. Retreat. Tate's body roared, aching for a deeper connection. Still, he merely kissed her. Gorging on her. As if he'd been too long denied her taste. Finally his hands grasped her shoulders. His thumbs slid across her damp skin to press the pulse racing in her throat.

She took that as a sign. Allowing her hands free rein, she smoothed her hands down his chest, needing to find a single patch of his bare skin to assure her this was really happening.

He braceleted her wrists and brought them by her sides. He lifted his mouth.

At the loss of contact, she whimpered, "Nathan—"

"Ssh. I may be slow on the uptake but make no mistake I'm in charge. Rule number one of this lesson." His lips toyed with hers. "Keep your hands against the wall unless I tell you differently." He positioned her hands palm side down, next to her thighs, taking a moment to run one wayward finger up the center of her body.

She swallowed hard. "Okay."

"Good. Now, where were we?" he murmured.

"On the way to the bedroom?" Tate suggested. She curled her hands into fists against the tiny kernel of fear that he'd stop touching her.

"Mmm. Not yet." His hair tickled her nose. "I'm not done kissing you." His breath exploded over her lips and she drank him in. "Lips like these gives a man all sorts of ideas." He drew the tip of his tongue across the seam, slowly, tiny flicks of flame urging her to surrender to the heat.

When she gasped at the erotic sensation his clever tongue dashed inside for a quick taste. Her interior muscles clenched.

"I think about this mouth." He nibbled her top lip from corner to corner. Then he ran his tongue along the underside near her teeth. "Fantasize really." He used the wet inside rim of his bottom lip to trace thrilling circles over her lips. "About things I'd like to do to it. Things I'd like to see this pouty mouth doing to me."

Tate trembled against the near orgasmic experience of simple mouth on mouth. She was drowning in sensuality with every lazy sweep, every suctioning pull of his tongue. Helplessly her head fell back against the wall.

Nathan kissed her again, growling deep in his throat, "Don't move."

Hot open-mouthed kisses trailed down her cheek, her jaw line, the tip of her chin. His labored breathing heightened her awareness, releasing a delicious shiver down to the marrow of her softening bones.

Tate moaned. Electric shock therapy. That's what it felt like, his moist mouth feasting on her tingling skin. Turning her head to sample him, she lost her mind in his raw taste. He swung away from her explorations with a muffled curse.

Blazing a damp path down her neck, he flicked his tongue to the beat pulsing in the hollow of her throat. Soft nibbling kisses on each side of her collarbone. The graze of his teeth. His mouth ventured lower. His fingers skillfully feathered up her wrists, her arms, her shoulders to rest on the curve of her neck.

She was afraid she'd beg for a firmer, faster contact. "Nathan—"

"Remember you telling me to have patience? Same goes, sweetheart." Nathan's big hands slid through her hair, gripping the short tresses. His callused fingertips casually stroked her nape. His thumbs traced every sensitive section of her ears. Then he splayed his hands wide. Gradually those thick, open palms descended to her breasts.

Her breath hitched, yet she stayed still. She ached to press the hardened tips into his too-patient hands. She craved the first intimate heated sensation of his slick mouth on her skin.

Hot puffs of air gusted over the scrap of bikini top. Her nipples pebbled to near painful points. He suckled the nubs through the silky triangular fabric with deliberate slowness, until tremors radiated from her cervix. She cursed his patience as he caressed the bottom swell of her breasts with barely-there touches of his fingertips. Another jolt of electricity arced through her blood when he captured her lips in a voracious kiss.

Panting, Tate broke away. "Please, why don't you—" Arching into him, she rubbed against the rough fabric of his shirt, wishing it were the muscled contours of his naked chest.

"Why don't I what?" He nuzzled the skin under her ear, sliding his jean-clad leg up and over her bare thigh. "Tell me."

"Touch me with your mouth."

"Where?"

She glanced down.

But Nathan latched onto her earlobe. "Imagine this," he repeatedly flicked his tongue over the small flap of skin and sucked hard, "is your nipple, tight and hot against my wet tongue. Is this what you want?"

His mouth tormented her. His clothing rasped over her exposed skin. She wanted this man more than her next breath. "Yes."

Nathan retreated and she moaned her disapproval. When their gazes collided, he demanded softly, "Then offer them to me. Take off your top. Now."

His cheeks were rosy, either from desire or the stifling heat. Tate didn't know. Didn't care. Whatever strange magic caused her to go insane with lust around him had finally taken hold of him, too.

Thank God.

Nathan's ardent gaze locked onto her shaking hands as she reached behind her back to untie the strings.

Her bikini top fell to the floor.

Chapter Ten

The minute Tate bared herself in front of him, Nathan couldn't think. He softly ran the rough pad of his thumb over one pink tip, then the other. Cupping her right breast, he sucked the peak firmly into the wetness of his mouth.

Dear God, she tasted like heaven too.

Tate groaned but kept her hands clutched at her sides.

He didn't rush. Each glorious breast deserved a thorough exploration. Using his hot mouth in tandem with his hands, he lapped his fill of her sweet bottom curves. Pressing the globes together, Nathan lightly flicked his tongue back and forth, pursed his lips over her rigid nipple, and suckled carefully, reluctant to use his teeth on such delicate skin.

She bowed, thrusting out her dampened breasts. "Please."

He nestled his chin in her cleavage as he savored her smooth feminine skin against the hardness of his jaw. "Please what?"

"Harder." Her voice was scarcely a whisper. "Suck harder."

An answering growl rose from his throat. Nathan latched on to the puckered nub with his whole mouth and drove her shoulders against the wall. He clutched her ass, outlining the crease where hip met the thigh. While his tongue continued to lick and tease, his hands traveled the tiny scrap of material to the small of her back.

Tate's hips pushed closer.

Nathan wanted to drop his pants and drive into her. Feel her silken heat gripping his cock. He grasped the bottoms of her bikini in front and back, gently rubbing the slippery fabric between the velvety softness between her legs.

Suddenly Tate grabbed the waistband of his jeans.

He pulled back. If she touched him, he'd last about two seconds. "Your hands are supposed to be by your side."

"Nathan," she whispered. "I'm dying to touch you."

"The feeling is entirely mutual," he murmured, removing her hands from his pants. "However, I was touching you first and I'm not done. Turn around and face the wall."

Her eyes went wide and she stammered, "B-but—"

"I won't hurt you. I'd never do anything you don't want." He used drugging kisses until once again she seemed boneless. Helpless as he was against the purely sexual heat that exploded between them. "Trust me, Tate. You want this."

A spark of passion darkened her eyes. She turned around.

"Place your palms against the wall and spread your legs," he urged, eliminating the space between them.

She inhaled sharply when his groin rubbed against her butt.

He smiled. The abrasion of denim on her bare skin drove her wild. His hands roamed the flat plane of her stomach. Reaching those luscious breasts, he squeezed her nipples between his knuckles. He burrowed his chin into the susceptible curve where her nape met spine, continuing the rocking of his hips. His erection grew harder at the salty taste of her sweat coating her skin. "Tate," he breathed, "tell me what you want."

"Oh God. Touch me. Just touch me, please."

Nathan shifted his body away. Prolonged contact with her perfect ass and he'd embarrass himself. Hell, he was close to self-detonation now. He followed the contour of her spine with tongue, lips and teeth. His hand sought the soft curls between her thighs.

Tate's head dropped back at his first intimate touch. She shuddered from her blonde head to her pink toenails.

He chuckled. "Is this the kind of surprise you had in mind?" The scant fabric of her swimsuit bottoms were no challenge. His finger found and stroked those slippery and oh-so-feminine folds. His groin had a mind of its own and reconnected with her bottom. Playfully, he nipped the slope of her shoulder. "Open your eyes, sweetheart. Watch my hand between your legs."

Her breath caught. "I don't know…"

"Do it." Nathan rubbed her wetness up and over her sweet spot until she writhed. He positioned the pad of his thumb on top of the pouting bundle of nerves and felt her blood gather and pulse. A groan rumbled forth when he plunged his middle finger in and out of her slick entrance. "God, you are so hot. So wet," he whispered roughly against her hair. He thrust higher, harder when he realized she'd gone on her tiptoes in anticipation.

Her internal muscles greedily clamped around him.

Tate reared back, her neck slick against the moisture on his. "It's too intense. I can't. Oh please, I'm gonna…"

"Don't tense up. Let go, it'll happen." He wiggled another finger inside to reach—Ah yes!—her G-spot while his open palm pressed down hard where she most needed it. "Come for me Tate. Come hard. Come now."

And she did, with a small surprised scream. Her drenched sex convulsed and pulsed. She gasped as her climax intensified by the calculated speed of the rhythm of his fingers. Her essence poured into his hand, as the spasms slowed, then stopped.

Beads of sweat dripped down the side of his face. The back and forth grinding motions against her sweet behind almost proved too much. He carefully removed his painfully hard cock, concentrating on tasting Tate from her hairline to her shell-shaped ear. "You okay?" When his voice cracked he realized her release had shaken him to his very core.

"Okay? I'm better than okay," she purred. "And this was much better than romance, don't you think?"

Her words snapped him out of his sexual daze and spread panic. There was not one romantic thing about shoving her against a wall and fingering her to orgasm. Hot as the sun, but not what he'd envisioned for their first intimate encounter. He eased his hand from between her thighs. Swept his palm up her still quivering belly to linger on her plump breasts.

Apparently sated, Tate rubbed her temple alongside his cheek, then nipped his jaw. "Your turn."

"No. That was my turn and, believe me, I enjoyed it." Nathan inhaled the heady aroma of Tate: coconut suntan oil, the vanilla scent of her shampoo and the sweet musk of her arousal with a hint of sweat. "Although I am sorry. I wanted the first time I touched you to be—"

"Romantic." She sighed wearily.

"Wasn't how it ended up, was it?"

"Oh please." She burrowed into his arms. "Those moans I made were really screams of agony because I hated every vibrating second—"

"Smart aleck," he said, smothering her sarcastic protest with a kiss. He explored her mouth tenderly, using the rough tips of his fingers to memorize her silky skin. Amazing that a woman so small fit him so well. What a pair. He cursed his lack of finesse and she gave him grief for not taking what he wanted.

"Hell of a surprise, Mr. LeBeau," Tate mumbled against his mouth.

Nathan planted a chaste kiss on her forehead and moved back. Way back, toward the door. He tripped over the rattan umbrella stand in his haste to escape from the sexual tension that still crackled in the room like heat lightning.

"Why are you acting like you're leaving?"

"Because I am."

"Why?" Her bewildered expression nearly undid him. "We have all night to finish—"

"Not tonight. I have a mountain of paperwork to finish that can't wait."

She said dryly, "Gee, glad to know I rank right up there with dreaded paperwork."

"Dammit Tate, that's not the case and you know it. Trust me. It's a helluva lot harder to walk away than it is to throw you on the ground and satisfy the…" he floundered and swore, "…the damn cravings you bring out in me. Besides we are under a deadline."

"I don't even think about the damn deadline whenever we're together."

"Well you'd better think about it."

"Why?"

"Look at me, Tate." His arms spread wide so she could get a good look at his well-worn 501's and faded Henley. "I am not a gentle, easy man, in or out of the bedroom." Why didn't pacifying words come as easily to him as pipe dimensions and plant classifications? "I don't know if I can be. You're soft and sweet and nice… You'd better be damn sure you can handle my rougher edges, because once we start this, we both know there'll be no turning back."

Tate rose to every inch of her five-foot-two height and her blue eyes spit fire. She closed the gap between them in one giant step. "Newsflash: I don't want to turn back *now*. It might be good for you to remember something too, mister." She speared a finger into his chest. "I'm not a child nor am I as soft, sweet and nice as you believe. I know what kind of man you are."

Yeah, she was a real tough chick, spewing the kind of words that made his heart—not his dick—swell. "Speaking of agreements, we need to finalize financial arrangements for plants—"

"I'm not talking about plants, dirt and rocks, and you damn well know it, Nathan LeBeau."

He opened his mouth but her shrewd look stopped comment.

"Be warned. Next time we're together I'll have a few surprises of my own. And they won't have a blessed thing to do with landscaping."

Heat zinged straight to his groin. "Yeah?"

"Count on it," she said with a saucy smile.

Nathan grinned. "I can hardly wait."

໕ ໕ ໕

Tate hadn't seen or heard from Nathan in days.

When the doorbell chimed at five-thirty, she practically skipped from the parlor. She imagined his sexy body complete with killer grin filling the threshold, not another neighborhood kid selling magazine subscriptions or raffle tickets.

But Val sagged against the doorframe. She wore a neon orange maternity smock. With her belly larger than last week she looked like a pissed off pumpkin. "Hi!" Tate said with false enthusiasm. "Come in and sit down. You look exhausted."

Grunting, Val waddled to the couch. Tossed her bag next to the fireplace, right on top of Aunt Bea's ceramic pig. "That's because I am. What I wouldn't give for a shot of caffeine."

"No can do. And the only caffeine-free drink I've got is water."

"Then make mine on the rocks."

Tate set two frosty glasses of ice water on the sandstone coasters. "So what brings you here?"

"I'm here because you haven't called me." Val crunched a piece of ice and studied Tate critically.

Tate self-consciously smoothed the curled edge of her tattered, once-pink shorts. There was nothing wrong with going braless and skipping the underwear when stuck inside slopping paint.

"There's no smug smile of a satisfaction on your face so I'm assuming you and Nathan haven't done the deed yet."

"Valerie!"

"What?" Her eyes widened in a mock innocence. "You going to tell me to mind my own business, too?"

"Too?" Tate echoed.

"Yes *too*. Nathan told me to butt out when I asked him."

"I'm sorry, those are the rules." Tate held up her paint-stained hand and recited, "And I promise not to divulge graphic details about our agreement to anyone." Her shoulders slumped, sending the stretched out strap of her purple camisole sliding down her arm. "Truth is, there's nothing to discuss."

Val bobbled her ice water. "You're kidding, right?"

"I wish."

"Apparently my anger at being left in the dark is my problem, since nothing is going on in the dark or otherwise." Val rubbed a swollen hand over her equally swollen abdomen. "Let me get this straight. Nathan hasn't made any moves on you at all?"

Like Tate was going to confess the one time Nathan had touched her, she'd gone off like a nuclear reactor. And she'd practically begged him to do her in the foyer. Right before he hightailed it out the door. At this point the benefits in *not* divulging details didn't seem so bad. "I don't know about moves, but we've umm…kissed. And talked."

"You've talked?" Val repeated the word "talked" in hushed tones like it was a communicable disease.

"Yes. We even went out for ice cream. And he took me to the fair. Oh, we had dinner one night too." Geez. Things were the polar opposite of the wild sexual adventures she'd expected.

"Tate, what is really going on?" Val leaned as close as her belly allowed, grabbing a handful of lemon drops from the candy dish. "Don't you find Nathan attractive? He's got that whole ethnic thing going on, even if he's a bit rough around the edges—"

"I find him unbelievably attractive," Tate reassured her. She half closed her eyes and Nathan's likeness floated into view. The picture that lingered wasn't his delicious he-man physique, his raw male power and sexiness, but the aura of sweetness she'd uncovered. The all-too familiar loneliness she glimpsed in his eyes. That sadness made her want to tuck his exhausted body in bed and minister to him, not necessarily in a sexual manner. Tate frowned at that odd thought and it immediately snapped her out of her reverie.

"But didn't you want sex without strings?" Val demanded. "What's the problem?"

I don't know. Val's advice would prove invaluable but Tate wouldn't break her promise to Nathan. A feasible fib slid into her mind. "No problem, except I really like him. And I've umm…chickened out as far as wild uninhibited sex. So we're taking it slow. He really is a nice guy, but I guess you knew that." She smiled uneasily when she realized every word she'd said was true. She did like Nathan in ways she'd never anticipated.

Too bad *she* hadn't warranted the same tender consideration from him. He hadn't bothered to call her all week. Tate gritted her teeth and added to the white lie, "He's been swamped and feels guilty that he's cancelled our ahh…dates."

Val tapped her chin as if sensing Tate had perjured herself. When Tate blinked innocently, Val snorted. "Something fishy is going on but I'll pretend I don't smell it. Since he's too busy to come to you, you should drop in at the jobsite for the new Community Center on Creek Drive."

Tate scrutinized Val for ulterior motives. Val's her face remained blank. "You don't think he'd mind?"

"Nah. He could use the break. Man works like a slave. Half the time he forgets to eat." She snapped her fingers. "There's a thought. Take him dinner. He's partial to beef lo-mein and hot and sour soup."

"Thanks for the tip."

"Don't mention it." Val picked up her sketchbook from the coffee table. "What's this?"

"Just some doodles for art projects at the Girls Club."

"How is that going?"

"Good. Grace and I put our heads together and came up with a really cool curriculum before I started last week. The kids have been so pumped up that teaching them doesn't seem like a real job." She debated on telling Val about Grace's troubles. Val had dropped hints things were rocky with Luke and Grace. Except Tate didn't want to break Grace's confidence. Seemed her only choice was to hope her covert attempts to unearth answers from Val weren't hopelessly juvenile. "Unfortunately, I don't see Grace much. Have you talked to her lately?"

"No, I haven't talked to her but that wasn't a very subtle segue in the conversation." When Tate didn't smile Val turned serious. "What happened?"

"Grace started *crying*. That's what happened."

"Omigod! Why?"

"Guess Luke applied for a new position in Rosebud without telling her. He expects her to move." Tate took a big swig of water. "She was so lost and confused and didn't act anything like the efficient Grace we both know and love. I wish you had been there because I sure wasn't much comfort."

"Just having someone to listen to her had to be a huge relief. Heaven knows, she never calls me up and whines the way I do with her." Val tossed the sketchbook back on the coffee table. "She hasn't said anything else?"

Tate shook her head. "It's a fine line. She *is* my boss. But I don't want to press her for details about the situation with Luke if she's not ready to talk."

"I'll call her. Maybe between the two of us we can figure out how much support she needs." The line between Val's eyebrows puckered. "I can't believe the marriage would be over. They've always been one of the happiest couples I know. Even if they are both hyper-focused on their careers."

Did Val realize Nathan fell into that same "the job is everything" category?

Val heaved herself up, slinging the tangerine-colored canvas bag over her shoulder. "I'll call you tomorrow and let you know what I find out from Grace." At the last second she spun on her Keds and pinned Tate with a look. "Even if you can't give me the dirty lowdown about you and my brother you can give me a few general hints, right?"

Tate smirked. "We'll see."

& & &

Ginger and garlic scented the inside of her car as Tate navigated the unfamiliar dirt road. After one particularly hard bump, she'd expected to see bean sprouts and egg ribbons strewn across the floorboards. Miraculously the soup had stayed lodged in the seat.

She spied Nathan's truck among the other pickups, all big rigs with toolboxes and mysterious machinery poking out of the beds. Piles of building material littered the ground, but she didn't see anyone wandering around.

Damn. Where was he? She doubted he was the only one here, but she didn't want to feed him in front of an audience. She hadn't the foggiest idea what he'd said to his friends and co-workers about their relationship.

Relationship. Wrong word choice. Theirs was a business agreement with fringe benefits, plain and simple. She left the food in the car and skirted the piles of plastic pipes, sheet metal and fine powdery dirt, scouring the motley group of men that had just appeared. A tap on her shoulder nearly made her scream.

A blond man with a dusty beard stepped in front of her and smiled. "Can I help you?"

"Umm, yes. I'm looking for Nathan LeBeau. He still around?"

"Yeah. Last time I saw him he was over by the stockpile of gravel." He pointed to her red flowered flip-flops and added, "Kinda rough terrain for those shoes. Tell you what. Give me your name and I'll go fetch him for you."

Tate stayed put, torn with indecision.

"Nice try, Steve." Nathan's voice drifted from behind her. "But I'll take care of this."

Her first reaction was to leap into his arms. Probably the macho guys watching them from the clearing with unabashed interest would rag on him forever if she did something so typically female. Instead, she smiled brightly. "Hi."

"Hi yourself. What brings you here?"

Not the warm welcome she'd expected. "Val stopped by. Said you might need a break."

"I imagine she asked you a zillion questions."

"Yep, but I didn't crack under pressure. I'm a tough cookie, remember?" She reached for a chunk of pine bark clinging to his faded denim shirt. When her fingers brushed across the soft fabric, lingering a beat too long on the warm flesh beneath, his hand engulfed hers.

He met her shocked gaze before slanting his mouth over hers for a steamy kiss that fogged up her insides. "You're a tasty cookie too. I'm glad you came."

"Aren't you going to introduce us?" asked the blonde man who at some point had sidled up alongside them.

"Nope." Nathan's tone half-teased, but his eyes never left hers. He made no move to dislodge her hand. "Go away, Steve."

The man grumbled good-naturedly, leaving them alone.

Lost in the way Nathan kissed her, Tate almost missed the deep fatigue lines carved around his eyes. But when she leaned into him, he held her at bay.

"Tate, honey," he said, his thumb rubbed her jaw, "you don't want to do that. I'm dirty, sweaty and most likely I stink."

"I don't care." She wrapped her arms around his waist. Resting her head against the sun-warmed skin and firm muscles of his chest, a strange peace passed through her. "Mmm. Hard work, pure man and the great outdoors." She tilted her head back to look at him in the fading daylight. "Besides, you'll feel like hugging me when I tell you I brought you dinner."

"You did?"

"Yep. Chinese. It's in my car."

"I think I love you."

"So food *is* the way to a man's heart."

Something resembling hope danced in his eyes. "You looking for a way to my heart, *winyan?*"

"Nope. I'm looking for a way into your pants. Unfortunately my mother didn't have a clever saying for that scenario so I'm winging it."

"Glad Steve wasn't around to hear that one."

She froze. "Does it bother you that I'm here?"

"Not at all. Hope you don't mind if I don't introduce you around. I don't feel like sharing you." Behind a wide cottonwood tree he kissed her again. Sweeping his hands over her body as if touching her had healing properties. How she wished it did. He followed her across the glorified goat path to her VW bug and helped her unload.

Tate set up a makeshift picnic area, spreading an old velour blanket inside a grove of pines. She dumped the soup in bowls and opened the other square white cartons, spooning the noodle concoction on his plate. While Nathan devoured every morsel with his chopsticks she barely choked down an egg roll.

After they'd cleaned up, he settled back against a spruce trunk. His ever-present clipboard hit the rocky ground. "Come here."

Tate dropped beside him, trying to avoid the pine needles. She didn't need to turn her bare legs into an acupuncture experiment.

"I said come *here.*" He lifted her between his outstretched thighs, aligning his front to her back. "Comfy?"

She scooted backward until her butt met his groin. She wiggled suggestively until his breath hissed out. "Now I am."

His low chuckle sent the hairs on the back of her neck to full alert. "Wanna take a peek at the changes I added to your landscaping project?"

No, I want to take a peek at your package.

Focus, Tate. "I'm sure they're fine. I trust you."

Nathan's body went absolutely still beneath hers. A black crow screamed high above them and another answered in kind. His callused fingers stopped drawing lazy feather-light circles on her upper arms. "Then why are you really here?"

"If I tell you I don't know, will you believe me?"

"Possibly." His boots hooked under her ankles, bringing her thighs directly over the top of his. With his hands splayed over her legs, he stroked the same path of skin from the line of her shorts to the dimple in her knee. "But plying me with food is a highly romantic ploy."

"It is?"

"An impromptu picnic? With my favorite foods?" Stubble tickled her nape as his chin skated across her bare shoulders. "Admit you're liking this romance stuff."

"Maybe." Tate wondered how hands so strong hands could also possess such infinite gentleness. "But not more than sex."

A pinecone crashed behind them. "You'd rather we were on top of the picnic blanket? Going at it wildly like a pair of squirrels?"

Tate couldn't help but laugh even when his constant touches made her squirm. "I don't want to think about squirrels having wild sex. I want to think about *us* having wild sex."

"You didn't answer the question." Nathan nipped the upper part of her ear. Tingles raced the length of her body, inside and out. "You don't like this? Letting me touch you like I've dreamed all week?"

"You dreamed of me? Then why didn't you call? Especially since I know you're surgically attached to your cell phone?" She almost kicked herself with his big boot the minute the words left her mouth.

"Because I'm a lousy jerk. I've had little time to act on my wild squirrel impulses or anything else the last few days." His warm wet tongue dipped into her ear.

Tate promptly turned to mush. "I can't think when you do that."

"Then stop thinking." He traced the rim, bit the lobe, sucked on the hypersensitive skin between her jaw and ear. "God, woman," he breathed, "what you can do to me in two seconds flat with my clothes on is obscene."

She offered the other ear. "Do it again."

Nathan sigh was full of regret. "I can't. Dinner break is over. I've got to finish up before it gets dark." He left a trail of promising kisses along her shoulders. "But I did enjoy the surprise. Thank you."

She twisted to face him. "This wasn't your big surprise. You'll just have to wait."

They stood. Golden light streamed through the tree branches creating misshapen shadows on the forest floor. Birds, animals, even the bugs were quiet. The eerie silence signaled the fading of day into evening. Nathan didn't seem to notice. He only had eyes for her.

He framed her face in his hands. Lowered his mouth and the gentle, tender kiss became rough and needy before he withdrew. Pressing his lips to her knuckles, he said, "Thank you for showing up here. Most people are afraid they'll find me knee-deep in sewage. I never get visitors."

"Never?"

"You're the first."

"Glad I could be your 'first' at something, too."

He smiled wearily. "Tomorrow night?"

"Sure." She smoothed her fingers over the lines of exhaustion imprinted in his face. She wished she could erase them, if only for a little while.

"I'll call you. I swear."

Tate watched him walk away. Confused again by his sweet, romantic actions and her own tangled emotions.

Emotions she was finding, much to her chagrin, that couldn't be blamed only her desire for red-hot sex.

Chapter Eleven

The phone rang and Tate answered it with a yawn. "Hello?"

"Hey, sexy girl. It's Nathan."

"You really did call me."

"I said I would." Heavy machinery sounds echoed in the background. "Look. I don't have much time to talk. What are you doing tonight?"

"I'd planned on going to Tanner and Tyler's Little League game." Not on the off chance he might show up. The twins would be snoring in their bunk beds long before Uncle Nathan quit working. "Why?"

"I've got a more tempting offer," he said.

That possibility jolted her from her lethargy quicker than a caffeine injection. Did this offer involve her body draped around his while the fan cooled the sweat from their naked, satiated selves? Yeah right. Might as well imagine being named artistic director at a Madison Avenue ad firm, 'cause it seemed neither scenario was happening anytime soon.

"I could swing by and pick you up, say at 7:00? The nursery is open until 8:00—"

She gasped as panic set in. "Val had her baby? When? Why didn't anyone call me before now—"

"No, not the nursery at the *hospital*, the *greenhouse* nursery. Where we need to pick up trees and bushes for your landscaping?"

"Whew," she laughed. "Had me worried there for a second." A loud grinding noise flowed from the receiver followed a stream of curses. Then silence. "Nathan?"

"Sorry," he said. "Eight, then? After I get the nursery business out of the way, I'd like to...well, I've got a surprise."

A surprise? She remembered the *last* time he'd surprised her. In mind-blowing, orgasmic detail. Were they finally getting down to the nitty-gritty, down and dirty terms of the deal? "What kind of surprise?"

"The kind which requires swimwear. The thong suit would be nice," he added with a low male chuckle.

"My thong swimsuit? Why am I not shocked that this 'surprise' entails more mystery and romance?"

"Bring a towel too. See you later." He hung up.

Without doubt, she'd be unable to accomplish another thing today. Luckily she'd already drawn up her lesson plan for tomorrow's art classes.

Nathan showed up promptly at eight. Before he uttered a syllable, he tugged her against his solid frame. He wrapped his strong arms around her in a bone-crushing hug. Then he pulled back and studied her face as if he hadn't seen her for years, instead of days. He brushed a roughened fingertip down her cheek, then across her bottom lip.

She breathed him into her lungs. Felt him in every pore.

He kept their gaze locked until the breathless moment their lips finally touched.

It was a devastating kiss. Amidst the sparks short-circuiting her brain, Tate suspected that a man who poured such pure emotion into a mere kiss was a man worth keeping. Too bad that wasn't an option.

"It's strange. I hardly know you and yet I missed you."

Not so strange, since she felt the same way. "We could remedy that." She slowly ran her hands down his wide back. "Let's stay here," she latched on to his hips, bumping his pelvis to hers, "and get to know each other a whole lot better."

Almost immediately he stepped back. He gave her an indulgent smile and a quick peck on the forehead. "Tempting. But your surprise awaits."

She sighed, grabbed her stuff and followed him outside.

"Where are we going?" Tate asked vaulting herself into his truck.

"To the lake."

"At night?"

"Yep."

When he downshifted at the stoplight she was fascinated by the raw power in his muscular legs and the way his sheer masculinity seemed to fill every bit of the confined space.

He gave her a curious sideways glance. "Ever been on a moonlit boat ride?"

Tate pictured Nathan, half-naked with his long raven hair flying behind him as they skimmed the water's surface. Then the violent rocking motion of the boat on the water as their bodies slapped together, moonlight bathing their wet skin. She clamped her legs together to stave off the gathering heat.

"My friend Steve," he continued, oblivious to the added hitch in her breathing, "offered us the use of his boat. Said it's amazing to watch the moonrise over the water on a summer night."

"I'm sure it'll be spectacular." She directed her gaze out the window away from the sexual thoughts Nathan inspired.

"He did lend it to me on one condition." He paused and turned down the red dirt road leading out of town. "That I bring you to his annual pig roast. Are you interested?"

His uncertainty was sweet. Looking at big, macho Nathan LeBeau, she couldn't believe the man was actually shy on occasion. "Sure. Sounds fun."

The soft twang of county music filled the truck cab. They remained quiet for the rest of the drive. Nathan entwined their fingers and Tate's skin prickled from the way his rough thumb grazed over her knuckles. Talk about depraved. She was extolling the sexy virtues of his *thumbs*.

"I've got snacks in the cooler," he said as they pulled into the marina. A bait shop/convenience store sat prominently on the hill across from the nearly empty parking lot and the line of porti-potties.

Tate stared at him. "Okay now *I'm* the one who's frightened. A picnic and a moonlit boat ride? You're still serious about this romance angle, aren't you?"

"Did you think I'd changed my mind?"

"After what happened the last time we were alone together? I'd definitely hoped." She directed her gaze over the lake to watch the sun's last golden rays flash brightly across the blue-green water.

Nathan grabbed her chin, forcing her to meet his eyes. He used the same gentle stroking motion on her jaw that he'd perfected on her hand and she felt herself melting again. "Regrets about that, Tate?"

"Only that you left. But then again, that part wasn't a surprise."

"Small steps," he said softly. "Remember?"

Irked that he believed it was his right to call the shots, Tate reinforced her determination something had to change. Tonight. "Being a person of small stature, I'm more in favor of a giant leap."

"*Winyan*, you'll be the death of me." He hefted the enormous cooler on one broad shoulder and headed toward the docks.

Nathan had barely begun unhooking the boat tarp when a man stomped across the floating planks and stopped behind him. "Hey, Tonto, this here is private property."

Nathan's back went rigid.

"I ain't seen you before," the sneering man continued, "so that means you got no business messin' around here. Now take off before I call the ranger. Or the sheriff."

Slowly, Nathan faced the man. Tate's own cheeks burned hotly when she saw the humiliation etched in hard lines on Nathan's face. How often did he have to deal with insults and insinuations because of the color of his skin?

"Excuse me, *sir*," Nathan said through clenched teeth, "but I have permission from Steve Campbell to use his boat tonight."

The man snorted his disbelief.

From the pocket of his swimming trunks, Nathan extracted a boat key attached to a black lanyard. He dangled it in front of the old man's rheumy eyes. "See? Official and everything. But if you'd rather, you're welcome to call Steve and make sure an *Injun* isn't making off with his prized boat." He paused. "Or better yet, go ahead and call Deputy Black Wolf since he's a friend of mine."

Weighty silence followed, only punctuated by the vindictive man's agitated breaths. Finally he turned on his heel, muttering, "Lazy damn Indians oughta stay on the rez where they belong."

By the time the man threw his last dirty look over his hunched shoulder, Tate was fuming. "I can't believe—"

"Just forget it, okay?" Nathan rolled up the green tarp and stowed it.

She leveled her breathing and regained control of her temper. "How often does this happen?"

"More often than you want to know." He gave her a calculating look. "You sure you don't mind being in the company of *kicisica*?"

Startled by his lapse into Lakota, she demanded, "What does that mean?"

He shrugged. "Bad one."

"Oh, don't be ridiculous, he's the..." she didn't dare try to repeat the difficult to pronounce Lakota word, "...the bad one."

"Glad you think so." With a hard jerk he untied the boat from the moorings and motioned for her to climb aboard. "Besides, I refuse to let him ruin our night." With that said, he guided the hull around the end of the dock and jumped in the driver's seat at the last minute.

The boat was one of those low-slung models; sleek, sexy, shiny red with an engine that purred. Once they'd putted away from the docks, Nathan opened the throttle.

Tate leaned over the bow as cool water sprayed her face, rolling her body into the cresting waves as if she were part sea nymph. Despite the previous confrontation, the night seemed ideal: a gorgeous man, a little romance and her inhibitions tossed to the wind. If not perfect, damn close to it.

Last hints of golden sunlight glinted across the water. Besides a fishing boat on the far side of the lake, they were alone.

The boat swayed in the soft swells as the sun set. Nathan dropped anchor. The day fell deeper into twilight. The low moon started ascending into the evening sky.

Tate sighed and wiggled her bare toes on the roughly pebbled surface of the boat's bottom. "I wish I could paint this."

Nathan rummaged in the cooler and spread a picnic across the back seats. "Why can't you?"

"I can. I mean I just don't have enough time. Most of my day is spent doing the type of art that pays the bills. Then I'm too tired and sick of it to create the type of art that fills my soul." She glanced at him, wondering if that admission made her seem hopelessly...hokey.

He tossed her a Diet Pepsi. "And yet you chose art for a career. Why?"

Tate squirted cheese on a cracker, added a fat green grape on top and grinned when he grimaced at her concoction. "Who said I chose *it*? *It* chose me, much to my mother's dismay." She made a wry face before she popped the morsel in her mouth.

"Really?" he said, snatching the cheese canister. "She had a specific career in mind for you?"

"Just a business degree."

"That doesn't seem too bad."

"Followed by a master's with an emphasis in international finance. So not me." She rolled her suddenly tight shoulders. "Of course, I haven't told her I'm teaching art classes at the Girl's Club." Or the deal she'd struck with Nathan. She couldn't fathom how her mother would react to that bit of news. "I'd never hear the end of it."

His eyebrows lifted. "You're a natural for teaching."

"Thanks. I love it. The kids are great. I don't remember ever having that much enthusiasm. It's contagious. Makes me wish…" *That I'd followed my own dream instead of my mother's.*

"So what did you want to do, when art chose you?"

"At the sophisticated age of eighteen?" She smiled, thankful he hadn't pursued the topic of her strained parental relationship. "Move to Paris, of course. Suffer for my muse. Wear a velvet beret, sketch on the street for francs, drink strong coffee everyday in the same little sidewalk café. Embark on a torrid affair with a much older French man. Then settle down with my one true love to paint and teach."

"Sounds romantic."

"You would say that." When Nathan blushed, Tate was completely captivated. "Unfortunately, that's what my mother decided too. I applied to The Art Institute of Denver, and was expected pursue the path she picked…" Tate fiddled with the tab on her soda can. "See, my mother didn't have a career, so she was determined that I would. We compromised. I did it her way and I have a bachelor's degree in graphic arts." She pushed the immediate burst of anger aside. "Anyway, Ryan claims she wants me to be successful since he is the rebellious one."

He frowned. The Triscuit stopped halfway to his mouth. "Who is Ryan?"

Did she detect a smidgen of jealousy? "Ryan is my know-it-all older brother. Seems I've spent my whole life, even adulthood, arguing with my mother about what's best for *me*. She is appalled that I'm here, not in Denver fighting for my career."

"Fighting for your career?"

Not time for confession or for Nathan to believe she was still under her mother's thumb. "Long, boring story. So enough about me not living up to parental expectations. What about you?"

By the sly grin tugging at the corners of his sinful mouth, he was amused by the abrupt subject change. "Spent eight years in the Army. Wanted to be in the field fulltime. Covert operations, all that cool stuff. Mostly they stuck me inside behind a supply desk. After my dad's heart attack, I came back here to help out. Only, he wanted to retire so he sold the business to me. I've been here ever since."

"Was building utilities your first career choice?"

"Working for myself was a long time dream, even if I do spend most of my time in the dirt. I like being my own boss."

"Your boss is a slave-driver."

Something like guilt narrowed his eyes. "You sound like Val. I like working. I've maintained my dad's business, regardless if it isn't glamorous or if it leaves me little time for other pursuits."

She didn't comment on the specifics of those pursuits, he didn't need her judgment of his hectic schedule. Plus, he'd sensed she didn't want to discuss her parents or her stalled career in Denver, so she returned the favor. "How often do you see Val?"

He scowled at the grape he'd inadvertently smashed between his fingers. "Not near enough. It's been fun, watching her brood grow, and weird seeing my little sister as a mother. Her bossy streak comes in handy with the monsters. I'm jealous as hell of her family and social life." Nathan shifted, as if embarrassed by his admission.

"I thought you'd have tons of friends since you grew up around here."

"A few. Mostly work acquaintances, now. I don't have much contact with the people I went to school with."

"Why not?"

He turned his profile to her as he looked at the sandstone cliffs on the other side of the lake. "It wasn't easy growing up being an Indian in a school of white kids."

Although Nathan and Val's parents were considerably older than hers, they'd never seemed out of touch. Or hadn't they known their oldest child had been so conflicted? "I can't imagine that Bev and Tom didn't encourage you to explore your heritage. Aren't there lots of other Native American families in Spearfish?"

"Neither of my parents grew up on the reservation. Since my dad is only half Sioux we didn't follow any of the Lakota traditions. Most of his immediate family has gone on to the 'happy hunting grounds' and I've never bothered to look for my birth parents."

She ignored his sarcasm. "But you speak Lakota."

"Not really." He turned back around and faced her. "I've picked up a few words here and there."

"Does it bother you—"

"That I'm a redskin in a white man's world?"

She lightly smacked his knee. "I'm serious. You should explore your heritage." Tate grinned when a brilliant idea popped up. "You know my friend Grace?" He nodded. "Well, she told me her husband, Luke Yellow Hawk is in a support group for Native American men."

"I think it's called Alcoholics Anonymous," he said.

His self-deprecating bit was getting old. "Would you stop?"

"Actually, I have heard of that group." He drained his soda and tossed the empty can in the cooler. "This engineer I do some work for, Jim White Feather, has been bugging me to join for about a year."

"So why haven't you?"

Nathan gave her a droll look. "When would I have time?"

"Point taken."

A fish jumped about five feet from the hull and a bird swooped down a second too late. A frustrated screech echoed. "I know I live in the Rocky Mountains, I just never seem to make it outside the city limits. I forgot how beautiful it is here," she murmured, watching the white bird take wing across the black sky.

"I'll say. You couldn't pay me to live in a large city."

A warning sparked in Tate's mind like an emergency flare. No matter how much she liked Nathan, emotional attachment was out. He had roots here. She didn't. This was nothing more than a temporary fling left on the South Dakota border the minute she hit the Colorado state line.

124

After a bit Nathan seemed content. Peaceful. They were as comfortable together as an old pair of shoes.

Which normally she would have taken as a good sign. But his relaxed nature irked her. She'd worn the tiny bikini he'd gone gaga over, yet he remained sprawled on the bench, apparently unaffected.

Tate shifted when her bare legs stuck to the leather seats. Blaming the deep-seated itch on the way her swimsuit chafed beneath the denim shorts was a cop out; she knew differently.

This distinct itch was courtesy of Nathan LeBeau.

A shiver worked loose. Lord, she wanted to climb out of her too-tight skin. Or…maybe…she should climb out of her clothes. If that didn't shake his complacency, nothing would. She stood and stretched, adding a heartfelt moan for good measure. "Ever been skinny dipping?"

Without pause, he said, "Yep. Have you?"

"Of course. I love it." Reaching behind her back, she tugged at the strings on her bikini top.

"Tate," he warned, his gaze glued to her chest, correctly sensing her intention to strip. "I don't know if that's such a good idea."

"Why not?"

"We're in an extremely public place."

She pointed around the deserted lake. "One boat, clear on the other side. If those geezer fisherman can see this far then they're in for a helluva show. Unless I'm that repulsive to you naked." After completely dispensing with her top, she added, "Although I'd argue that you have a serious thing for my breasts."

Nathan closed his eyes and said tersely, "You aren't repulsive in the least and you know it. As far as your breasts…nope. I'm not even going there."

Taking advantage of his unease, Tate quickly divested herself of her bottoms. Take control and seduce him, her inner temptress chanted. Standing on the bow, she tossed the two pieces of her suit in Nathan's face and dove in.

The clean water chilled her bare skin. Swimming at night seemed secretive and intimate. Perfect for seduction.

When she resurfaced Nathan was leaning over the boat edge so far the end of his braid skimmed the water's surface. "Dammit! You might've warned me you planned on abandoning ship in the dark."

"Sorry," she offered half-heartedly. "You coming in? The water is awesome." She floated to her back, giving him a brief glimpse of her bouncing breasts and the blonde curls between her thighs.

Holding her breath, she dove beneath the surface, plunging deeper into the darkness. At the sudden influx of bubbles, she reversed course, speeding back toward the faint light dancing above her. Tate popped up right next to Nathan. Damn. He still wore his conservative swimming trunks.

"Glad you decided to join me," she said huskily.

"Hard to resist when you're naked."

"You've done a fine job of it so far."

"That was before you reminded me of all my suppressed mermaid fantasies," he said with a grin. Treading water, he tilted forward, outlining her lips with his tongue before scrambling her brain with an ardent kiss. "You taste good." One fingertip glided over the water before it dropped to trace tiny, patient circles on her breastbone.

Tate trembled.

"Since you're the skinny-dipping expert," he asked mildly, "have you ever been kissed underwater?"

"No." She withheld another quiver as those clever fingers moved to lightly stroke her breast. "Is it like scuba diving?"

"Not even close." He inhaled and dipped below the water.

Desire rocketed through her as his hot mouth fastened on her cold nipple, working magic on her lake-cooled skin. Mesmerized by the licks and tugs of his sharp teeth and warm tongue, she forgot to tread water and promptly sank like a rock.

Nathan's large hands circled her hips and he hauled her back up. He kept them both afloat while she shivered and coughed. "You okay?"

Nodding, Tate coughed again. "Maybe we should save that kissing experiment for next time." She swam around to the back of the boat. "You coming?"

"I will be if I see you climbing up that ladder naked. Don't know what I was thinking. Get dressed."

The warm night air dried her body quickly. Tate wrapped the towel around her middle and called, "You're safe. I'm covered."

"Safe, yeah right," he muttered. The boat rocked as Nathan scrambled up the ladder. He froze when he noticed her swimming suit spread on the boat's bench seat. "You said you were dressed."

"No. I said I was covered," she gestured smugly to the boldly striped beach towel, "which I am."

Tate braced herself for the impending debate, but was utterly charmed when he threw back his head to the stars and laughed. He dropped into the seat closest to the steering wheel and hung his head. "I swear you'll be the death of me."

"Not tonight." She plopped right beside him, making sure her skin brushed his. "We'll just sit here and moon-gaze. I'll behave."

He grunted but didn't retreat.

They watched in silence as the moon arced across the sky, sending silver flashes of light rippling over the water. The boat rocked. A soft warm pine scented breeze wafted over them. Nathan dropped his arm behind her neck and gently pulled her against his shoulder.

Seemed they could just exist together—neither felt that odd compunction to destroy the serenity by filling the quiet air with mindless chatter. Not that the previous conversation had been banal. His admission of envy over Val's life had struck a chord in her. As did the underlying sense he too, was following a career path that hadn't been his first choice. Somehow she just knew he'd never shared that secret with any other woman. It gave her a newfound sense of purpose to share something equally intimate with him.

Tate's wiggling toes came in contact with Nathan's bare foot. Ah. Was there anything sexier than the soft top of a man's foot? Especially when every other part of his he-man physique was rough and hard? She rubbed her big toe over his, across the bone, around his ankle before replacing her foot on the boat floor. He hadn't moved a muscle. On the verge of expanding her tentative touches, Nathan stopped her explorations by picking her up and straddling her on his lap.

"Trying to play footsie with me, Tate?" He held her captive with his hungry eyes as he unhooked the towel inch-by-inch. The moment she was bared before him he filled his hands with her breasts. "I don't have a foot fetish but you were right about one thing."

His warm palms on her chilled nipples sent her blood tripping. Tate pressed her hips closer, literally thanking the stars above. "Right about what?"

"I have an obsession with your gorgeous breasts." Dark eyes fixed on her wild-eyed expression; he pressed the mounds together, raising her torso higher so both nipples were at his mouth level. His tongue darted back and forth and he sucked at protruding peaks hard, like a starving man. Lifting his head at her uncontrolled moan, he kissed her mouth with recklessness. His hands inched closer up her thighs to her core with each controlled thrust of his talented tongue.

Rocking against him, she clutched his shoulders for support. She rubbed her breasts over his broad chest, desperate to feel the rasp of his hair and muscle against her ruddy, sensitized nipples. His mouth fed at hers. Insistent, greedy, then slow and languid, making her dizzy with desire, wet with need.

"You drive me wild, Tate," he groaned, scattering heated kisses across her skin, until his thumbs breached the line of curls.

She pressed her thighs together, even when she wanted to leave them splayed open to his questing fingers. "I'll show you wild," she panted against his throat. Tate moved, but not the direction he'd expected. She slid down between his legs, hooking her fingers inside the waistband of his trunks. "Lift up."

He grasped her wrist. "What are you doing?"

"What do you think?" She tugged, but the wet material wouldn't budge. Damn. Val's comment about erections and swimsuits had been right on target.

"I don't think—"

"That's right. Don't think." Tate brushed her bare breasts over his shin, loving the erotic sensation of running her tongue over the coarse hairs on his legs. Her teeth sank into his muscled thigh. "Time for your surprise. Your choice. Take them off or I'll tear them off."

"You're serious?" Nathan peered into her face; half-hopeful, half-afraid. "You don't have to do this."

"I know. I want to." She kissed him, sucking at his tongue in a carnal preview. He groaned when she broke the kiss and licked a trail of hot kisses up and down the pulse quickening in his throat. "I really, really want to. So take them off. Now."

Another feeble protest tumbled from his lips before he disposed of his trunks with unsteady hands. His breathing turned rough when Tate dropped to her knees.

She didn't care that she was nearly crammed beneath the steering wheel. Her desire to finally touch him superseded all reason, even comfort. Her hands glided up the tops of his legs to pass over his narrow hips. She spread her hands wide, fingers squeezing the outside of his smooth, tight butt. Mmm. Small yet firm. Unlike the rod jutting from the dark springy curls that nearly reached his navel. Not small at all, she thought wickedly, but definitely firm.

She laved his belly button and the sculpted ridges of his abdomen, letting her warm breath follow the wet path, evoking tiny shudders and his encouraging growls. When his erection nudged her breastbone, Tate abruptly changed teasing tactics, desperate to feel every inch of that male hardness in her hands. In her mouth. Scooting back, one hand dropped between his thighs to fondle his balls while the other circled and pumped the satiny rigid length of his cock.

He sucked in a sharp breath when the pad of her thumb swept across the tip to spread the single drop of fluid.

An answering rush of moisture dampened her thighs. She bent forward and tasted him, reveling in the secret male scent pouring from his most private places. Places she intended to explore to her own curiosity and his satisfaction. She savored his salty, musky taste hidden under the clean tang of water.

Tate looked up to see Nathan watching her. His eyes were heavy-lidded and black with desire. His face flushed, breathing ragged. Maintaining eye contact, she took him deep, hollowing her cheeks, opening her jaw fully until the tip of his penis met the back of her throat.

A deep hum of approval erupted from his lips. His nostrils flared.

Slowly, she swirled her tongue around the silky length as she released him.

One inch at a time.

"Sweet Jesus."

Hiding her smile, Tate used the flat part of her tongue to stroke the thickly pulsing vein running up the front of his shaft. At the glans she flicked little whips of her tongue all the way around. Suckled the knob with just her lips. Repeated the process back down. Softly cupping his balls, she pulled his penis entirely into the wet heat of her mouth again.

Nathan's grip on the seat increased and he hissed.

Incredible, the power it gave her to pleasure him. The twitches, the moans, the sexy sucking sound of her tease and retreat. The feel of him lengthening in her mouth. The trust he placed in allowing her this intimacy. Tate kept a steady rhythm with tongue, hands and teeth, loving the way Nathan's tentative fingers had changed from gripping her shoulders, to fiercely digging into her scalp to hold her head in place.

Not that she had any intention of leaving him high and dry. She silently marveled at his astounding control, then in a blink of an eye, it disappeared.

His hips bucked twice and he groaned right before his balls lifted from her hand. With his cock curved against the inside of her cheek, his essence released in hot spurts. She sucked hard to his escalating thrusts, dazed by the way his ferocious orgasm had caused a throb in her internal muscles. She soothed his pulsing organ with her hot mouth and lips, tonguing the tip until the spasms slowed, then stopped completely.

A contented gust of air released from his lips and his body trembled one last time.

Tate swallowed, gradually easing back, letting a smile curl the corners of her mouth.

As far as surprises went, she was pretty sure now they were even.

Chapter Twelve

Darkness permeated the edges of Nathan's awareness. He worried the fuzzy feeling meant it had been a fantasy: Tate's blonde head between his legs, working him with her hot mouth, cool hands, and wicked tongue.

He cracked his eyes open at a soft, feminine sigh. She stood by the bow. Her legs braced apart, arms high overhead in an indolent stretch. The taut muscles of her naked back gleamed from the moon's reflection on the water, casting intriguing shadows over the curves and slopes of her lush body. His breath caught at her resemblance to a water nymph, sleek, luminous. Beautifully uninhibited.

Not a dream, thank God. Just the most stunningly erotic experience of his entire life. The unselfish show of Tate's generosity held him speechless. Breathless. He wanted to touch her. Taste her in the same mind-bending manner. Not because turnabout was fair play, but giving back to her even a smidgen of the sweet surrender she'd lovingly bestowed on him filled his soul with a sense of absolute rightness.

"Nathan?" she called softly as she donned her clothes.

"Helluva surprise, Ms. Cross," he said raggedly, managing to yank up his trunks on the first attempt. When he stumbled to his feet, he knew the reverberations coursing through his body weren't from the rocking motion of the boat. But the aftereffects from a coma-inducing orgasm courtesy of a woman with a heart as large as her wild streak.

Instead of retreating and ignoring the emotion clogging his throat, he went to her. Nathan held her face gently to let her see how profoundly she'd affected him. He dove into her mouth with a languorous kiss, tasting the remnants of her soda and his spent passion. "Thank you. I'd come up with something more original, but the synapses in my brain aren't firing yet."

"M-m-my pleasure." Tate smiled shyly then shivered.

He rubbed his palms up and down her arms. "Cold?"

"Yeah." She wrapped the towel tight. "And it's getting late."

Nathan pulled anchor, stowing it in the boat's floor compartment. The throaty growl of the engine made conversation difficult, but he was so stunned by the turn of events he found himself speechless anyway. Once he safely docked the boat and secured the tarp, he looked around to see if the insulting man from the bait shop still lurked about. God, that had been humiliating. Fortunately the lights were off and his truck was the only vehicle in the parking lot.

Tate's flip-flops dragged as they trudged uphill to the pickup. Why did he have this urge to swing her into his arms and hold her close until her face was slack with sleep? "You tired?"

Her smile was slightly embarrassed. "Must be past my bedtime."

"Sleep on the way home." He unlocked her door. "I'll take a rain check on dinner."

"I'm afraid you'll cancel if I don't get it in writing," she teased without her usual gusto.

"I promise to take you wherever you want to go." He kissed the inside of her wrist, locking their gazes while he gentled a hand over her face. "You are beautiful."

"Thanks." She closed her eyes but a pleased smile remained.

Half an hour later Nathan shook her awake. "Tate, you're home." Her eyes opened with that sexy, slumberous look he imagined she'd sport first thing in the morning. A whip of lust tightened his groin.

She leaned over the console to give him a quick peck. "Thank you. I had fun. Good night."

He stopped her retreat with long heated, kisses. Her moist lips shuddered and clung beneath his. "When can I see you again?"

A low, seductive laugh emerged as she nipped his bottom lip. "Nathan," she chided, "I am not the one with the overloaded schedule."

She had a point. He'd cancelled two dinner dates with her this week. "Friday night? I'll pick you up at seven."

"Pick me up?" she echoed. "Why do we have to go someplace? Why can't we just stay in and…"

Have wild, screaming, raw sex that wakes up the neighbors?

Neither had uttered that sentence, yet it hung in the dark confines of his pickup. Nathan cleared his libido from his throat. "Because I play in a men's pool league on Friday nights."

Her eyes widened.

She wasn't one of those snooty types that thought league pool was hopelessly blue-collar? Or worse yet, had the encounter with the idiot on the dock seeded doubt about them spending time together in view of public disapproval? "You got a problem with that?" he asked defensively.

"No." She mollified his flash of temper with a sweet kiss. "But since we'll be in public that means strip nine ball is out of the question." She grinned saucily before jumping out of the truck.

Nathan decided it was high time he stopped making any kind of assumptions about the very surprising, very engaging Tate Cross.

& & &

Two nights later, feeling uninspired by her artistic attempts or the television, Tate baked a batch of her Aunt Bea's famous sugar cookies. But the sweet confection didn't offer its usual soothing properties nor did the baking process ease her restless spirit.

She bit off a chunk and sighed. Sitting home alone wallowing in carbs seemed pathetic. But where to go on a Thursday night? Grace declined her offer of margaritas and Richard said Val was napping. She was sick of her own company. Her thoughts drifted to Nathan. What was he up to? No brainer. He was probably still working.

But the man had to go home sometime, right? She brushed crumbs from her chest. Speaking of home…why hadn't he invited her over to his place? Visions of a swinging bachelor pad appeared, complete with satin sheets, mirrored ceilings and a pleasure swing. The more she considered his oversight, the more outlandish were the scenarios that developed. It became imperative it that she discover just what Mr. Romance was hiding.

Like most small town people, she imagined Nathan didn't bother to lock up his house. She'd sneak over to his place, leave a plate of warm cookies to tempt him and be back home in time to watch the end of *ER*. No sweat.

Tate zipped across the quiet town in her yellow VW, cruising his street slowly so as not to miss his house number. The small, deserted-looking gray one at the end of the cul-de-sac with a three-car garage surrounded by a six-foot high chain link fence. Just as she suspected. No lights on inside or outside.

She parked in the driveway and debated. Should she knock first? Nah. That might ruin the surprise. She grabbed the plate of cookies and hurried to the gate on the other side of the garage. She shivered when the latch squeaked loudly in the too-still darkness. As she quickly rounded the corner for the back door, a huge black muzzle materialized from out of nowhere.

The beast snarled, spit frothing from a cavernous mouth that snapped shark-like teeth. Black fur stood on end. Growls alternated with low, menacing barks. It lunged, sporting razor sharp incisors that gleamed in the dark. Tate screamed and froze in place in terror, imagining those fangs sinking into her throat or ripping her leg from the hip socket.

The chain clanked, jerking the monster back.

She breathed again, without moving, afraid her heart would leap from her chest and the blasted animal would gobble it up for sport. Fat lot of good it did the beast was shackled. She couldn't move forward or back to the gate without knowing how far the chain reached. He'd lured her with his silence. Seemed they were at a standstill.

Stay calm. Think. Granted, she didn't know much about animals. The phrase "they sense fear" popped into her head. If she acted like she was in control the demon might believe it. Tate stared at the two eyes glowing red in the darkness. After a few minutes, the beast whimpered. It whined. The tail wagged.

The tail wagged?

Her ruse had worked? Praise cable TV and the *Discovery Channel.* With an alpha leader attitude, she commanded, "Sit." Miracle of miracles, it sat. And looked at her expectantly for some kind of reward. A long string of drool plopped noisily on the ground. Eww. She tossed over a cookie. The beast practically swallowed it whole. She threw another toward the cacophony of slobbering and chomping.

Tate sighed. Why hadn't Nathan told her he owned a trained attack monster?

Because you don't want to know anything about him besides his endurance in the bedroom.

Not true, her subconscious argued. This arrangement—for lack of a better term—was turning into something neither of them expected, a relationship of sorts. So why was she skulking around in his backyard in the dark, lobbing cookies to a creature that'd like nothing better than to tear her to shreds?

Because she had missed Nathan, plain and simple. Not in a tear-his-clothes-off and ravish him way, but in a snuggle-up-and-talk-about-our-days way. Wow. Somehow that was a much scarier thought than being eaten alive by this beast.

Tate nibbled on a cookie and considered her options. The beast whined. Sat. Begged. More amused than she'd admit, Tate said, "Roll over." The animal complied. She flipped it another cookie, grumbling, "He probably gave you some stupid name like 'Sweetheart' or 'Tiny'. If you were my mine, your name would be 'Killer'."

It barked in agreement.

"My God. I'm actually holding a conversation with a dog."

Headlights swept the garage. An engine idled briefly before a door slammed shut. A dark shadow raced through the open gate. The beast yipped and jumped, nearly choking in its joy for the master. We'll see who's the master now, Tate thought, chucking another cookie on the ground. The happy barking turned into loud crunching.

"Tate? Where are you?" Nathan sounded panicked. "You okay?"

"Peachy." Warmth flooded her and a reluctant smile broke forth. "Afraid I'm trapped over here."

At once she was crushed into his arms, the he wildly searched her body for…what? Bite marks? Missing limbs? Signs of demon possession? "What are you doing here?" he asked, peppering her face with kisses.

"Short version?" Tell him you missed him, her conscious prodded. She ignored it, not wanting to seem lonely and pathetic. Although she definitely fit that description and she suspected Nathan did too. "I baked you some cookies, but I'm afraid I sacrificed some of them to the beast so it wouldn't attack me."

"What beast?" He turned in the dark and pointed at the dark shape jerking the chain. "You mean Duke? He's just a dog."

Duke. She rolled her eyes at the macho name. "Someone played a nasty trick on you. That's not a dog. That's a rabid bear."

Nathan chuckled, which didn't earn him any points. "He's harmless."

"Try telling him that."

"Tate, Duke is a Rottweiler. He just looks mean. He's barely a year old. He does get overexcited sometimes—"

"Overexcited?" she repeated. "That thing tried to eat me!"

He grinned. "Can't say as I blame him much. You look awful tasty to me." He seemed to drink in her features before his warm mouth covered hers. Sweet, supplicating, he submerged her into the deep soul kiss like a drug.

The powerful addiction of his kisses and his reverent caresses seeped into the marrow of her bones. With the reluctance of a junkie forgoing a fix, she pulled away. "Not in front of the beast," she murmured. "He scares me."

Nathan waited a beat. "Seriously?"

The gentle caress of his thumb on her cheekbone made her feel safe enough to admit, "Most dogs scare me."

"Didn't you have a dog growing up?"

"Not for lack of trying."

"What do you mean?"

"See, I meticulously planned how I'd trick my parents into buying me a pet. I begged them for a pony *first*. Then a dog. But my scheme didn't work because I couldn't convince them to let me have even a small Persian cat. When I got my own place, it seemed cruel to leave an animal locked up all day." She winced, realizing what she'd implied. "But I didn't mean—"

Nathan cut off her apology with a soft kiss. "I know. The truth hurts. I feel guilty about leaving Duke penned up. Not his fault that I work so much. Val thought if I had a dog, at least maybe I wouldn't hate coming home to an empty house." His hands dropped to her shoulders.

Tate watched the play of emotions in his eyes before she cuddled closer. "Come on. Let's go inside. I'm dying to see your house."

He tipped her chin up. His eyes roamed her face. "Why? Did you think I lived in a tipi?"

"Hardly. While I contemplated the end of my life at Duke's ferocious jowls, my imagination ran wild on why you've got a guard dog in the first place. Got a cache of kinky stuff hidden in your closet?" She brushed tender kisses over his jaw, his lips, the corners of his mouth until he released a sigh. "Pity we can't sample anything tonight, but you look exhausted."

"I am. Although I am up for sampling those cookies."

Tate stopped when they moved toward the source of loud excited yipping. "So Duke is coming in, too?"

"Why? Don't you like him?"

"Even though we bonded in a Pavlovian way," she faltered, deciding for once to give Nathan more than a flip answer. "I don't like him nearly as much as I like you."

Nathan hugged her to his chest at her small confession. "The feeling is mutual."

"Besides, he slobbers," Tate pointed out.

"One whiff of you and I slobber, too. But Duke does need to come in. He's probably hungry."

"Not after all the cookies he ate."

હ હ હ

Friday night, cigarette smoke and country music clouded the air in the jam-packed bar. It'd been ages since Tate had spent an evening out with a date. Not that she and Nathan were dating. Still…something crackled in the air between them tonight. He ambled back to the pool table and she zeroed in on the yummy view of his killer backside.

"I saw that," a husky voice whispered close to her ear.

"Saw what?" Tipping the beer bottle toward her mouth, Tate studied Nancy's amused expression.

"The way you checked out how nicely Nathan's butt fills out those Wranglers." Nancy slurped the last bit of her Fuzzy Navel. "Mmm. Mmm. Don't be offended when I say he has the most extraordinary buns."

"Amen," two voices chorused from across the table.

"Does your husband know you ogle other men?"

"Yep. As long as all I do is look." Nancy grinned and chomped on the red and white striped straw. "So tell me, how long have you and Nathan been together?"

We aren't. The immediate denial popped into Tate's head, but she played along, convincing herself the little white lie hurt no one. "A couple of weeks."

"Funny how he hadn't mentioned that to any of us," Nancy said. "How did you two hook up?"

Initially, Tate had been nervous about meeting Nathan's friends. But when they'd welcomed her into their group, she'd relaxed and pretended just for tonight this was an actual date. "He's doing some work for me."

Nancy batted aside her sleek bob. "Of course it had to be business related with Nathan. That man works like a dog."

"Never has time for anything else," Tina added. "I, for one am thrilled to see him dating again. Someone nice this time, especially after—" She broke off when Vickie elbowed her.

"Especially after," Nancy interjected, "Nathan hasn't dated for awhile."

"I know," Tate said.

Vickie's jeweled fingers fluttered at her tanned throat. "You *know* about Kathy, the Indian princess?"

First time she'd heard her called that. Did Nathan prefer dating women with a similar ethnic background? It made sense, but the thought didn't sit well with her. "Not everything," Tate admitted with a tiny shrug. "Just the basic break-up story. Did you all know her well?"

Tina scowled, tracing the condensation from her highball glass with a violet fingernail. "Enough to be glad she didn't get her hooks into Nathan, although she tried."

"And she's still trying," Vickie pointed out.

"Yeah, she sure bitched about him working all the time but she was more than willing to spend his hard earned money. Luckily, Nathan wised up."

Nancy signaled for another round of drinks. "Let's not waste another breath on her when I want to hear the details about you and Nathan."

Over the chorus of oohs, Tina winked. "Fair warning. As Nathan's friends we feel entitled to ask you anything."

"And I thought Val was bad," Tate grumbled.

"No, I think Nathan's got it bad. He can't take his eyes off of you," Vickie said slyly. "And either he's got a broken pool cue in his pocket or he is very happy you are here."

"He does look more relaxed." Nancy gestured with the mangled straw. "How you managed to get him to borrow Steve's boat this week is a major miracle. Did you guys have fun?"

Tate nearly choked on her beer. Surely Nathan hadn't confessed to one of their husbands what had transpired between them on the boat? "Umm…"

"Are you are or are you not…" Vickie gestured vaguely.

"Sleeping with him," Tina supplied, when Tate looked baffled. "We're curious how that killer bod moves between the sheets."

How was she supposed to answer? If she couldn't spill the particulars to Val, Nathan wouldn't appreciate her telling the skimpy details to them. She shifted on the barstool. "Umm—"

"He's probably sweet, tender and romantic," Nancy offered.

Tate gave her a wry look which was completely lost on her.

Vickie's bleached-blonde hair stuck to her Miller Lite bottle as she vehemently shook her head. "No. Nathan has too much raw male power. I'll bet he's an animal."

"True. With his Native American genes I'll bet he has the single-minded concentration of a warrior on a buffalo hunt," Tina said dreamily.

They looked to her raptly and waited. Tate kept her expression bland. "He's very sweet and only exhibits animal behavior when I tie him up. He hates that."

By their raucous hoots, she knew she'd given the right answer. Tate laughed herself silly listening to their exploits. Although she spent time with Val and occasionally Grace, she realized how much she'd isolated herself since leaving Denver. There was nothing on earth like female camaraderie. For a while she'd even forgotten she was on a pseudo date.

But Nathan hadn't forgotten.

Tate was distracting as hell. Her bare legs dangled enticingly from the barstool, making him ache to run his tongue from toe to hip. Her conspiratorial laughter drifted on the smoky air and brought to mind her soft gasps the one time he'd allowed himself to pleasure her. The marathon pool game finally ended and he yanked her back toward the jukebox, amidst the lewd suggestions and wolf whistles of his friends.

In a darkened corner of the dance floor he dropped his lips over hers and devoured her. Yearning dulled his senses. Nathan didn't know how much more he could take and not take her right there in the dimly lit bar.

Tate pulled back and blinked up at him with drowsy satisfaction. "What was that for?"

"For looking so damn sexy that you totally blew my concentration. We lost. You are hell on my pool game, Tate."

She smirked. "Sorry."

"No you're not." He backed her against the wall. One whiff of her shampoo crowded reason from his head. Bracing his hands next to her shoulders, he kept his mouth a mere kiss away.

Panic momentarily flared in her eyes. "Let's dance so it doesn't look like we're screwing in the corner."

When she tried to duck under his arm, he boxed her in. "Does it bother you what my friends might think?" *Or have you noticed I'm the only red-skinned guy in the place?*

"No." A tight smile didn't quite reach her eyes. "I implied we were boinking like bunnies anyway."

"Why would you do that?"

"Remember?" Her eyes became unnaturally bright. "That's part of what this deal is about, right? To prove that you're not lousy in the sack?"

He stared at Tate for a moment with an acute sense of loss, forgetting that *was* what she believed: he was using her to recoup the supposed crushing blow Kathy had leveled to his manhood.

His eyes burned and embarrassment tinged his cheeks. God, he was a heel. No, lower than a heel. The lowest worn down tread of his cheapest pair of cowboy boots type of heel. A liar that had taken advantage of the sweetest, sexiest woman he'd ever known.

Without waiting for his reply, Tate wrapped herself around him and they swayed to the wailing steel guitar.

"I like touching you." His hand pressed into the small of her back. "All over body touching."

"Not here," she murmured. "However I'm not surprised that slow dancing appeals to your romantic streak."

Tate stared up at him with blue eyes so deep and clear a man could dive right in and never get out. "It does."

"Mine too," she whispered, snuggling closer.

The slow song segued into two, then three. They remained entwined. But the minute "Boot Scootin' Boogie" started, Tate leapt back. "No way."

A slow grin spread across his face. "Opposed to fast dancing?"

"Nathan, Nathan," she chided. "The only fast moves I want to witness from you are done horizontally in complete privacy."

It was the soft, unsure girlish kiss on the cheek that undid him. He wanted her. She wanted him. The path of romance could only carry them so far and they'd finally reached the end of the road. Instead of regretting his utter lack of willpower where Tate was concerned, anticipation fired his will to show her how much she'd come to mean to him.

Nathan clasped her hand and led her back to the table, nearly tripping over his own cowboy boots in an attempt to drag her out of the bar.

Except his friends wouldn't let them leave. The women he'd affectionately dubbed "The Trio of Terror" whisked Tate to the other end of the table before Nathan could protest.

While discussing an upcoming job with the guys, Nathan glanced up at the clock impatiently and saw Kathy surveying their table. He froze. Her quizzical gaze flicked from Tate back to Nathan. She sneered.

The women bent their heads together and Tate leaned back slightly to give Kathy a once over that was anything but casual.

Nathan stood and knocked his stool over in his haste to reach Tate. He ignored her startled look, hauled her to her feet and crushed their mouths and bodies together so tightly a flimsy bar napkin wouldn't have fit between them. He kissed her, and kissed her and kissed her until all the oxygen exited his body, rendering him lightheaded.

Tate broke the kiss with a huge gasp for breath and staggered backward, her face and chest the color of an over-ripe tomato.

Applause broke out. Steve shouted, "Way to show the rest of us how it's done, LeBeau. Better check her butt to see if your brand took." Deep rumbling chuckles mixed with feminine giggles.

Nathan swallowed his automatic grin at Tate's furious eyes.

"Take me home. *Now.*" She grabbed her purse, spun on her heel and stormed outside.

He followed Tate to his pickup keeping a safe distance from the purple handbag she'd started swinging like a mace.

The warm night breeze was a refreshing break from the stale air in the bar. Inside the truck, he left the windows open but turned off the CD player, waiting for Tate to chew his ass.

But she remained aloof. After he shut off the engine in her driveway, he started to apologize for his idiotic behavior. "Tate—"

She raised her hand to forestall any further comment. "I'll see you later." Within seconds, she'd bolted from the truck cab.

At the arbor, Nathan caught her shoulder. He took a step back at her hard expression when he spun her to face him. "I'm sorry I acted like an ass. I don't know what else to say."

Confused, hurt, blue eyes studied him for an eternity. Again, she started toward her front door.

Nathan turned her around again. "Where are you going?"

"Inside. It's late and I'm sure you're planning an early start in the morning."

His stomach churned at the sight of her usually sweet mouth drawn into a grim line. "I planned on staying with you tonight."

Incredulity flashed through her eyes. "Why would you think that?"

"Because—when—"

"When what? When a mere fifteen seconds after you spot your ex-girlfriend this whole 'you-need-romance' line of bullshit isn't enough anymore? *Now* you're anxious to burn up the sheets with me?"

The heat of her anger sucked the breath from his lungs and his hope for the evening whooshed out right along side it. His jaw tightened. His hands curled into fists against the urge to grab her and make her see reason. "That incident has nothing to do with me wanting to stay with you tonight."

"No?" she challenged. "But then again it's always been about what *you* want, hasn't it? Have you ever wondered what I want? How I feel?" Her eyes glittered with unshed tears. "Let me tell you. I feel like the most undesirable woman on the planet. You can't even bring yourself to have sex with me when I am a *sure thing*. Forget the humiliating way you conk out when I'm touching you, or that you can't be bothered to call me when we've made tentative plans." Her chin quivered briefly, but she firmed it and defiantly thrust it out. "Dammit Nathan, I know this isn't a relationship, but I entered this...*deal* in good faith."

Nathan was speechless.

Her voice dropped another octave. "If you didn't want me, or weren't attracted to me, you should have said 'no' to the landscaping proposal and the rest of my stupid suggestion in the first place."

Frustrated, he kissed her. All thrusting tongue, knocking teeth, a wet, hot, carnal swamping of the senses that left them both weak and clinging. Through his uneven breathing, he demanded softly, "Did that feel like I don't want you?"

She stepped away and swiped her mouth with the back of her unsteady hand. She wrapped her arms around her upper body in a self-hug.

Guilt flooded him. She looked small and fragile. Hurt. It was entirely his fault. He pleaded, "Then let me stay tonight and make it up to you, Tate."

"I can't," she said, finally raising her miserable blue gaze to him. "I need to respect myself more than I need an orgasm."

He could only watch helplessly as Tate raced up the sagging porch steps, slammed and locked the heavy oak door behind her.

Now what should he do?

Beating on the screen hollering her name, ala Brando in *Streetcar*, would never seem romantic from a schmuck like him. It'd smack of desperation. Instead he climbed into his truck and burned rubber like the finest NASCAR driver.

Harsh reality slapped at his conscience. Her anger was not misplaced; his was. He'd known exactly what Tate had wanted—what they'd both agreed to—with her every hot look, sweet smile and tentative touch. And he'd completely disregarded it, choosing his own agenda. The wave of sickness intensified as he remembered her troubled eyes, her wounded expression, her voice filled with pain. Pain he alone had caused.

Even now he couldn't tell her the truth. She'd be even more distraught if he confessed entering the Maxwell Contest was the impetuous of striking the bargain with her, not the promise of free art lessons or free-for-all sex.

A souped-up orange Camaro screeched up beside him at the red stoplight. He glanced over at the teenaged couple who'd taken the opportunity to plaster their mouths together in a full-body kiss. Hormones, he scoffed.

Yeah, like he had room to pass judgment. Male pride, testosterone, whatever it was called, the Neanderthal behavior he'd exhibited in the bar proved *his* idiocy. He didn't own Tate. They weren't really even dating. What right did he have to embarrass the shit out of her? He had *no* rights with her, that seemed to be the crux of his problem.

The light changed and he hit the gas. His grungy silver thermos crashed to the floorboard. No, the crux of the problem was Tate wanted hot sex and he wanted the silly things that defined a normal relationship: coffee, conversation, a few stolen kisses and promising touches before they became intimate. Late night phone calls, long walks in the park, leisurely dinners where heartfelt discussions weren't used as a precursor to lovemaking.

Had he made time to attempt many of those things he professed to need?

No.

He scowled and turned the music up. From he moment they'd met, Tate had brought feelings to light he didn't believe existed. Why? Why her? Why now?

Nathan didn't need a high-priced shrink to point that gem out. Tate was unattainable. She didn't want a relationship. So by denying her the only thing she craved—lots of steamy sex—he retained the upper hand.

Add in the fact he'd entered her landscaping project in the Maxwell Memorial contest *without* telling her and purposely mislead her about his true purpose in the deal... Ah hell. Was he really such a controlling bastard?

Damn. Nothing with Tate could be long term, no matter if he longed for a permanent connection. She'd hightail it back to the Mile High City the day her landscaping was finished and passed inspection. With his business based in Spearfish, moving was not an option for him. He doubted she'd consider a long distance relationship.

Not that she'd hinted that direction. Tate hadn't pretended for even one brief shining moment that there was—or ever would be—anything but hormones and hot looks between them. She'd offered little of herself because in the end it didn't matter. She was leaving.

Real cool, convincing himself that he could handle anything besides a purely sexual relationship.

This wasn't a relationship, no matter how much that idea appealed to him. Nope. He mustn't forget this was a business arrangement. No way was he letting this deal fall through. These strange, unwanted feelings would disappear the minute he climbed out of her bed. Yeah that's all it was, he assured himself angrily, as he blew past the carnival lights on the edge of town, just lack of sex.

Nathan decided he'd rectify the situation tomorrow. To her complete and utter satisfaction.

Chapter Thirteen

The first load of dirt landed right beneath Tate's open window at 6:00 a.m. She tossed back the duvet, intent on chewing Nathan out for his uncivilized wake up call.

Except he probably expected histrionics. Well, she'd show him her civilized side by not rising to the bait. Hunkering back in bed, she shut her eyes and leveled her breathing in hopes of drifting back to sleep. Unfortunately neither the comforter nor the puffy pillow over her ears blocked out the grinding machinery. She hurled back the flannel bedcovers with a resigned sigh.

Impossible to ignore the scattered thoughts racing around in her head anyway. Tate wasn't sure which of them was the bigger idiot. Her, for agreeing to his stupid, slow pace regarding the bonus sex lessons in the first place. Or him, for using Kathy as the catalyst to act on his supposed undying lust.

Tate had been tempted to scream at him last night and demand answers. She, who had always prided herself on her even temperament. How she managed to leave the situation with her dignity intact remained a mystery. However the reasons for Nathan's behavior had become abundantly clear: he'd repeatedly held her off because he could. Not necessarily in a power play. Evidently the frequent invitations to her bed didn't mean much to him. Add in the wanton way she'd been acting, and well, he probably assumed she issued the invitation lightly.

Not so. The number of men she'd entertained all night and into breakfast the following morning numbered a whopping three. Should she have confessed her sexual inexperience from the start? Had he guessed? Was that the problem?

Tate sighed. Pondering the male psyche was pointless.

Sex with Nathan was inevitable. He'd be chomping at the bit to prove her accusations wrong, probably tonight. Traitorous tingles of anticipation aside, she felt the perverse need to hold him off. Play hard to get. Drive him to the brink and leave *him* hanging. Being one hundred percent accessible hadn't worked so far.

She deserved some control in this situation. How could she experience delicious sex *and* keep him at arms length?

An idea clicked. If she insisted on banning their sexual antics from her bedroom and proclaimed herself a restless sleeper—which wasn't entirely untrue—Nathan couldn't argue with her refusal to let him spend the night. Most likely he'd be relieved. In her limited encounters men searched for the closest exit right after the action ended anyway. Besides, waking up together was the ultimate intimacy in her mind. God forbid she got used to having him in her bed or in her life.

Clouds of dust floated under the window shade on the brisk breeze, reminding her that Nathan wasn't the only one with work to finish this morning.

A pot of strong coffee and two bowls of Cap'n Crunch later, Tate hauled out the old, ugly extension ladder to prep the dining room ceiling for paint. Once the stained tarps were spread out, she cranked The Smithereens on her boom box and got to work.

Lost in the tedious task and the loud music, she didn't notice Nathan's presence until he shouted, "What the hell are you doing?"

"Baking cookies," she muttered, realigning the paint-filled brush she'd nearly dropped on his head.

He switched off the music. "What are you doing?"

"Working." She dipped the brush into the can, arcing a cream swath over the grungy gray-white ceiling. "Why?"

"Because you shouldn't be up that high. You could easily slip and fall—"

"—especially when someone barges in unannounced and scares the crap out of me?" she said sweetly.

"Oh, you're hilarious. I'm especially busting a gut about the funny way you're teetering on that rickety-ass ladder." Heavy footsteps shuffled across the crinkly blue tarp. "Why didn't you ask for my help?"

Tate's single handhold on the ladder increased. "Because I don't want it. I can do this. Since you're the landscaping expert isn't your work supposed to be done outside?"

A breath hissed between his teeth. "Low blow."

"Sorry." She glanced down and was rewarded with a glimpse of his steel-toed work boots and his yellow hardhat. Plus the rippling muscles straining at the seams of his tight T-shirt. Damn. She'd be better off focusing on his physical attributes and not the way his unsure eyes threatened the wall she'd erected around her resolve, not to mention her heart.

"Did you need something else?"

"Yeah, to tell you I'm leaving."

Her aggressive brush tapping sent paint splattering. "So the deal is off?"

"No, the damn deal isn't off," he snapped.

"Are you coming back?"

"Later." His booted feet tapped impatiently. "You'll be here?"

"Hopefully not right here, stuck repainting the same section of ceiling." She stirred absentmindedly, wondering what else to say. Yet she didn't feel the initial apology about last night's fiasco should be hers.

Nathan made it to the living room before he expelled a low curse. "Tate?"

"What?" She held her breath. *Please say something sweet. Any kind of that romantic stuff you specialize in.*

"I'm sorry about last night. It's just," he paused, "you were right, okay? It's time I stop acting like you shouldn't have a say in our…lessons. I never meant to hurt you." His heavy tread echoed through the silence and the screen door banged shut behind him.

Tate grinned at the empty room. "Good answer."

ଧ ଧ ଧ

Late that afternoon a glass of icy lemonade sweltered on the sideboard when a dusty, but damnably appealing Nathan sidled inside the kitchen. She handed him the cold drink and watched him drain it in one long draw. He held her gaze and smiled shyly.

Her residual anger dissipated like the last of the paint fumes.

"Thanks." He wiped his brow with the back of the cool glass. "It's hot out there."

"In here too. You want to sit down?"

He shook his head, scowling at his dirt-covered clothes. "No. I'm headed home to clean up." Tension filled the already stifling air as he rattled the ice in his glass. "Thought I'd better check to see if you're still going to Steve's with me tonight."

Tate took her time pouring another glass for herself. "I guess. Why?"

"Figured you might've changed your mind. You still mad?"

She measured him. His sweaty, earthy scent and vulnerable expression created thoughts of flinging herself into his strong arms, damning the dust clouds, paint splatters and misunderstandings between them. "I'm not mad. Let's forget it, okay?"

His jaw dropped. "You aren't going to make me beg to get back in your good graces?"

"I do enough begging for both of us," she said. "I'll go to this party with you since your friends are expecting us. But I'm warning you, this is our last social event."

Nathan's eyes sharpened. "Why?"

"Because it wasn't part of the deal. I never agreed to weekly pool games or barbecues."

"But you agreed to no-holds barred sex," he stated coldly.

"That was the arrangement. If you want to change it, tell me now because I'm running of out time. I need to be back in Denver in three weeks." There. She had reminded him of her temporary status.

Mouth tight, Nathan slammed the glass on the counter. "We're not changing a damn thing. I'll be back in an hour. You'd better be ready."

The door crashed behind him and he was gone.

Hot and sticky from sweat and paint, Tate indulged in a long, cool shower. She cursed the heat melting her freshly applied makeup and slipped on her skimpiest sundress, grateful the floral rayon fabric allowed her skin to breathe.

Half an hour later, she descended the stairs the same time Nathan stormed inside without knocking. Her stomach dropped to the tips of her red toenails. Oh man. By the set of his shoulders he was still spitting mad.

He lifted his head, sending his dark, untamed hair flowing down his broad back. Those honey-colored eyes, usually soft and gentle, were dark and filled with a dangerous glint.

Tate gripped the newel post. She felt as unbound as his hair, freefalling without a net.

His nostrils flared as his glance swept her. He exuded pure male power.

Lord, how had she ever imagined she could handle him? The way his gaze burned through her, the way his hunger clawed at her, Tate wondered why she'd bothered dressing at all.

"Tate."

That one, half-growled word, said everything. She waited without breathing, without thinking, without moving.

By her side in two short strides, he hauled her into his arms. His mouth swooped down and overwhelmed. Hard, unrelenting, his tongue demanded her total surrender. Gone were the gentle coaxing kisses, the soft exploratory touches. The hands holding her head traveled over her throat to claim her breasts, down further yet to caress with single-minded accuracy the aching spot between her legs.

She was helpless against the passion that flared to life. Moisture pooled low, dampening her thighs. Heart pounding, she clung to his brawny neck, breathing in his clean scent, immersing herself in his glossy hair.

His kisses destroyed her. His questing fingers created a flash of heat in her groin that owed nothing to fabric friction.

Nathan nudged her toward the living room. "You're driving me crazy, *winyan*," he muttered against her mouth. He wrenched the straps of her sundress down her arms until she was bared before him. "Stark raving mad with wanting you." His thumb lightly grazed the pebbled tip. "With remembering how these feel in my mouth."

"Nathan, please."

Ignoring her entreaty, he feasted on her nipples until they were stiff and rosy. Until she arched and moaned, thrashing against him, wild with an elemental need.

He ripped his avid mouth away to lick a teasing path to her ear. "I want to fuck you. Right now."

His rough words were meant to shock her, but they didn't. Her hand continued sifting through the silken tangles of his hair. "What?" she whispered through the colors whirling, growing, building a frenzy in her brain. She needed to hear those potent words again.

"You heard me. That's what you want, isn't it?" Teeth scraped over the sensitive chord in her neck, followed by hot breaths over her moist skin. "No more pretty phrases. No more hesitation. No more pathetic attempts at romance. I want you, right here, right now, on the couch, coming hard on the end of my cock until you scream my name."

She trembled. Not from his crude tone, but from the blinding heat of desire. From the seductive combination of his magical hands and impatient mouth on her body which turned the throbbing ache between her legs more sharply pronounced.

When the back of her knees hit the couch, she grabbed his shoulders. The heat rising from his skin nearly scorched her fingers. "Wait," she whispered, fighting for control.

His eyes were dark with passion. His mouth was wet from suckling her. He shook his head; his soft hair fanned over her taut nipple. She bit back a cry at the erotic sensation. Those reddened lips lowered again as his hips ground into hers.

Tate turned her head away from the wonders of his mouth. If he kissed her again she'd be lost. But he was relentless. He moved to lick the pulse tripping erratically in the hollow of her throat. Heat spiraled across her skin. She moaned, wanting his expertly flickering tongue in uncharted territory.

"God, I've been such an idiot," he panted. "You are beautiful. Let me have you, Tate. Let me make love to you right now."

Her head spun, yet she managed to remember they had other obligations besides orgasms. "Stop."

Nathan's hands paused in the rhythmic squeezing on her butt. "Why?"

"Because we're going to be late for the party."

"I don't care about the damn party," he snarled, then tugged and twirled her nipples while his greedy mouth sought her skin. His teeth sunk into the upper swell of her breast, he sucked hard, then used long sweeps of his tongue to soothe the love bruise. "Come closer."

"Dammit!" She shoved his shoulders. "Will you listen?"

He went utterly still.

Tate stumbled back, attempting to straighten her dress. She fiddled with the spaghetti straps to avoid looking at him. "As long as I've waited for this Nathan, I deserve better than a quick coupling on the couch. Weren't you the one who insisted our first sex lesson should be romantic? This sure as hell doesn't fit the bill."

Dead silence.

His eventual laugh was low and not amused. "Guess that comment about needing romance turned around and bit me on the ass, didn't it?"

Warily, Tate watched him drag his hands through his hair in sheer frustration.

"What do you want from me, Tate?"

Everything. She willed her voice not to wobble. "Can we just go to this party like planned? We'll talk about this later, okay?"

His tightened jaw made his smile a grimace. "Fine. Let's go."

& & &

Tate surveyed her surroundings while she nursed her warm ginger ale.

Their late arrival caused the expected catcalls and wolf whistles. That hadn't bothered her. The way Nathan had retreated into polite, disinterested mode bothered her far more.

Sure, he'd introduced her to his friends and sat with her during dinner, fielding questions about their "relationship". But that was all. They hadn't exchanged one personal private word. The minute Nancy, Tina and Vickie had descended on her like long lost friends he'd bailed with a profound look of relief.

Still, she couldn't keep her eyes off him. Although he hung out with the other men surrounding the barbecue pit, he didn't join in their eruptions of laughter. Did he ever relax? Or was *she* the cause of his disgruntled demeanor?

When Roger handed Nathan a fifth beer—yes, it was pathetic to admit she'd been counting—she sighed, wondering how she'd fare driving his big rig home.

Cold fear curled in the pit of her stomach.

Unless that was part of Nathan's plan? Get drunk and have one of his buddies to drop her off at her house to prove he still had the upper hand?

Part of her didn't believe it. A rational voice insisted there was more going on between them than the bouts of tease and retreat.

He turned. Their gazes collided and he glanced away again without so much as a smile. His indifference brought tears to her eyes and a sting to her soul. Right then Tate decided the deal was off. She'd suck up her stupid pride and borrow the money to finish the landscaping. Listening to Ryan berate her for her shortsightedness didn't seem nearly as awful as the dismissive expression in Nathan's eyes.

But isn't that what you did? A little voice piped up inside her head. Dismissed Nathan? By telling him you'd have no part of more social situations? Can you blame the guy for distancing himself?

Her stomach roiled as that bit of knowledge settled in. This time it was her fault. Confused, she fled to the house in search of solitude.

Inside, piles of barbequed chicken and ribs, potato salad, fruit and relish trays leftover from dinner were spread out on the marble kitchen countertops. Tate popped a green grape into her mouth and searched for a glass. Her stomach rumbled at the same time she found the ice bucket and bottled water.

She considered her situation. She could march out there and demand someone take her home. Or call a cab and sneak away, letting Nathan explain that to his friends. She could walk… Yeah, maybe she could sprout wings and fly. A bottle of Absolute Pepper vodka rattled on the bar cart as the door slammed shut.

Nathan stalked into view.

Lordy, lordy, looked like they were going to scrap this out, right here, right now. Tate sipped the water, wetting the dryness in her throat when she met his angry gaze.

The door slammed again and the house teemed with people. Amidst the chaos, she tried to slip away, but Nathan caught her elbow and dragged her to the secluded entryway.

Every annoyed breath he pulled into his lungs echoed in the small space. But he didn't speak. His hands were shoved in his shorts pockets as he paced.

"Can you find someone to take me home?"

He quit moving. "Don't want to be seen with me?"

"Why is that always the first question you ask? You must think I'm shallow."

"If that's not it, then why are you so hot to leave?"

"Because you've been hitting the beer pretty hard."

"Two beers, Tate," he held up his fingers in a 'V' shape, "two."

"No. I watched—"

"You were watching to see how much I drank? Got a high opinion of me, don't you?"

Tate bristled. "When I'm riding with someone else I make it my business to watch. And I've seen your friend Ross bringing you beer. Five," she mimicked, holding up her palm, fingers splayed wide, "five at my last count." Upending her glass, she sucked a large ice chunk into her mouth to keep from spewing any more angry words.

Nathan hauled her closer by the front of her dress. "You're right on the count, but how many did you actually see me drink?" His dangerous laugh touched her every open nerve. "Who'd blame me if I used beer to erase the nasty thoughts I'm having about you? It's making me nuts."

Tate blinked at him.

He muttered, "Hell with it." His lips slammed down on hers and he thrust his tongue inside her mouth.

The demanding tip of his tongue met the ice cube. He froze for an instant, and began slowly sucking the ice cube simultaneously with her tongue.

Chills coated her body. Warm lips, hot tongue, cold ice; the sensations assaulted her. She melted into his embrace while he seduced her with the erotic play. Tender tugs, teasing sips, the velvet slide of his lips followed by the cool hardness of the ice. When the freeze became too intense he passed back the cube back into her mouth and her warm tongue absorbed the cold. But nothing cooled the need in his every touch. When the ice cube was reduced to liquid, he backed off.

Tate nearly toppled over, reeling from the loss of his hard body against hers.

His tight grip on her shoulders softened into a caress. "Do you have any idea how hard it's been staying away from you?"

She held his gaze. "I don't want you to stay away from me."

"That's not what you said earlier."

"Sorry." She wound a wayward strand of his dark silky hair around her pinky. "Is that why you stayed away?"

"No." His gaze seared her, made her breath quicken. "Because I get one whiff of you and I'm instantly hard. Images of what we've done, what I dream of doing to you, start a continual loop in my head. I want more."

"More what?" Her finger quit twirling his hair. She studied him, needing absolutely clarity on what he wanted before she offered him anything. Or everything.

"More of you and me exploring the nuclear reaction between us. You said it the first day we met—what could be better than pushing our sexual boundaries?"

So, Mr. Romance decided he'd accept their overwhelming chemistry. Big of him. *But that's what you wanted, right?* Lots of burning hot sex without strings. Without promises. Without love.

Why did her victory feel hollow? A tiny part of her deflated. Wouldn't it be ironic if it were the part that didn't believe she needed romance?

"Tate?" He nuzzled her neck, bringing her back to earth pronto.

"Mmm?" She gasped when his cold tongue flicked across her clavicle, turning her skin into a mass of gooseflesh.

"You smell good," his palms rasped over her nipples, "you feel good. Know what else I've noticed?"

"What?" Then he sucked the air from her ear and every coherent thought clean out of her head.

"How good you taste." His erection teased her stomach as he pressed her against the wall. "I want you right now."

Her eyes glazed over. "Okay." When Nathan all-but inhaled her, Tate wondered how she'd stayed clothed in the aftermath of his consuming kiss.

"Did you forget we are in Steve and Nellie's foyer?" he muttered into her hair, sliding a hand around to cup her bottom.

The blush crept down, increasing the heavy ache in her breasts. "Let's go back to my house."

"Don't think I can wait that long." His eyes glittered a challenge. "Remember when you said you wanted to be daring?"

Her heartbeat zoomed to warp speed. "You just said—"

"Not here specifically, but around here."

"Like a coat closet?" Forbidden, erotic visions of her bare back rubbing against mink. Nathan's hot mouth muffling her cries as he pounded into her sent another surge of heat rocketing through her system.

"No. Downstairs would be more private." His nostrils flared. "Admit it. You are just as turned on by this idea as I am."

As if to prove his point, he bent his head and sucked her nipple hard through the thin material of her dress. "I can make it romantic."

No doubt he could make anything romantic.

"You want this."

She did. Desperately. No more games. "You've got a condom?"

"Baby, I've got two." His hot breath fanned over her breast. "Want to hear my idea?"

Tate stroked his sex through the material of his shorts, flicking her tongue back and forth over his bottom lip. "No. Show me. Show me now."

He removed her hand, propelling her at breakneck speed down the darkened circular staircase. The ice in her glass rattled with every step.

Downstairs Tate's eyes adjusted to the light waning through the slatted blinds. Her palms were clammy, her heart raced, the inside of her thighs were soaked. Just sex, not love, she reminded herself. Take what he's offering.

At the end of an endless hallway, while kissing her senseless, he pushed her backward through a doorway.

"Where are we?" she whispered.

"A bathroom."

"How do you know about—"

"I helped build this house, Tate. I've played poker here every week for the last five years. I probably know Steve's den and this bathroom better than my own. Okay?"

"Okay." Desire for the unknown ripped through her. Once inside the small space, he shut the door, locked it and didn't bother flipping on the lights.

The black void was absolute.

Tate couldn't see, but she sensed Nathan's uneven breathing matched her own. "It's awfully dark in here," she whispered. She withheld a moan as his tongue skated up her arm light as a butterfly kiss.

"Don't worry," he said, working the soft straps of her dress down her shoulders with his teeth. "I can feel my way."

"I'll bet you can." She set the glass beside her, wanting no more distractions.

Amidst heated caresses, hungry kisses, muttered words against her mouth, her dress finally fell to the floor.

His large, skilled hands raced over her bared flesh. Then stopped.

She laughed softly when his hand encountered her naked butt.

"Tate?" he said in a strangled voice.

"Surprise."

Chapter Fourteen

Tate wasn't wearing any underwear.

Nathan's brain repeated the phrase like a mantra. *Tate wasn't wearing any underwear. Tate wasn't wearing any underwear.*

He reined in his control. "Did you plan—?"

"N-n-o," she stuttered. "I... I was so flustered..."

"I haven't even begun to fluster you," he growled, settling her bare backside against the counter.

Her hands curled around his face. Her sweet breath drifted over his jaw as she tried to find his lips in the dark. "Then show me."

This was the moment. No turning back. His blood began a slow, steady burn. Talk about performance anxiety.

Nathan swept his thumb across her bottom lip, following the teasing motion with his tongue. "Every inch of you is so tempting I don't know where to start."

A beat passed. She set his hands on her breasts, rising and falling with each ragged breath. "Start here." Her nipples were beaded and her heart beat wildly beneath his palm. "I love the way you touch me. Touch me any way you want."

Floored by her complete surrender, Nathan captured her mouth, drinking from her honeyed lips. He licked at her sweetness until he was drunk on her taste. He slid his leg in between hers, delirious at the satiny feel of her bare thighs brushing against the coarse hair on his. The wetness he encountered tore a groan from his throat.

"You don't need to see me to make me crazy."

But the complete absence of light proved a challenge. He couldn't witness her beautiful face lost in pleasure, see her eyes glaze over, watch her body language. He might miss the usual signals.

Tate's muscled legs locked around his knee, holding him still while she rubbed her molten core over his thigh.

No mixed signals there.

So he worshipped Tate in darkness. He savored her sweetly scented curves, from her petite collarbones to the sonnet provoking breasts. Against the supple skin of her abdomen, he inhaled the scent of her arousal. It made his head spin, how their aromas combined to create one that was new and unique to them. Where his diligent hands glided, soothed, teased with a slight pinch, his hungry lips followed. Drawing his fingertips from hipbone to hipbone, he suctioned his mouth to the skin below her ear in the manner that drove her mad.

Her needy moan sang through his system.

"Ever had wild squirrel sex during a party?" he said, blowing into her ear. "Where you've been so hot and impatient you don't care who hears you scream?"

"No." She broadened her stance, urging him with tiny hips thrusts to take advantage of unfettered access to the heat taunting him. Her head turned to seek his lips.

He denied her that sublime mating of hungry mouths, skating his hot breath over her temple instead. "Do you really want me, right here, right now?"

"Yes." In her zeal to drag him closer she accidentally knocked over the glass she'd placed on the counter.

Icy water splashed on his hand. Nathan fished a chunk of ice from the cup, keeping Tate distracted by slipping his tongue inside her mouth.

Her soft feminine sigh increased his already raging erection.

He palmed the lower swell of her breast, amazed at the supreme softness beneath that fiercely pebbled tip. As he turned up the intensity of the kiss, he rubbed the ice back and forth over her rigid nipple, never holding it in place too long.

She gasped in his mouth and pulled away. "That's cold."

"Mmm. But it feels naughty. You like it." Tate inhaled sharply and shivered when he blew across the frozen tip. "I can tell."

He scattered kisses over her face, drawing ever larger, ever wetter circles around her breast as her hot skin seared the ice to a small sliver. Her surprised shriek echoed in the small space when he tugged the cold nub inside his warm mouth.

"Oh. My. God." She arched closer for more.

Nathan suckled hard, arcing the ice to the other breast. Water ran down her body. Damn if he didn't long to trace that wet path with his tongue before it turned into nothing but a vapor trail.

Grabbing a larger piece, he moved the frosty cube down her center with painstaking precision. Not one quivering section remained untouched. Or dry. He stopped at the dampened curls, letting the cold water mingle with the hot slick moisture between her thighs.

"That's freezing," she said. "You're making me shiver."

His heavy whisper hung in the darkness. "I want you shivering. I want you aching. I want you so mindless with need that when I'm inside you, you'll understand why the wait was worth it."

She whimpered.

"Nothing exists outside these walls." A trickle of moisture ran between her breasts, an offering he lapped at greedily. "Spread your legs."

She trembled. The tremble morphed into a full-blown shudder when he moved the ice cube down over her pouting sex. He rubbed that swollen female flesh until she rolled her hips with a needy cry. Hot. Wet. All for him.

A heady sense of male satisfaction yowled in his head, rumbled in his blood, and increased the throbbing in his groin. Sweat ran in rivulets down his body.

Balancing the small cube between two fingers, he parted her slick folds and pushed the ice inside her, covering her gasping protest with a plundering kiss. He flicked his thumb over the tangle of nerves. The cold sensation of the ice coupled with the friction of his fingers made her writhe, whimper and buck.

Her fiery sheath clamped around him as he brought her to orgasm. She let loose a long moan, digging her fingers into his biceps. Her body shook violently from the vibrations.

He growled, "I want to drop to my knees, bury my face between your thighs. Lick every drop off water from the inside of your body out." She strained against him as he tried to level his breathing.

Tate nearly ripped his shorts in the struggle to depant him.

His belt buckle clanked against the tile floor as she succeeded.

"Now," she pleaded, yanking at his briefs.

"Whoa. Hold on. Let's just slow down for a sec—"

"Too late." She frantically kissed the corded muscles in his neck, punctuating her need with a tiny nip.

Nathan caught her hips when she lifted the lower part of her body off the counter. He drew one finger slowly down her cleft, through the quivering wetness. "I love the way you heat up for me."

"Heat up?" Tate echoed, rocking her pelvis forward. "I'm on fire. If you don't get that condom out I swear I'm going to kill you."

He smiled in the dark, pausing to sample one velvety nipple. "Death threats are not going to get you what you want."

"What I want, Nathan, is what I've always wanted since the day we met. You." Tate pressed hot openmouthed kisses to his sternum, swirling her tongue through his scant chest hair.

"Our options are—"

"I don't care," she said. "Pick one. Pick one now."

He chuckled, tasting the salty dew gathered on her neck. "If my memory serves me, the counter is too low." He shoved his groin forward, bumping into her breastbone. "The door is flimsy. It can't withstand the thrusting power I have in store for you."

Tate whimpered when he cupped her still molten core and again slid one finger inside. Her sex clenched one time.

"Not enough room to stretch out on the floor," he offered as the fierce pulling of her internal muscles tugged his finger deeper. In between sips of her heated, fragrant flesh, he changed the angle of his hand, pretending a conversational tone he no longer felt. "We've got two options left." He stroked her clit faster. "Choose. The shower stall or—"

"The shower!"

"Excellent choice." He withdrew his fingers to trail her sweet-scented moisture up her torso and followed the path with his mouth where they shared the taste of her.

Tate tried to simultaneously rub her nakedness over his, scale up his body and eliminate his shirt. She broke the kiss on a gasp. "Nathan, tell me what to do. I've never—"

"Ssh. We'll start out slow. But it won't stay slow for long because I want you so bad, Tate..."

"God, yes. I want you too."

Her musky female scent surrounding them in the tiny, humid space made him feel as if he'd climbed inside her. He fumbled for the condom from his shorts pocket before kicking his clothes away.

Scattering kisses on her face, he whispered roughly, "Place your knees on the edge of the bathtub and grab onto the acrylic bar inside the shower on the far wall."

Her nervous swallow was audible next to his ear. "But—"

"Trust me, this will blow your mind." The words spilled from his mouth as a primitive growl. Fire raced through his blood as the need to mate, to brand Tate as his consumed his every thought and colored his every action.

Hungry, harsh kisses, tender touches, heat from his hardened body until she became as mindless and frenzied as he.

"Let me help you."

Yanking the shower curtain aside, he angled her forward on her knees, caressing the long line of her supple body from hip to where her fingers curled tightly around the bar. "You feel so sexy, stretched out before me like some primal goddess." Tracing the heart-shaped curves of her ass, he stood behind her and flattened his palms over the satiny surface of her back.

Nathan probed her wet, ready opening with a hard-on that rivaled his strongest piece of rebar. He glided his rigid sex through the silky flesh between her thighs. Gripping her left hip with his left hand, he plunged inside.

Hot. Tight. Perfect. He hissed his pleasure. With forced patience he let her snug walls adjust to the deep angle, gritting his teeth against the desire to surge into her without finesse. To rut like the beast she'd released with her eager hands, hot body and pleading demands.

She instinctively rocked back into him and moaned.

Nathan moved with torturous strokes at first, half in, then all the way back out. The mouth of her sex gripped him, trying to keep his pulsing thickness inside. He circled the tip of his cock around her wet opening before plunging in again. The thrusts became shorter, harder, each concentrated stroke brought him deeper until he withdrew fully and sank to the root.

"Oh God," she gasped, widening her stance.

The aroma of her damp skin taunted him. Stretching over her back, he aligned their bodies thigh to shoulder, rough flesh to soft. The sensation spun his control to the breaking point. He snaked an arm around to trace her feminine contours from this angle, to taste the dew gathering on the curve of her neck. Her lush breasts swayed to the pumping of his hips.

Her tightness dragged him deeper as repeatedly pushed to the hilt. This position was a raw, sexy, ancient mating that fed the desire coiled between them. Yet he missed the thrilling feel of her hungry mouth on his.

Nathan slipped his hand past the bounty of her breasts, down her softly rounded belly, into her tight curls. While continuing to drive into her with

167

sure, steady strokes, he spread her wide to caress the swollen pearl begging for his attention.

Immediately she wailed, "I can't wait. Nathan, *please*." His finger began stroking until several keening sobs broke free and she arched. The spasms of her internal muscles clamping around his cock matched the blood pulsing under his finger. She screamed and it nearly undid him. His balls lifted, but he clenched his butt muscles tightly and regained control.

She stopped thrashing beneath him and went boneless with a final shudder. He gently bit her nape. Then blew in her ear and swept his finger side-to-side across her swollen clit.

It set her off again and the pulses milked his cock until he gritted his teeth.

"Tate, honey, I can't hold out any longer." Sweat beaded between his shoulders to run in a line down his back, between his ass cheeks directly to his overheated balls. "Brace yourself cause this is gonna be hard and fast."

With that said, he pounded into her. Spirals of heat shot up his spine. His legs, usually strong from hours of physical labor, trembled. Fingers dug for purchase on her slick hips. An intense wave started a slow roll, then crashed over him. Blinding whiteness roared through his head. A ball of fire exploded in his groin. Every muscle in his body went high and tight, groin, abdomen, buttocks, jaw.

Nathan threw back his head in ecstasy, groaned, and let go.

Tate came apart again. Her internal muscles clamped around him like a steel vise.

After the raging in his head dulled he opened his eyes to utter darkness. The air was heavy with the sounds of labored breathing, the scents of sex and sweat. Sated beyond belief, he felt like he'd finally found the one place he belonged.

"Tate?" he murmured.

"I'm still here." She snickered. "At least I think so."

Smoothing his unsteady hands across her damp back, he trailed kisses on her bared skin and slowly withdrew from her body.

After he helped her stand, he cradled her in his arms. "You are incredible." A lingering, tender kiss later, he said, "I wish I could see your face."

"Trust me, I'm smiling." Her small fingers traced his jaw, his cheekbones, his nose, and his forehead before stopping at his lips. "I guess you are too."

"Was there ever any question?"

"No. Especially not after you howled." At her small laugh, her breath tickled his chest hairs as her cheek rested against his thundering heart. A shiver of possession rolled through him. "If your friends wondered where we'd disappeared to, I'm sure they know now."

"Same goes, jungle girl. I had to stop from coming about three times. Those very sexy noises emerging from your wicked mouth 'bout did me in."

Content, Nathan held her loosely. This was too strong a feeling to be a simple mutual slaking of lust. The sex between them was astounding. True, he'd had satisfying physical relationships before. But he'd never felt the urge to belong completely to a woman, heart, body and soul as he did with Tatum Cross. His hold on her increased. "You really are okay? I was kind of rough."

"I am now. But truthfully, at first, I didn't know how…"

"How what?" He stopped drawing lazy circles on her luscious butt. "What do you mean?"

"I've never, umm… Oh, shoot." She sighed. "Okay, so I've never exactly, umm…done it that way before."

Nathan's stomach dropped. His feeling of afterglow dimmed. "Why didn't you tell me? Jesus, Tate, I would have been—"

"That's *why* I didn't. I felt…I don't know. *Powerful* knowing that you wanted me so much that you forgot to be romantic." A wet tongue rounded his nipple before she lightly bit it. "I'm not some delicate flower that requires soft words and candlelight. I'm just—"

"—not as sexually experienced as you'd led me to believe." He paused, tipping her face back as if he could read her eyes in the dark. "Tell me something else. That night on the boat, have you ever…"

"Not with much success," she admitted with a soft, embarrassed laugh. "Was it that obvious I was a novice?"

"No! My God, then where did you learn—" He swallowed, aware that merely thinking about Tate's hot, wet mouth on his dick would make him hard again.

Nathan clamped a hand on her bare butt when she tried to wriggle away. "Tate? You gonna tell me?"

Her answer was somewhat reluctant. "Porn is a great source of information."

He went hard anyway. "You watch *porn*?"

"Strictly for educational purposes." She wreathed her arms around his neck and breathed a hot challenge, "Wanna watch one with me sometime and act out the good parts?"

"You are trying to kill me, aren't you?"

"Only if we can die in bed."

"Speaking of bed." Pressing his forehead to hers, he fought the fear that she'd think he was needy. But man, he wanted to be with her until the sun rose tomorrow. Truth was, he longed to spend every night, every waking hour with her until the moment she skipped town.

"Speaking of bed, what?"

"Can we try out your bed tonight?"

"Mmm." Tate licked the line defining his pectorals. "We'll see. Some other places might be more interesting."

Relief soared through him. "But that's a yes?"

"Don't act so surprised."

At that moment, Nathan knew the strange sensation banding his heart went deeper than eagerness for more hot sex. And it scared the shit out of him. Although next time they made love it'd be chock full of all the romantic frills she didn't claim to need. "Can't help it," he muttered. "You continually surprise me."

"I can't think of anything I'd like better than to take you home right now and indulge in wild squirrel sex all night long." She playfully bit his lobe. "Was that a more romantic proposition?"

"It'll do. Come on. Let's get out of here."

Chapter Fifteen

The air whooshed from Tate's lungs as Nathan's weight, combined with hers, plastered her against the wall in her foyer. Not that she had much air left with the breath-stealing way he kissed her. She hitched her shoulders back. The velvet-flocked wallpaper abraded her skin as he impatiently tugged the thin straps of her sundress down her biceps.

Nathan eased the slinky dress over her hips until it pooled on the rug. "I love this outfit but I love the body under it more." His hands took a curve filled detour. "Soft. Warm. Wet in all the right places. Gimme."

She giggled. The sight of his large, tanned fingers kneading her pale breasts sent a thrill through her. "Right here?" A moan tumbled forth as he thumbed her nipples and his silky hair brushed over her stomach, her hips.

"No. I'd like to make it to the bedroom at least *one* time tonight," he mumbled, lapping with exquisite pressure at the bottom swell of her breast.

Tate unbuttoned his shirt, throwing it on the dried cattails arrangement in the corner. Her hands glided over his pectorals to pinch his nipples. "Beds are highly overrated."

"You haven't been in bed with me." Fastening his mouth to hers, he kept their gazes locked as he began an unbearably slow, but extremely thorough journey down her body with those wickedly talented hands.

The phone rang.

He pulled away a fraction of an inch. "Ignore it," he said, continuing to play with her lips.

172

He'd answer it, a tiny voice reminded her before she snarled at it to disappear. The phone continued to peal.

Tate closed her eyes, focusing on the sensation of his rough hands trailing over the soft inner skin of her thighs. Every cell vibrated under his seductive touch. The slow simmer he'd started in her blood changed, heated, and began to boil. Her ears rang.

No. Dammit. That was still the phone.

Who would be calling at eleven on a Saturday night? Her mother? Definitely didn't want to chat with her. Didn't even want to *think* about her mother when Nathan was doing such naughty things with his tongue.

"Tate. I'm losing you." He did some maneuver with his hand and thumb that made her gasp. "That's better," he murmured, nuzzling her hairline with light, barely-there breaths.

The ringing stopped. She breathed a sigh of relief. Probably a wrong number. Her fingers inched down Nathan's flat stomach to the line of dark hair when the phone started in again.

He thunked his head on the wall above her. "Fine. I give. Answer it. Quickly."

She slipped from beneath his curtain of hair and snatched up her dress, using it as a cover as she raced for the phone. "Don't go anywhere."

"Trust me. I'll be right here."

"Hello?" Tate said. "Wait... When? Val... Val! Slow down. Well, I'm here now." Her startled glance moved to Nathan. "Yes... He's here too... You really want to talk about this *now*? No... That's fine... We'll be there in ten minutes."

"Let me guess."

"Yep. She's in labor. We have to go. Now."

Nathan's head hit the wall two more times. "As usual Val's timing is impeccable." With a sigh, he grabbed his shirt off the floor, reaching in the front pocket for a ponytail holder. "She was looking for me?"

"Yes, when she couldn't get a hold of you—" Tate grinned. "No wonder she panicked. You must've been in an awful hurry to get back here if you forgot your beloved cell phone."

"You have no idea how much I wanted to get back here to you."

Back here to you. Just for the sex? She glanced at him, but his face was unreadable. Disgusted with the twisted straps on her dress, she threw it on the couch. "I can't wear this."

"You haven't actually had it on all that much," he said with a very satisfied, very masculine smirk.

"Funny. I'll be right back." Tate ran up the stairs naked.

She slipped on clean underwear, a relatively stain-free pair of gym shorts and a Metallica T-shirt. Grabbing the overnight bag, she stuffed in two changes of clothes. She tossed in pajamas, wondering if she'd even need them. Hopefully Nathan planned on keeping her naked.

In the tiny, dimly lit bathroom, she swept everything off the counter into the bag's side compartment. Packed and ready to roll in two minutes flat.

She flew down the staircase bag in hand. "Let's go." She hesitated, watching him pace a hole in the hallway runner. "Unless you want to take separate cars?"

"No." He hit the light switch in the living room and herded her toward the foyer.

"You okay?"

"I know it's her fifth kid and all..." He expelled a slow breath and clasped her hand tightly. "But she's still my little sister and I worry. How far apart are her contractions?"

Touched by his concern for Val, Tate kissed him and pushed him out the door. "She didn't say. Let's go find out."

∝ ∝ ∝

Since every light was on at Val and Richard's house they didn't bother to knock.

In the far end of the living area, Val, wearing lime green pajamas, paced the wooden floor, clutching the small of her back. Richard still clad in a suit and tie, sat glumly on the circular staircase with his elbows propped on his knees, watching her like a hawk.

Startled from his daze, Richard rushed toward them. "Thank God." He shot a glance over his shoulder before he muttered, "Look out. She's a demon when she's in labor. And she's gunning for you two right now." A boyish smile flashed. "Glad it's not me, but my turn is coming, so I'm warning you: You're on your own."

"Gee, thanks," Nathan said.

Val charged forward. "'Bout damn time. Where have you two been?"

Tate withheld her surprise at the wild look in Val's normally calm brown eyes and the scowl marring her usually serene face. "We were at a party."

"A party? Have you been drinking?" Val sniffed Tate's breath and glared at Nathan. "Or was this a party for two?"

"Knock it off," Nathan said, edging closer to grasp Val's hand. He stroked her knuckles, then her cheek. "Does it hurt?"

Stuck in the moment, Tate watched Nathan's tender care and patience with Val, feeling her heart skip.

"How far apart?" Nathan murmured, drawing his hand over Val's shifting belly.

Val closed her eyes, seeming to bask in Nathan's comfort before she blew out three short breaths. "Five minutes."

Nathan gave Richard a puzzled look.

Tate was confused. What was wrong? Wasn't five minutes a good thing?

Richard said, "Her water broke a half hour ago. Not much has happened since then."

"Except I feel like I'm peeing my pants every two minutes," Val added crossly.

"Why don't you sit down?" Tate offered.

Val, Richard and Nathan all chorused, "No!"

Tate shrank back. Evidently she was the only one that didn't have a clue about childbirth. It wasn't her fault she'd never been around a woman in labor. She squared her shoulders and asked, "Why not?"

"Walking helps the labor progress naturally," Richard said.

"Takes her mind off the pain," Nathan said, ambling back to her side with a reassuring smile. He brought Tate's hand to his lips. "She's done this before. Don't worry."

Val started exhaling rapidly. "Time."

Richard glanced at his watch. "Still at five."

"Damn. Oh God, it hurts." Richard was by Val's side immediately, forcing her eyes to meet his, breathing in tandem with her until the contraction ended.

It seemed to last forever. Tate stayed motionless, save for the death-grip on Nathan's hand.

Val wiped her brow before meeting Tate's wide-eyed gaze with a grunt. "Tate, you should see your expression. Absolute horror."

"Well, what do you expect?" She was damn tired of being the resident idiot. "You're the one who's been waltzing around touting the ease of pregnancy. And I get here at the crucial time to find your previous Madonna persona was a big fat lie. You're hardly recognizable under that snappish attitude, Val."

"That's because it *hurts*! And this is the worst part." Richard smothered a chuckle with a cough when Val glared at him. "Okay, the next few hours are hideous." She stepped closer. Her probing gaze turned perceptive. "But I take my earlier statement back. You look terrific. You positively glow."

Afterglow? Not a myth after all. Tate fought the surge of color rising to her cheeks. She tried to remove her hand from Nathan's as unobtrusively as possible.

But his grip increased and he just smiled at his ill-tempered sister.

"I know I'm not supposed to be privy to the intimate details of your agreement. But by the satisfied expressions on both of your faces I don't have to guess what's been going on tonight. Which leads me right into…" She groaned and bent forward.

"Val, sweetheart, can we do this later? You should get to the hospital," Richard said calmly.

She straightened up, giving her husband an arrogant sneer. "Since *I'm* the one having this baby, *I'll* be the one that decides when we go to the hospital. I have something to discuss with Tate." She turned an accusing finger on Nathan. "And you might as well stick around because now it involves you, too."

"Have you called Mom and Dad yet?"

"No. They'd just worry. I'll call when it's over. Besides, that's not what I wanted to talk about."

"Sis, I'm sure whatever is bothering you, Tate and I—"

"No." She leaned back and Richard rubbed her shoulder, pressing his other hand into the small of her back. "Thank you, honey. No, lower. Yeah, right there." She zeroed in on Tate and Nathan. "I want to be absolutely clear on this. I'm over the moon that you two…finalized the terms of your deal. But that deal and anything associated with it is null and void in this house."

Nathan started to argue but Val held her hand up.

"Hear me out. Nathan, the kids worship you." She looked at Tate, "And you're my friend. For those reasons, I want both of you to promise that you will not have sex in this house while you're caring for our children."

Tate's jaw dropped. Not what she'd expected at all. "But—"

"No buts. This is non-negotiable. No sleeping or waking up in the same bed. No mysterious absences. No kissing or cuddling in front of the TV. Strictly friends while you're here." Val paused. "We know your association is temporary. The kids don't. Fielding questions from them about Uncle Nathan and Tate…well, you get the gist. What you do in your houses is your business. What you do in our house is mine."

Richard cleared his throat and Tate noticed Nathan's clenched jaw. Val's uneven breathing echoed in the sudden silence.

"Come on. Say something," Val demanded.

Val's tone made Tate take a tentative step toward her, mindless of whether or not she'd charge like a wounded buffalo. Using her most comforting smile, she said, "Of course we promise. You don't need to worry."

Val squeezed her eyes shut and said, "Time."

Richard checked his watch. "We're at four minutes. Can we please go now?"

Fascinated despite her fear, Tate watched Richard patiently work through breathing techniques with Val again. When the contraction ended, he and Nathan scooted Val to the car but not before Val handed Tate a four-page list of typed instructions.

When Nathan reentered the room it appeared to have shrunk. They stared at one another warily. Tate wondered exactly how they were supposed to pass the next few hours alone.

Good thing she packed those pajamas.

ଥ ଥ ଥ

It figured that his sadistic sister would find a way to frustrate the hell out of him. Dangle Tate as the world's tastiest treat and just when he'd finally taken an addictive bite—YANK, right out from under him.

Yet he hated to admit Val's logic was valid. But damn, why did she pick tonight of all nights to start making sense? When she should've been concentrating on the impending birth of her child? An act she'd claimed was the most beautiful and powerful known to mankind?

With the possible exception of the act of making a baby.

Oh how he'd wanted to get some intense practice in on *that* particular act tonight with Tate.

Don't go there. Not only can you not have sex with Tate for—God how long did it take to deliver a fifth baby? An hour? Two? He glanced at the grandfather clock. Hmm. Richard, Val and baby Westfield would be home Monday— which meant he and Tate could be naked, sweaty and utterly satisfied by that evening, which wasn't too bad considering—

"Nathan?"

His guilty gaze flew to Tate. Possibly he should focus on something besides getting laid.

Tate gnawed on her bottom lip. Her nervous glance darted upstairs. "Should we wake the kids?"

Nathan shook his head. "Rule number one. Heard of 'let sleeping dogs lie'? Double goes for sleeping kids. If Val would've wanted them awake they'd be tearing the place apart."

"I'll defer to you on that since I haven't had much experience with little kids."

"Why not?"

Her shoulder lifted in a half-shrug. "Ryan isn't married and neither were any of my friends in Denver. My mother, well, you can imagine she'd be horrified if I confessed a burning desire to reproduce. Not a good career move for me."

He hid his shock. "Seriously?"

"What about you? Ever wish a Nathan Jr. was trailing after you on the jobsite?"

"Sometimes. There's a definite hole in my life that even Duke can't fill, large as he is." He frowned. Why was he telling her this? "But if I feel the urge to be tormented I just borrow one of Val's kids. She's got plenty."

Her blue eyes clouded. "Truthfully, that's why I was surprised Val suggested this trade—"

"You made a trade with Val?"

"Not with Val, per se, with Richard. He did legal work for me regarding the Beautification Committee. Val came up with the babysitting gig as an alternative payment."

Val had sneakiness down to an art. She'd already asked him months ago to stay with the kids when she went into labor. But as usual, his sister's big heart was in the right place and Tate's pride was intact. "Trust me. Richard got the better end of the deal. The kids are a handful."

"Then I'm glad you're here Nathan, even if we can't..."

"Me too." He felt a stirring in his belly that had little to do with desire.

They stared at each other across the wide expanse of the Westfield's great room. Tate rocked on her heels, apparently studying the opulent space. "Should we go to bed?" She winced. "What I meant was—"

"I know what you meant." He offered her a smile. "Take the guest bedroom upstairs. I'll crash on the couch. That way I can hear when Richard calls."

"You'll wake me? Right away?"

He nodded, shoving aside the immediate visions of a naked, sleepy Tate stretching her arms above her head. Exposing those pert nipples as the satin sheet slipped down... Man. Get a grip. Tate was dynamite. He was a match. An explosive combination they couldn't set off right now.

She lifted her bag. "Good night, Nathan."

"Night," he muttered to her disappearing back.

&. &. &.

A sharp knee nicked his groin then scored a direct hit in his stomach. A wet smacking kiss on his forehead followed. He peeled one eye open and grunted.

Chelsea kissed his nose. "Wake-up, wake-up! Tate made breakfast!"

Nathan yawned. "Chels, I'm tired. Go away." He put the pillow over his head.

180

"But it's waffles! And not the toaster kind. Come on." When he didn't budge, Chelsea pounced on his calves, yanked up the blanket and tickled his bare feet.

He jerked her to his chest and blew raspberries on her tummy until she screamed, "Uncle!"

"No fair," she said between giggles and gasping breaths.

"Sure it is." He nuzzled her soft blonde hair, momentarily lost in a burst of love for Val's troublesome daughter. "That's what happens to little princesses that disturb papa bear's beauty sleep."

Chelsea sighed. "You mixed them up again, Uncle Nathan."

"Made-up fairy tales are more fun."

"Nuh-uh." She leaned forward and whispered, "Don't tell mommy, but my favorite book is the one you gived me for Christmas with the Indian stories. Especially the stories about *Iktomi*, the trickster. Will you read it to me later?"

"You bet." He stood. "Come on short stuff, let's have some waffles."

She raced ahead while Nathan dragged his feet, trying to work out the kinks from sleeping on the couch. Not that he'd gotten much sleep. When Richard called at two a.m. and said Val had undergone an emergency C-section, falling back asleep had been nearly impossible. Even after Richard assured him Val and the newest baby Westfield were fine.

Chattering voices and the rich smell of coffee and bacon lured him to the kitchen. But once inside the arched doorway, he froze.

Pure longing clouded his senses making it difficult to breathe. Or think. He just wanted.

Tate looked completely at ease, laughing with the twins while she scurried around the enormous kitchen with Hannah perched on a hip.

Blood roared in his ears and through his body but for once not straight to his groin. Nathan wanted her. But not naked in his bed. In a far more intimate, far more dangerous way. Instead of wanting Tate tangled in his sheets he wanted to step into this life and make it his. Theirs.

That thought jarred him to his core.

He imagined standing behind her, kissing her nape while she cooked. She'd be wearing his T-shirt, one that still carried the scent of their shared passion. Romantic notion indeed, the sarcastic part of his brain scoffed. But his jumbled emotions didn't have a blessed thing to do with sex.

Therein was the problem because that's all Tate wanted.

Sure Nathan could make her ache. He could even make her beg. But what would it take to make her completely his?

A move to Denver.

Not in the cards. Somehow, he closed the last few feet to the counter, mulling over his surprising revelations. Was this confusing feeling the beginning of love? He shook his head hard. Nah. Just residual lust.

But when Tate gifted him a smile filled with sunshine, he understood his heart was giving him trouble, not testosterone.

"Hey, sleepyhead," she said brightly. "Coffee?"

"Sure." He reached out to stroke a finger down Hannah's cheek but she burrowed into Tate's shoulder. "What? No kisses for Uncle Nathan today, Hannah Banana?"

Hannah made a small disgruntled sound, pulling the corner of the purple lace blanket and her thumb into her pouting mouth.

"Somebody's missing momma this morning, huh, sweetie?" Tate kissed Hannah's red-gold crown.

Nathan's feeling of longing increased tenfold. For not having much experience with kids, Tate had worked wonders with Hannah, who up until this morning was very much momma's girl. What did Hannah sense in Tate that Tate herself was unsure she possessed? His eyes half-closed as he considered the possibilities. What if it was *their* daughter clinging to her? What if her belly were round, ripe with his child?

Tate's voice broke into his strange reverie. "The kids are anxious to hear about…"

Nathan snapped back to attention. "You haven't told them?"

"No. I thought it'd be more appropriate coming from you."

She gave him a look that was sheepish and completely endearing.

Damn. This had been simpler when it was only about romance and winning the landscaping competition. How could he alternate between wanting nothing and everything with her? Had to be Val's pregnancy hormones lingering in the house. Contagious, dangerous emotions, wreaking havoc on his senses. Normally these ideas never crossed his mind.

Then again nothing about the situation with Tate was normal.

She stood on tiptoe reaching for a cup. Her straining calf muscles distracted him for a second before he said, "Let me." Pressing his front to her back, much in the same intimate manner he'd done last night, he reached into the cupboard and snagged a mug. Her breath caught at the unexpected contact, just soft and feminine enough to stir his loins. He nearly dropped the cup on poor Hannah's head.

Eschewing further body contact, Tate stepped aside, murmuring to Hannah and pouring thick batter in the waffle iron.

Chelsea demanded, "So. Tell us. Boy or girl?"

Nathan sipped slowly, knowing it'd drive his niece crazy. When Chelsea sighed with exasperation, he grinned. "Girl."

"Yes!" She played hopscotch across the tile, raced over and pulled Hannah from Tate's arms. She danced Hannah around in a speeded up version of ring-around-the-rosy. "We win! More girls than boys."

Tanner and Tyler exchanged a glum look and a low five before Tanner scoffed, "So? We're the biggest. We're boys. We get to do everything first."

Tyler sneered, "Did Mom give her some stupid girly name?"

"She's not stupid. Boys are stupid," Chelsea said.

"Tupid, tupid," Hannah mimicked.

"That's enough," Nathan warned. "Your sister's name is Maddie. I know for a fact your mom doesn't let you guys use the word 'stupid' so knock it off." He rubbed his hands together with glee. "Now where are those waffles?"

Properly chastised, the kids focused on their food for about thirty seconds...before starting in again.

Tate slid a steaming waffle in front of him. The sweet batter tempted him until he got a whiff of her bare arm. Mmm. The scent of ripened apricots clung to her. He imagined nuzzling the bend in her elbow, searching for the source of that elusive scent. A peaked breast brushed his shoulder as she refilled his coffee, bouncing him back to reality. A harsh reality, where there was no touching at all. Her husky morning voice murmured a low apology in his ear, sending shivers down his spine.

Living through the next few hours where even innocent contact held promise, would probably kill him. Glancing up, he managed a rough, "Thanks."

"No problem." She smiled sweetly. A little *too* sweetly in his opinion. His eyes narrowed when she slowly moistened her lips. "Anything else I can do for you?"

Aha. He recognized that challenging expression. She *had* purposely rubbed her breast on him as a reminder that he couldn't touch her, even when she was within arm's reach. Nathan withheld a chuckle. Tate wanted to play. Good. But how far could they take it?

He smiled. "Not right this second."

Another round of waffles disappeared before she shimmied into the chair next to him. Her silky knee brushed his, sending his knife clattering to the plate and his blood racing. She smirked. "What's on the agenda?"

"Who cares? We're in charge, so we get to decide."

"Cool!" Tyler said. "Can we play cowboys and Indians?"

"You wish," Nathan mumbled around a piece of bacon.

Tate gave Nathan a wry smile. "I'm guessing you get to be the Indian?"

"Always. Seems they forget they've got Sioux blood too."

"Then what are we gonna do?" Chelsea demanded. "Let's play princesses."

Tyler and Tanner looked horrified.

184

"I think we should hang outside and play some games." He gave Tate a pointed look. "You like to play games, don't you, Tate?"

"What kind of games?" she asked with a touch of wariness.

Nathan shook the canister of whipped cream, squirting a generous line on the waffle square perched on his fork. With his pointed tongue, he swirled the whiteness into a peak. He lapped noisily before sucking it clean. He offered a casual shrug, even when his stomach tightened at her soft gasp. "Something new, I think." He sprayed another dollop, slowly licking off the sweetness with long strokes of his tongue.

Her eyes darkened. Her breath quickened. Nathan noticed she wasn't nearly as confident as she'd been a minute ago.

"I'll warn you," she said. "I don't like to lose. I won't play fair if it means I have a shot at winning."

"Sportsmanlike conduct be damned?"

"You're on."

He grinned before he popped the waffle in his mouth. "Let the games begin."

Chapter Sixteen

Tate contemplated the kind of games Nathan had in mind while she loaded the dishwasher. True, she'd purposely brushed her breast over his shoulder. But only because he'd sneakily pressed his groin into her behind, disguised as "helping" her retrieve a coffee cup.

They'd promised Val no hot kisses. No lingering looks and no sex. Especially no mind-boggling-multiple-orgasm-inducing-sex.

The silverware clanked in the basket as she sprinkled in soap and latched the dishwasher door. She faded out for a minute, reliving the inferno they'd created last night.

Everything had been magical. The absolute darkness. The rough texture of his hands smoothing over her damp skin. His sharp teeth, the rasp of his beard on her spine. His hard thrusts as he'd lost himself inside her. Passion, followed by sweet kisses, loving caresses. Her toes damn near curled now, recalling the sheer erotic pleasure of them caving into their caveman instincts. The flush spreading over her cheeks owed nothing to the steamy water rising from the sink.

The dishwasher kicked on, startling her into dropping the twisted dishrag right to the floor.

Normally she didn't have sex on the brain. Then again, she'd never had sex with a man like Nathan LeBeau. Whenever he waltzed into view, in person or in her mind's eye, Whammo! Her circuits went haywire. What caused this reaction? His overwhelming masculinity? His insistence on romance when he had little time for it?

186

Tate sighed, realizing it was a combination of all those things. He was so…devastatingly male.

A shout permeated her thoughts. Outside the bay window she saw all four kids hanging on Nathan, trying and failing to wrest the water hose to the ground. He'd make a wonderful father. The kind who'd take an active part in child rearing and enjoy it. The kind of man she'd imagined settling down with.

She squashed that thought immediately.

Warning: this was strictly a summer fling not a prelude to a real relationship. Her longing for more with Nathan had increased only because of Val's moratorium on sex. Plus, the happy family aura in this house would skew anyone's judgment. She didn't want forever. Neither did he.

Her gaze was drawn back outdoors. In the yard, amidst shrieks and pleading bribes, Nathan surrendered, taking in a face full of water and a soaking to the skin.

And Nathan soaking wet was a sight to behold.

Mmm. Those sopping wet clothes definitely had to come off now. Tate drifted into the fantasy of peeling the black tank over his head. Leaving a trail of hot kisses on his cool skin as she gradually headed south. *Pop pop pop* went the snaps on his jean shorts, until his briefs were exposed. Inside the damp cotton, she'd wrap her warm hand around—

"Tate, come on." Tanner's exasperated voice cut through the sliding glass door and knocked her from her wet dream. "Uncle Nathan said if you didn't get out there he'd drag you out."

"I'll bet," she said, tossing the rag on the counter before following a dripping Tanner on the patio.

The minute her feet hit the hot concrete, she faltered.

Nathan stood armed with the hose, wearing a grin just a shade shy of evil. "Hello, Tate. Nice that you could join us."

Tate shivered despite the early morning heat. "Nathan, please."

"Please what?" He arced cold water over her bare toes.

The stinging sensation galvanized her into action. "Please do not spray me," she pleaded, sidling across patio, over the ceramic bricks toward the grass.

He followed her, splashing water up her calves. "You're asking a lot." Craftily, he asked, "What do I get if I don't spray you?"

"A hearty thank you?"

He shook his head. "Try again. The rest of us are wet, it's not fair that you're dry."

"But I wasn't playing."

"You're playing. You started it."

Tate ignored his double meaning and gauged her chances on making it to the shelterbelt where the hose didn't reach. If she ran like the devil was chasing her... She glanced up at the devil himself. "Okay. What do you want?"

His gaze devoured her head to toe. "What I can't have, at least not today." After a sly grin, he cocked his head toward the trees, sending his braid swinging. "I know what you're thinking, jungle girl. You can't outrun me."

"Says who?"

"Says the record I set at basic training for the hundred-yard dash." Nathan gestured with the hose. "But give it your best shot."

Tate took off. When the first blast of icy water hit the back of her knees, she screamed. Outraged kids rushed Nathan and she hightailed it across the yard until another wet explosion soaked her backside. He *was* fast. She took shelter behind a small mountain ash tree.

Nathan advanced.

Her pleas for mercy were lost as he doused her, loudly touting his superior warfare skills.

Wiping the water from her eyes, she glanced up at his sudden silence.

Nathan stared slack-jawed at the thin material of her tank top. The hose, now limp, drooped forgotten by his side.

A ripple of desire hit her like a blast furnace when he licked his lips.

Her nipples hardened, aching for the heat of his mouth to take away the chill. And was that water dripping from his chin? Or drool? No matter, she decided, wantonly raising her arms, reaching with cat-like languor for nothing in particular. Chewing her lower lip, she moaned into the stretch, her breasts pushed together higher, testing the limits of the flimsy fabric. She lowered her palms in a "don't-shoot-me" gesture. "I surrender completely. Do with me what you will."

Nathan hung his head and groaned.

She smirked. Game one winner: Tate.

After a rousing game of Duck Duck Goose, the kids scrambled off to the swing set and jungle gym area, leaving them alone.

Tate flopped on the ground, gasping for breath. "Now I know how Val stays so thin, chasing after kids."

"She loves it. These hooligans are her life. She's probably pacing the hospital corridor, wondering what horrors we let them eat for breakfast. I'm surprised she hasn't called a hundred times." Nathan plucked at the lush grass. "Thanks for cooking, by the way."

"No problem. I like to cook, but it seems pointless for one."

"Tell me about it."

Tate's eyes closed to the sun's light, relishing the decadent warmth on her damp skin. Stretching her arms overhead, the lazy move lifted her tank top, exposing her belly.

Next to her Nathan sighed his apparent contentment.

She smiled, ignoring the prickles of grass on the backs of her legs and arms and inhaled the dank smell of earth. A tickle moved over her stomach. Thinking it was a bug, she brushed it away.

It happened again several seconds later.

Tate opened her eyes to see Nathan rolling a long blade of buffalo grass between his blunt fingers, dragging it over her bared skin with unwavering concentration.

"That tickles," she said.

189

"It's supposed to." Resting on his elbow, he swirled the tip over her navel, glancing up to witness her reaction.

"Stop that," she said half-heartedly.

"I'm practicing."

"For what?"

"For when I use my tongue on you this way."

Heat shot straight to her core but she didn't move or even think beyond imagining it *was* his tongue tantalizing her.

He zigzagged the green strip across her shorts, hipbone-to-hipbone, lower, down to the slight rise of her pubic bone.

"Nathan." Tate scrambled onto her elbows. "Stop. We promised Val we wouldn't..." Her wary gaze drifted to the loud argument coming from the sandbox.

"We're not doing anything, just sitting on grass enjoying the heat." He blew gentle, coffee-scented breath across her bare midriff. "Can you feel the heat, Tate?"

Every inch of her body flamed with desire. Any coherent response dried up in her parched mouth.

"Besides," he continued, "they can't see us." Rotating the stem, he traced a path between her inner thighs. "I'm wondering how you taste here." He crisscrossed just the tip over her knees, down her shinbones to the tops of her bare feet. "And here. And everywhere in between." He wove the strand through her toes like the finest silken ribbon. "Would you like that?"

In her mind's eye, Tate saw his large callused hand circled around her slender ankle, as the tip of his pink tongue slowly licked between her toes. The scrape of his white teeth and the urgent suckling as he immersed each toe into the hot slickness of his mouth. Followed by the raspy stubble of his strong jaw against her vulnerable instep, the oh-so-sensitive ball of her foot, the susceptible tendons above her heel. A low moan escaped before she stopped it.

He chuckled and moved to the other foot.

She kicked at his hand and leapt away out of his reach. The anticipatory beating of the pulse between her legs and the answering pull in her nipples felt like a string stretched to the limit.

His heavy-lidded gaze raked over her. "What's wrong?"

"Nothing," she said, her voice sounding breathy and aroused even to her own burning ears. Dammit. Playing footsie with him was not on the list of options today.

Yet she admitted game two definitely belonged to Nathan.

Thumb in mouth, Hannah loped over. She held her arm above her head and Tate swung her onto her hip. "What's wrong?"

Hannah removed her thumb long enough to say, "Want momma," before she tunneled into Tate's neck with a little heartbreaking sob.

Tate sent Nathan a panicked look.

He rose to his feet. "I'm thinking we'd better use some diversionary tactics. Got any ideas?"

"What's on the list?"

Nathan scowled. "Don't know and don't care. Sometimes Val's stupid rules go too far."

Amen to that. "I checked out the art supplies here but they're pretty dismal." She shifted Hannah to the other hip. "Want to take them over to my house for a change of pace? Let them paint and do crafts for a while? They love that."

"That'd be good." His eyes brightened. "Can I bring Duke?"

Just what she didn't need, monster mutt in her newly repainted interior. Her eyes narrowed over Hannah's head. "Why?"

"He adores the kids. Plus the poor thing's been alone since yesterday. Do you think you can handle them for a few hours?"

"You're leaving me alone with four kids and a wild bear?"

Nathan laughed. "Duke will be the least of your worries. I'll be right outside. I've got to get the last dirt pile moved today." He stroked Hannah's crown. Tate's heart swelled at his loving gesture, before she tamped it down.

"With any luck, next week I'll start planting. You can help me then. Would you mind?"

"I'm sure we'll be fine."

Hannah squirmed and scampered off.

He ran a hand over his stubbled chin. "I need a shower."

"I could always get the hose," Tate suggested sweetly.

"I'll pass."

"Your choice." She gave him an appreciative once over. "Still, doesn't take much for me to imagine you naked." Tate ventured closer. "Think of me when your hands are circling your—"

"Tate," he warned.

She traced a beaded droplet of sweat from his temple to where stopped on his jaw. "Wouldn't it be romantic, creating our own sauna under the pounding spray of water? Suds. Steam. Your body becoming my own personal slip and slide? Mmm. I feel dirty just thinking about it, don't you?"

He forced a laugh as he turned away. "I would've been better off if you would have hosed me down."

🙒 🙒 🙒

The twins helped Nathan outside at Tate's house until they realized no amount of cajoling would convince him to let them drive the Bobcat. After they disappeared inside, Nathan wondered how Tate was holding up. The four lovable monsters overwhelmed him most days. And he was used to them. Not to mention the attention his neurotic dog required. Best that he let Tate and Duke work out their differences without his interference.

He'd finished spreading the last load of soil when Tate stepped into view. "Hey," she said, pouring him a drink. "How's it going?"

"Almost done." Nathan knocked back the water and held the cup out for more. "Glad it's not blazing hot out here today."

"I'll bet." Tate lugged the cooler to a rickety wooden bench, frowning at the clipboard and drafting papers spread across the slats. She plopped herself on the ground. "Worked up an appetite yet?"

Not for food. "Nah. What're the kids doing?"

"They all crashed while watching *Beauty and the Beast,* They're pretty cranky." She glanced at him from the corner of her eye. "Did you know your dog snores?"

"Yeah. Sometimes he even wakes me up." Nathan wasn't about to confess it was because Duke slept at the bottom of his king-sized bed. Tate would never consent to spend the night if she suspected he kept the dog in close quarters out of sheer loneliness. He changed the subject before she thought to ask specifics. "You brought the baby monitor and movies along from Val's house?"

"Umm, not exactly." She emitted a tiny, self-conscious laugh. "If I admit I own a copy will you think I'm hopelessly juvenile?"

Pure sweetness. And Tate be thine name. He faced her, refraining from stroking the rosy flush along her cheekbones. "No. But it is a pretty romantic movie."

She frowned and scooted back into the bench, scattering papers. Scrambling to pick them up, she studied the drawing she'd replaced on the clipboard, angling it sideways. "What is this? A new project?"

He wanted to snatch away the clipboard holding the initial sketches for the landscaping for the new fire station. During breaks on jobsites, he'd been implementing some of the techniques Tate had taught him. "Why?"

She pointed to the bottom corner. "Just wondering what this scruffy green cat has to do with anything."

"What?" He leaned over, zeroing in on the area where her index finger tapped. "That's not a cat. That's a bush."

Her eyes widened. "Really? 'Cause no offense, but that is the worst looking bush I've ever seen." She squinted at the opposite corner. "So this row of spikes over here, resembling a medieval torture device is…"

"A stand of young aspen," he said irritably.

193

"Wow. Those are some horrifically deformed trees. Why—"

"Why don't you quit making fun of my drawing skills? I promised not to laugh at your penchant for sappy Disney movies."

Tate grinned and placed a small consoling kiss on the corner of his mouth. "Poor baby. Sorry. Don't take this personally, but I don't see how you can sell your landscaping services with these depictions." She jumped to her feet. "Hang on. I'll check on the kids and be right back."

Nathan brooded while she was gone, refusing to reexamine the primitive illustrations. He knew it didn't look like he'd spent any time agonizing over these plans, when in truth; he'd sweated bullets on this drawing. What if she was right? What if his lousy renditions would keep him from getting any landscaping business?

Tate bounded back and dropped beside him, setting the baby monitor handset within reach. She opened a plastic case, extracted an eraser and obliterated the sorry looking bush from existence. "There," she said. "Let's start from scratch."

"What are you doing?" He grabbed at the clipboard.

She held it aloft and pinned him with a haughty look. "I can't dig trenches with my bare hands or heft boulders like they were pebbles, but I can draw simple bushes and trees. Let me fix it."

"Okay." Nathan swept a finger along her furrowed brow. "Last night was amazing, by the way."

Another splotch of red colored her face, but she didn't break eye contact. "For me, too."

If they'd didn't have to worry about impressionable eyes and ears, he'd knock the clipboard from her hands, toss her on that luscious behind, kiss her until that sexy keening moan bubbled up. Touch her until their pesky clothes were hanging from the tree branches. Their naked bodies were covered in grass stains and their pleasure cries mingled with the summer breeze rustling through the treetops.

He cleared his throat as well as his mind. "So smarty, show me what a real professional would do."

"No problem." Rummaging around in the box, she withdrew four colored pencils. "This cat bush," she teased, "is it blue-green, grass-green, gray-green or forest-green?"

Nathan considered the pencils. "Grassy-green."

"Gotcha," Tate said and bent to her task.

Soon the rapid scratching of her pencil created a shape. Mesmerized, he suggested, "Think choke cherries."

Tate smothered a giggle. "That was supposed to be a chokecherry bush?" She deftly dotted the pencil and created small red-black berries, adding brown to flesh out the branches. "See? Doesn't that look better?"

"Couldn't have looked worse," he grumbled. "Okay, Picasso. Let's see you fix that spiky clump of aspen."

"Ugh," she shuddered. "Don't call me Picasso. I hate his stuff." She dug through the box with one hand while the other erased. "Are aspen leaves crimson-red or orange red?"

"Crimson, but they only turn that color late in the fall. Don't you want them yellowish-green to match the other greens?"

"No. It'll make a bolder statement to show them in autumnal colors."

Nathan cocked his head, studying her confident strokes. "So if you don't like Picasso which artist do you admire?"

Scratch scratch. "I guess Monet is my favorite." Black blended into the leaves, creating a small twig-like base. "His paintings are simple, yet complex." She reaching for the eraser and said, "Malcolm used to make fun of my peasant tastes. Tried to steer me in a more sophisticated direction...until our client admitted he was tired of contemporary art designs and favored realism too."

Silence.

No doubt if she'd had a free hand, she would've clapped it over her mouth for that admittance. Instead, she began sketching like mad.

A ball of jealousy lodged in his throat. "Don't think many art critics would refer to Monet's works as only appealing to peasants." He waited a beat. "So who is he?"

"Monet?" she said with contrived innocence.

"Ha ha. Not who I meant."

Her shoulders tensed but her tone stayed even. "Then who? Malcolm the Bastard?"

"Wow," Nathan said with false awe. "This Malcolm guy was titled? No wonder he had a bad attitude toward peasant art."

Tate snorted. Her strokes grew larger and bolder. "Malcolm was a royal pain in the... Well, let's say, he was a toad I kissed, mistaking him for a prince."

"Remained a frog?"

"Yeah. Unfortunately I didn't realize it until he'd stormed the castle gates. By then it was too late. Hand me the white."

"Enough with the fairy tale references. Tell me the truth, Pinocchio."

She started on the trees. "The truth is the bastard stole my project design and tried to pass it off—not only to a big-time client as his idea—but to the partners in our firm."

Puzzled, he asked, "You didn't put up with that, did you?"

"No." The lead on the pencil snapped but she didn't reach for a replacement, nor did she look at him when she muttered, "Look, it's complicated."

"Did kissing him make the complication?"

"In a way." She furiously sharpened a gray pencil.

He waited for her to elaborate. She didn't. He couldn't stand it. "Tate, what happened?"

Without missing a pencil stroke she said, "Malcolm was my supervisor. We became involved, against company policy. Stupid mistake. So when I discovered he'd only been sneaking around with me to get me to create designs for *his* client..." She laughed bitterly. "He lied to me, and used me and my artwork to secure his position as department head. Of course he denied everything, including our relationship."

Nathan paled. "Then what happened?"

"I went before the board and spilled the whole sordid story. We both ended up temporarily suspended and the client walked. Luckily, my labor rep was a lot shrewder than his and blamed my behavior on grief. Hence the unpaid trip back here and the time to settle my aunt's estate. I was damn lucky I didn't get canned, but it still might happen at my reinstatement hearing."

Sickness washed over him as he considered the parallels. Wasn't he doing the same thing? In keeping the Maxwell Competition a secret from her? Using her design to ensure a win? "So what now?" he prompted, curling his hands into fists.

"I wait. The hearing is in a couple of weeks." Another broken pencil rolled to the ground. "And I try not to make the same mistake ever again."

"Is that why you only wanted this to be a strictly sexual arrangement?"

"That was the original deal, right?"

Nathan took a chance. "Things can change."

The eraser stopped moving. "Why?" she demanded. "Do you plan on telling me that my bedroom skills need some work?"

"God no. Why would I ever think that?"

She glared at him. "You want to hear Malcolm's parting shot? I should have suspected he was using me because I wasn't exactly the type of woman men fantasized about."

Rage burned inside him. "He told you that?"

"Yes."

"Why didn't you tell me about this?"

"I'm sure you haven't told me everything that happened with Kathy. Frankly, I don't want to know. I figured my sob story didn't matter either." She met his gaze again but the defiance in the blue depths didn't mask the pain.

It ripped at him. Now wasn't the time to delve into this distressing part of her past. Or to admit he knew exactly how she felt. "It does matter, but not in the way you imagine." After he handed her another white pencil she ducked her head from view and attacked the aspens with renewed vigor.

Mired in his own guilty thoughts, Nathan let silence fill the uneasy void. No wonder she only wanted sex and scoffed at his ideas of romance. Her heart wasn't the major organ involved in a purely physical relationship.

Yet Nathan couldn't wrap his mind around the idea that Tate believed that she wasn't enough, sexually speaking, to fulfill a lifetime's worth of fantasies. As much as he loved the idea of never leaving her bed, he craved her fun, adventurous nature as much as her body. Her sweetness. Her honesty. He liked everything about her.

Hold on. He mentally backtracked. Wanting more from her than the agreed upon sex was dangerous. Admitting using her house as his entry in the Maxwell competition wouldn't make her happy. Add in the fact she was completing his schematics for the fire station as an added incentive for the committee to pick his entry for the contest...

No way could he confess now.

He grabbed a handful of pebbles and tossed them toward the street. He wished he'd never entered that damn competition in such an underhanded way. For the first time he wondered if losing Tate was worse than losing the contest.

"Ta-da!" she said proudly. "What do you think?"

Nathan took the proffered clipboard, studying the transformation. Her artistic skill, combined with his initial vision, had changed the drawing from ho-hum to va-voom. Color exploded everywhere. From the shrubs and trees on the corners to the new retaining wall. "I think you and I make a great team," he said, playfully nudging her. "Maybe you should quit your job in Denver and come to work for me as my personal designer."

"I'd think about it..." she pointed to the Bobcat, "...if I could ride that fun little thing?"

"*Drive*, not ride. But yes, I'd show you how to drive it. Piece of cake."

"Actually that's not a good idea. I'm inept when it comes to machinery." She frowned, "And animals. The only area I've had complete confidence in was art. And even now that's not a sure thing."

"Don't do that."

"What?" She'd started gathering the art supplies.

"You know what." Nathan tilted her face to meet his eyes. "The self-deprecating bit. You are a beautiful, capable, intelligent woman. Anyone who's said differently to you is moron."

A paused filled the void before her eyes snapped fire. "Don't feel sorry for me."

"Feel sorry for you?" he repeated, taken aback. "That's what you think I'm doing?"

"Yes," she said insolently. "Why do you think I didn't tell you about Malcolm? Now you're going all soft, sweet and romantic again, trying to change the parameters of our agreement. We both know that won't work."

"Why not?"

Tate's gaze never wavered. "Because no matter how much I like you, no matter how unbelievable the sex is, no matter how spectacularly the landscaping turns out, I'm still leaving when it's done."

The air seeped from his lungs until he felt he'd suffocate.

"See?" She poked him in the chest with the eraser tip, easily reading his defeated expression. "It's important we stick to the original plan, that way neither of us gets hurt."

Nathan then understood that he'd only scratched the surface with her today. Well, wasn't he an expert at digging? He gave her an encouraging smile, bringing the back of her small hand to the warmth of his mouth. "Tate, I'd never—"

His rebuttal fell aside as angry voices and a loud crash sounded from the baby monitor. Tate took off for the house. The naps might be over, but this conversation wasn't. Not by a long shot.

Chapter Seventeen

Two nights later, Tate leaned against the pickup's bumper, watching Nathan jog across the street. Even though the dappled sunlight bathed him in a golden glow, he exuded dark, sexy and dangerous.

Definitely dangerous to her heart.

The last two days had cast Nathan in a different light. His firm, yet loving demeanor when dealing with his nieces and nephews. The tireless way he pitched in with the endless household chores. Although she'd felt his burning gaze many times, he'd kept his word to Val. Tate respected him all the more for the fact that he *hadn't* touched her.

Something entirely too possessive rolled through her. She tried shrugging it off, chalking it up to the intensity of not acting on their animal impulses. Yet the nameless feeling lingered. The need for something more, something permanent with this man. Regret filled her soul. Under other circumstances things might have been different.

He offered her an apologetic grin. "Sorry it took so long."

"What's up?" she said, pretending indifference at his megawatt smile. Simply standing next to him filled her heart with joy.

"Richard is staying with the kids. Said he'd page us when they're tucked in so he can go back up to the hospital." Nathan studied the ground, shuffled his feet and thrust his hands in his pockets.

"What else?"

"Nothing." His boot heel traced a short crack in the sidewalk, displacing a patch of weeds. "Okay, there is one other thing." He looked at her curiously. "Want to ride up to Deadwood right now? I gotta drop off the Bobcat so Steve has it first thing in the morning and I hate making the trip alone."

Touched by his request, she casually set her hand on his chest. "We have time before our nightly duties begin?"

"Shouldn't take that long. Rich ought to call it a night right after the kids. Poor guy is dragging. He's gotten less sleep than Val."

Speaking of tired... Tate stifled a yawn. The past forty-eight hours had taken a toll on her. Besides dealing with four demanding kids, her job at The Girl's Club, a beast masquerading as a dog, the "no sex" rule, and tension surrounding said rule, she was wound more tightly than Nathan's ponytail holder.

"It's all right if you don't want to—"

"I'll go. I'm just tired. Can't fathom how Val and Rich do this everyday."

"Me either. Come on." He grabbed her hand, kissing the inside of her wrist as they crossed the alley to the flatbed. "You can catch a nap in the truck."

"What about you?" She frowned at the dark circles beneath his tired eyes. Not only had he helped out with the kids, he'd spent hours laboring on her landscaping.

"I'll manage," he said, giving her hand another peck.

He was sweetness personified, Tate thought sleepily. She jumped into the passenger side and nestled her head into the headrest. Whiny licks of steel guitar drifted from the speakers, covering the squeaking groans of the flatbed trailer, lulling her into the first relaxed state in days. She yawned again and closed her eyes.

Large, rough hands gliding up her bare thighs woke her. Every muscle that had been warm and pliant went hot and tight.

"Come on, sleeping beauty," he said. "Wake up."

Tate stretched slowly, aware of Nathan's intent focus on her breasts spilling out of her sundress. "Seems I recall something in that fairy tale about the princess being kissed awake," she challenged, pursing her lips in invitation.

His grip on her knees increased. "No kissing, remember?"

"Why? I don't see any impressionable kids running around, do you?" Her fingers leisurely followed the coiled muscles in his forearm to the bend in his elbow where her thumb stopped to draw lazy swirls. "When it's just us Val's rules don't apply, remember?"

"Damn. Must be more tired than I thought if I forgot that. Come here." He tugged her sideways across the seat toward the welcoming heat of his hard body.

She waited breathlessly for his lips to brush across hers in his usual gentle, captivating kiss.

Instead Nathan devoured her. Planting his lips firmly over hers, his tongue plunged inside, manipulating her mouth to meet his assault. Before she caught her balance, he'd yanked her from the cab and wrapped her legs securely around his lower back. His shoulder swung the door shut and he pressed her back against the sun warmed metal.

"Nathan—"

"No talking." He nipped the slope of her neck beneath her ear. "We can do that at Val's. Let me touch you." Fingers curled over her breast, puckering her nipple between his knuckles. His tongue traced the vein throbbing in her throat while hot breath seared a wet path over the dampness. "You feel so damn good, Tate."

While one hand unbuttoned her sundress, the other feathered loving touches across her jaw. Fingertips gentle as raindrops grazed the soft tops of her breasts until she arched into him, silently begging for more.

His expert ministrations left her weak. Tate ground her pelvis against his hardened sex. A rush of moisture soaked her panties when Nathan slipped a finger inside the elastic band. Need like fire slammed into her.

She wanted skin on skin. His hardness to her softness. She longed to feel his sleek chest rubbing against the cushion of her breasts. To watch his face lost in passion and to hear his growl of approval as he pushed into her moist core.

Nathan eased his hips back; his knuckles swept ever lower on her abdomen.

Carelessly her head fell back against the pick-up window as he scraped his teeth up her throat, pausing to give little suctioning love bites everywhere his busy mouth landed.

"Look at me."

Tate swallowed hard at seeing the passion that had turned Nathan's hazel eyes black with desire.

He brushed deceptively soft kisses around the vicinity of her trembling mouth. But she knew there wasn't a soft thing about this man right now. When his lips moved back and his panting breath tickled her ear, she nearly whined.

"Tate," he said on a groan. His head dropped dejectedly onto her shoulder. "Dammit, I don't have a condom. And your purse is at Val's."

The frustrated wail threatened to work loose from the depths of her womb. "Maybe if you pull out—"

"I won't take a chance on getting you pregnant, no matter how much I want you." His forehead rubbed over her cheekbone in a sweetly consoling gesture that melted her heart. "God. You have no idea how *much* I want from you," he said softly. "I'm so sorry."

She blew out a resigned sigh. "Not your fault."

Nathan's smile didn't reach his eyes as he set her on the ground. "I am sorry," he repeated.

"I know." Her gaze landed on the rise and fall of her naked breasts flapping in the evening breeze. She buttoned her dress, trying to regain her bearings. One kiss, okay, more than a simple kiss, and they'd both lost complete control. Okay, *she'd* lost complete control. Nathan had retained a cool head and put the brakes on.

Loud cursing followed a rolling thump. Tate watched as Nathan kicked a large rock halfway across the empty field.

Yeah, those brakes of his were definitely wearing thin.

His chivalry wasn't surprising. She found him the most sincere and appealing when he wasn't trying to bowl her over with romance. But by the rigid set of his shoulders, she doubted he'd appreciate her pointing the sentiment out, out loud.

As she straightened her clothing she took in their surroundings. Through the deserted clearing and the towering pine trees, she decided they were close to Highway 385, a main tourist thoroughfare. Quite a show they'd almost put on. "So," she said coyly, "I guess that ride you promised me is out."

"Not the kind of ride we had in mind." He angled his chin toward the machine a few feet away. "But would you like to..."

"Would I like to what?"

"Drive the Bobcat?"

"Seriously?" she asked with immediate skepticism. "You'd let me drive your cute little machine?"

He winced. "Yeah. My cute little machine. You said you thought it might be fun."

"You'd trust me with your two thousand horsepower precious baby?"

"Women." He gave a mock shudder. "Not two thousand HP, sixty HP."

She stepped closer and repeated, "But you'd trust me with it?"

"I'd trust you with anything." With infinite tenderness he traced her cheek, her throat, her shoulder and bare arm. Upon reaching her hand, he threaded their fingers together. "So is that a yes?"

His simple touch sizzled. Coupled with his sweet words and soft eyes, Tate was astonished. Did Nathan's complete trust in her include his heart too? She chalked up the answering thrill that went through her to his contagious romantic notions. "Yes."

"Come on then. It's almost dark."

Tucking away the cozy feeling to savor later, she watched Nathan unhook chains and the snake's nest of tie-downs that he'd so meticulously fastened earlier. He started the machine and backed it down the loading ramps. It belched a large cloud of black smoke, followed by a series of ear piercingly loud beeps. Once he turned around on the ground, he motioned her over.

"Climb in," he yelled. "I'll show you how to work the controls."

"Where am I supposed to sit?" she yelled back.

He patted his lap and grinned.

"No way. There's no room."

"You'd be surprised at the room in here. Come on. Don't be such a chicken. It'll be fun," he shouted.

Fun. Yeah right. Her parents never even let her near the riding lawn mower. If she told Nathan of her inexperience when it came to machinery, he'd recant his offer. Crashing the damn thing didn't seem as mortifying as admitting her ineptitude.

She cursed her sundress, crawled inside the cab, and perched on Nathan's knees. Her body slid down his muscular thighs until her butt met his groin. The unmistakable hard lump in his shorts revved her pulse back into overdrive. Turning her head, she lifted a brow.

Nathan beamed. "See what you do to me?"

"More like I can *feel* it. Maybe this isn't the best idea."

"Ah hell, Tate. What's a little erection between friends?"

"Not little at all," she pointed out, then pinned him with a curious look. "Friends? Is that what we are, Nathan?"

Something elusive skated through his eyes. "You even have to ask me if we're more than friends?" he replied with a tight smile. "Anyway, just ignore it."

"Is that what you're doing, my *friend*?" She pressed the issue, and her bottom, down firmly, wanting more than a short answer. Didn't seem likely they were only discussing an untimely erection. "Ignoring it?"

"At this point I don't have a choice. Neither do you. Now listen up."

Tate shifted forward on his legs. The cramped space, their raging hormones, and no condom weren't doing either of them any good. Ditto for the veiled conversation. She tried to concentrate but the cadence of his low voice brought to mind how those baritone sounds were ideal for whispering sweet sex talk in her ear. While he filled her over and over until they were both spent and covered in sweat.

"Tate?" he said impatiently. "Are you listening?"

No wonder her parents hadn't ever let her use the weed whacker; her concentration was nil. "Umm, sure."

Nathan demonstrated the lever's functions. With no steering wheel, gas pedal or brake on the floor, the little machine she'd deemed cute, seemed dangerous with the constant vibrations that caused a low level hum throughout her body.

After handling the controls under Nathan's watchful eye, she decided it was sort of fun zipping around. Powerful. No wonder men had such a hard-on for machines. Geez. Her brain affixed a sexual connotation to everything lately.

They circled the dump truck twice before Nathan jammed the levers in neutral and climbed out, leaving her alone in the driver's seat.

Tate tried not to panic. "Where should I go?"

"Behind that pile of gravel and park. Go slow," Nathan gave her arm a reassuring squeeze, then plopped a hideous orange hardhat on her head. He smirked. "You look sexy. Don't hit the floor control on the right because it drops the bucket. I'll be right behind if you need anything."

The machine lurched as Tate eased both levers forward. Somehow she managed not to scream. The gravel pile seemed to grow further away with every vanishing minute of daylight. She clamped a lid on her fear. Nathan would rescue her if anything went wrong. She sped up from her turtle-like speed, shocked by the increased humming vibrations in the seat.

Wow. That felt kind of good. Kind of kinky, but good nonetheless. She wiggled down, her flimsy sundress moved up, exposing her bottom directly to the seat. Slow tingles started at her epicenter, teasing all the way to the back of her bare thighs. Buzzing pinpricks like hot fingers danced across her skin. Helplessly lost in the erotic sensation, she bit back a moan. The hardhat tilted forward, blocking her vision.

Nathan's unexpected warning shout had her jumping out of her ultra-sensitized skin. Embarrassed, she turned around to see not concern, but a gigantic grin creasing his face.

Had he known the effect of the vibrations? Is that why he insisted on this test drive? Additional stimulation was the last thing she needed. Heat rolled over her body, from the tips of her tingling toes to the hairs standing on end and everywhere in between. Especially in between. She clamped her legs together to stave off another round of tremors, but the clenching of her outer thighs made the throbbing in her interior muscles much worse.

Tate threw the levers to full throttle and aimed for the gravel pile. Nathan's shouts fell on deaf ears. She ignored the aching buzz between her legs. The sooner she climbed out of this life-size vibrator, the better.

She circled the pile of rocks four times before she remembered how to stop the contraption. Needing to regain some semblance of rationality, Tate parked, left the Bobcat idling in neutral and wiped the guilty sweat from her brow.

"What the devil just happened? Why did you take off like that?"

Tate couldn't meet his gaze. Her insides quaked, her outsides shook and she was one twitch away from complete orgasmic meltdown.

He reached in and switched off the engine. "Tate? What's wrong?"

She sensed him studying her. Taking in her shallow breath, her suddenly rosy skin. She tried scramble away from him before he discovered the shocking truth. Then Nathan's rough-skinned hand coasted up her arm and nearly set her off.

Great. Now she was practically having orgasms from his accidental touch.

"Look at me." He pushed her back into the seat, tilting her face toward his. Recognition lit his eyes. "My God. You're turned on. From driving around—"

"As if you didn't know," she snapped. "This is not funny."

His eyes went wider. "You think I *planned* this?"

"Come on. You had me ready to...explode by the pickup before you tricked me into taking this crazy X-rated ride."

The fingers gently stroking the pulse hammering in her throat changed...into an insistent caress. "And now?" he murmured.

Tate would rather bury herself face first in the dirt pile than confess the truth. "It's worse, a lot worse, thanks to you." Or *no thanks* to you, she added with a mental raspberry.

"Gee, Tate," he said silkily, without an ounce of remorse. "What can I do?"

"Just ignore it."

"No. That came out all wrong. Let me help." Nathan boosted her up onto the back ledge of the chair. Her head nearly poked out the top of the machine. Her bottom was perched precariously on the edge of the vinyl seat. With little space to move inside the tiny cab, his long legs hung outside the open doors.

"What are you doing?" She gasped at the gleam in his eye.

He straddled the small seat, making his face level with her crotch. Tate felt his every expelled breath across her skin. His fingers traced a subtle path up and down her calves, front and back.

She shivered with abandon right before her toes curled.

Slowly, he opened her legs wide.

Tate tried pressing her thighs back together. "What are you doing?" she repeated.

Nathan's gaze dropped from hers as he deliberately nudged the sundress up to her hips, slowly revealing the bare skin of her legs a scant inch at a time. "Helping you." The husky intensity in his voice was unmistakable even over the steady thrum of her pulse. The heat in his eyes nearly scorched her skin through her dress.

"How is this helping?" she said.

No answer.

He scooted closer and didn't seem to notice he'd banged his knees into the metal. After removing her sandals, he flicked his tongue against the bones on the top of her left foot above her toes. Kissing his way up her foot, his naughty, talented tongue swirled around her ankle. His slight beard scraped the instep. He used his teeth for a tiny, impudent nip, which he immediately soothed with his hot mouth.

"Holy mother."

He smiled before settling her twitching toes on his broad shoulder. She nearly came at the touch of her heel pressing against the smoothness of his muscled flesh. Other foot, same procedure, but in no way was the erotic process tedious. Tate whimpered, afraid and excited by her lack of control.

Nathan lowered his dark head between her legs.

Reading his intentions, Tate's panicked tone nearly overshadowed the husky timbre of her voice. "We're in public—" The insincere protest died when he brushed wet, open-mouthed, drugging kisses on the underside of her thigh. Her nipples went rigid. Her leg started to shake like a dog getting its belly scratched. Except Nathan's gaze was nowhere near her tummy.

"I don't care," he said, dropping another prolonged kiss on the other leg, higher up. "Let me taste you. I'll make the ache go away."

Oh God. It was all she could do not to latch onto his ears and drag that marvelous mouth exactly where it needed to be. "Umm…this won't help you," she offered feebly.

His chuckle bordered on amusement. "I beg to differ. I've been dying to show you this lesson." He blew hot breath across her wet entrance. "And it happening in the Bobcat fulfills another longtime fantasy of *mine*."

Her breath hitched.

"You are my ultimate fantasy, Tate." His hands smoothed over her arms, raising them above her head. He placed one hand on each side of the black steel rollover cage surrounding them.

She clenched the metal until it bit into her skin. Halfway up her left thigh, his mouth stopped teasing kisses and he lifted his head.

"Do you trust me?"

"Y-yes."

"You still willing to push those sexual boundaries?"

"Y-yes."

His wicked grin had her fingers curling around the metal lattice tenfold. The pine-scented air turned thick and hot.

Tate couldn't think. She couldn't breathe. Mostly, she couldn't wait.

"Then hang on tight," he advised as he once again bent to his task. "I have a feeling this is gonna be one wild ride."

❧ ❧ ❧

Nathan forced his mouth to wander slowly up the silken expanse of Tate's thighs when he ached to race to her creamy core. The scent of her arousal tormented him. Along with the need to taste her, bury his eager tongue inside her where her juices were as sticky sweet as wild honey.

He drank in her face flushed with passion and gave her one defiant long lick right over her soaked panties.

Her eyes fluttered closed. She threw her head back and moaned. The hardhat crashed behind her but she didn't notice.

"Like that don't you?" He lapped at her again. Finesse be damned. Another vigorous sweep of his tongue. Followed by another. He yanked aside the flimsy barrier of her panties. Sure, strong, quick, he shortened his tongue strokes into tiny flicks.

Then he backed away.

She wiggled closer to his mouth, her gasp ended with a softly pled, "Don't stop. More. Faster. Please."

Nathan wasn't sure he didn't flat out growl at her sexy request.

He snapped the leash on the beast that sought to make her come over and over against his tongue until she begged for mercy. Drawing out her pleasure at this point wasn't an option. Still, he wanted to make his first intimate kiss memorable.

Like he'd ever forget the way her legs trembled. How her abdomen quivered. Her needy cry when his hot breath gusted over her swollen flesh. Or his first cherished glimpse of the glistening folds of her pink sex engorged with blood. God. She was gorgeous. Sweet. All soft and pink and wet for him.

Spreading her open with his thumbs, Nathan zigzagged his tongue up and down, around, inside her wet channel, rimming the outside, sucking the fleshy lips. Letting his tongue torment her everywhere except the spot pouting below her public bone.

Tate thrashed side to side, shaking the cage. "Don't tease. I'm so close that it almost hurts. Nathan, *please.*"

At her plea, Nathan settled his open mouth over her clit and sucked hard, drawing on that responsive bit of flesh until it constricted and pulsed. Until she twisted off the seat, her hands rattling the cage, sounding like applause.

Wind whistled through the treetops. Blue jays and robins chirped. Squirrels chattered and brown bats took wing in the warm evening air. He tuned it all out.

She came instantly, bucking, straining, grinding her wet, throbbing sex against his face. Then she slumped against one side of the Bobcat, her chest heaving in the aftermath.

Except the pulsating against his mouth slowed, but hadn't stopped. The erection straining behind his zipper twitched, fully expecting a turn at relief. He ignored it and fought for control.

"Again," he demanded, lapping at another rush of moisture.

"I can't," she whimpered, whipping her head side-to-side.

Somewhere in the distance a coyote howled.

"You can." He bit the soft inner flesh of her moist thighs, licked and soothed the bite with his tongue. "You will. Right now." Instead of backing off, he shifted, inserting his middle finger deep into her slick opening.

She gasped, pressing her mouth to her upper arm, biting her own skin to muffle the cry. Her abdomen clenched and pulled his finger higher inside her warm walls.

Patiently, Nathan used tiny whips of tongue, gentle nips of his lips until she was ready for direct contact. Adding another finger, he curled the tips against the inside wall connecting with her hot spot the same time his mouth fastened to her needy nub and suckled hard. He plunged and withdrew his fingers until she began to pump into his rhythm. His thumb drew her sweet wetness down to the crevice of her bottom and pressed against her rosy tight rear opening.

She stiffened up.

"Relax, baby. That's as far as I'm gonna go."

In the ultimate show of trust, she tipped her hips back and spread her thighs even wider.

Feeling her, tasting her, Nathan knew he'd never been this in tune with any woman. No woman had ever trusted him so completely. And for the first time, he believed he might be worthy of such a woman.

He continued to work her to an orgasmic frenzy. Tate's modest moans built into a full-fledged scream Her whole body convulsed at every contact point, around his fingers, his tongue, his thumb, strangely synchronized to the pulsing in his own groin.

Repeatedly rubbing his hips against the back of the seat while he pleasured Tate, his cock demanded release. His balls lifted, his brief pause for control was a tiny memory.

Nathan had no choice but to let go.

He came with her, hard, in a burst of hot satisfaction. Blood roared in his ears, blocking light, sound and motion. Time lost all meaning. Finally, he roused himself from where his cheek stuck to Tate's still quaking left thigh.

Normally he'd be completely mortified at his lack of restraint. But what just happened between them transcended embarrassment. It transcended logic. It even transcended sex.

Nathan had fallen hard for her. All of her; her sweetness, her sexiness, her stubbornness. Mostly her complete acceptance of everything about him.

God help him but he loved her like he'd never dreamed possible.

And there wasn't a damn thing he could do about it.

Or stop her from leaving.

If he told her how he felt right now she'd dismiss any declaration of love as the aftereffects of incredible sex.

When had his experiment with romance gone so terribly wrong? Why did everything between them feel so magically right?

Two quick vibrations broke through his daze. Reluctantly he glanced down to the cell phone attached to his belt.

Richard.

Perfect timing? Or lousy? Either way, he was saved from voicing his conflicting thoughts.

Which was a good thing. Because at that moment his ability to speak was lodged somewhere below the lump stuck in his throat.

Chapter Eighteen

"Yes, Mom." Tate withheld a bliss-filled sigh as Nathan's warm, rough tongue licked a path down her spine. "Don't worry. I'm being careful."

She eyed the half-empty condom box and grinned. She and her mother were *not* holding the same conversation. Nathan's chin dug into her tailbone. Tate squeaked, "What? Sorry. No, the TV distracted me. What did you say?"

"TV, my ass," Nathan grumbled, chomping her left butt cheek.

She clapped a hand over her mouth, smothering another squeal. "No. I haven't heard a word from the board. Of course I'd call you." An impatient breath exploded. "Geez, Mom, I'm *twenty*-nine, not nine... But—" Her protests died against her mother's usual rant.

Tate banged her head against the braided rug. Ouch. Nope, not a bad dream. She really was trying to have a normal conversation with her mother—as if that were *ever* possible—stark naked, sprawled face down on the floor after another rigorous bout of Nathan's lovemaking.

Not lovemaking, she mentally corrected, awesome sex. Phenomenal sex. Rug-burns-on-her-butt-till-she-couldn't-*move*-her-butt sex.

She waited for her mother's rebuttal to end, not really hearing any of it. "I'll call the minute I hear anything. Bye." She flung the receiver. It skidded across the parquet floor. "Shoot me if I answer the phone again."

Nathan's rough-skinned palms moved up her back to cup her shoulders. His warm breath crept across her skin, causing a decadent shiver of abandon. "Come on, Tate. It wasn't that bad."

"No?" She rolled over to face him. "I don't remember your mom bossing you around this week." Nathan and Val's mother's early appearance had ended Tate's babysitting gig.

"No. Being your own boss creates a whole different set of problems."

"Poor baby," she cooed. "Tell me all about it."

His gaze turned pensive as he absentmindedly stroked feather-light touches over her arm. "Since I'm in charge of everything, if a bid or a project gets screwed up, I don't have any one to blame besides myself."

"But if you do an awesome job, then you alone can take all the credit, right?"

Shame darkened his eyes before looked away. What was up with that?

"Have you considered hiring on? Find someone to share the blame and the workload?" Tate rested her chin in her hand. "Or are you one of those perfectionists who believes your way is the only way?"

He winced, letting her know she'd struck a nerve. "I guess maybe I am. It's easier to do everything myself than to rely on anyone else, especially seasonal workers." His sigh flowed across her skin. "By the time I get them trained, they're either sick of working in the muck or they head back to college, grateful they're not stuck digging ditches permanently. I don't kid myself that installing utilities is fascinating."

"But do you like it?"

"I don't mind it most days." The tips of his fingers moved south to caress the pulse point in her elbow. "Between the heavy machinery and the earplugs, there isn't much sense for conversation. Guess that's a hard habit to break once I leave the jobsite."

Her heart pitched at his easy acceptance of how his life had turned out. Even if nothing between them could be permanent, she had to convince him that spending his off hours in such isolation was a waste. "Is that the way you see the rest of your life?"

"No."

"Then what do you want?"

"A home. A life like Val's." Nathan paused, seeming surprised he'd voiced that answer. "Being alone never bothered me much before. But now…"

Tate wondered if she'd played a part in his transformation, but she didn't have the guts to ask. "Why do you work so hard?"

"Lately I've been asking myself the same question." Scooting sideways, he cradled her against his body. "Scary stuff, to think I'll be crippled up when I'm sixty years old because I was too stubborn to admit it's gotten harder to keep up this crazy pace." He smiled smugly. "I've come up with a back-up plan. If this latest project pans out, I can shift the focus of my business. Work less hours, hire someone I trust to run the utility end and spend less time belowground and more time on top."

"Mmm." She inhaled his familiar scent and slipped her knee between his thighs. "I like the 'on top' part very much." She yelped when he pinched her butt.

"You would like that, jungle girl."

"So are you going to give me specifics on how your great new business scheme will turn your life into a dream?"

"No." He developed a sudden interest in the stuffed pheasant on the fireplace mantel. "Your turn. What are your options if your job bites the dust?"

Her warm feeling of sharing disappeared. "I don't know."

"Uh-oh." He propped his head on his elbow. "I'm beginning to hate that look."

"What look?" she said crossly.

"The one that says I'll never know what's going on behind those beautiful blue eyes." Using slow, melting kisses, he left her lips tingling and her thought processes scrambled. "Tell me, my sweet Tate," he urged against the corner of her mouth, "how do you see *your* future?" He punctuated each word with a moist kiss, each one an erotic promise, dropping progressively lower down her neck.

Hedging any subject wasn't usually this difficult. Then again, Nathan's interrogation technique was highly distracting.

"Tell me," he warned, releasing the beaded tip with an audible pop, "or I swear I'll do something romantic that involves no touching at all."

"I can't think when you touch me like that, so you'd better stop right now if you want me to talk. This may be your only chance."

He blew a raspberry on her belly. "Fine."

Tate wondered where to start. She wondered if she had the courage not only to admit the truth to him but to herself. "My future, huh? Well, before the suspension, I envisioned a big office with a secretary and an assistant. And I was the epitome of chic in my Prada and Armani suits as I flitted from board meetings to client lunches. Of course with my many successes I had to get a larger office so I had more wall space to hang my numerous industry awards."

"And now?"

"Awards mean nothing." When Nathan blanched, she clarified, "I mean, now I'd trade every designer outfit and cheap plaque for one day of Val's crazy life."

"Seriously?"

"Yeah. Wouldn't my mother throw a conniption fit if she knew the source of my envy was a housewife?" She looked right in his eyes. "Val and Richard have it all, don't they? Love, happiness, great sex—"she frowned,"—however, the jury is still out on why they feel compelled to reproduce like rabbits."

His rich chuckle warmed her from the inside out.

"I thought Val would end up like Ally McBeal—you know a competitive, driven lawyer and not the type of woman content to settle for being a lawyer's wife."

"Much as your mother sees you as the career woman she couldn't be?"

"I guess."

"Val would have made a great attorney, but her focus changed once she met Richard."

Tate nodded. "I've never known anyone so truly happy with their life until I spent time with Val. She wants everyone on the planet to experience that same level of contentment. I think that's why she's pushed me so hard to try teaching art classes. She remembered how much I wanted to do it when I was younger. If nothing else comes from this mini-sabbatical, she showed me that if my graphic art career is over, my life isn't. I can move in another direction."

He went completely motionless. "Which direction were you planning on moving, Tate?"

A chirping sound echoed in the foyer. Nathan's cell phone. Thank God. For once she welcomed the interruption and leapt up to answer it.

Nathan grabbed her ankle and she tumbled back to the floor right on top of him. He banded those beefy arms around her. "Going somewhere?"

She wiggled and thrashed, but his long, muscular legs pinned hers as effectively as his dark gaze. "To get your cell phone."

"I'm not supposed to let you answer the phone any more today under penalty of death, remember? Besides it's probably just my mother checking to see if I'm still slaving away."

"You usually are," she retorted when the phone continued to trill. "Fine. Ignore it. But I can't loll around naked all night. I need to get dressed. Now let me go."

"Not on your life. Stop pushing me away, Tate. I care about you. Every part, even the stuff you keep hidden. Especially the stuff I'm finding we have in common."

Nathan's eyes answered every question she'd avoided asking him since the Bobcat episode. And it scared her to death.

The landscaping was nearly finished. She'd have no excuse not to list the house and get back to her real life in Denver. Why did that eventuality fill her with dread? Why was she wishing for the time to explore a relationship that wasn't based on sex?

His manhood twitched and hardened underneath her belly. A rush of moisture answered. Her heart might be confused about what it wanted, but her body wasn't.

She whispered, "Don't go all sweet on me now, Mr. Romance. I'd rather you made me scream."

He lifted a brow. "You said you were getting dressed."

"I changed my mind."

"Good. Then there's hope for me yet." He seared her lips with an avaricious kiss. Branded her skin with the feverish touch of his hands. Without preamble he slid her body down the length of his and fit himself inside her with one decisive push.

"Yes," she hissed, grinding into him.

"God. I can't get enough of you," he groaned. "Even when I've just had you I want you. Even when you're driving me crazy I want you."

He swallowed her moans like they were much-needed oxygen. His callused fingers burrowed into her buttocks as if the sweat sheening their bodies weren't enough to hold them together. He broke away and growled in her ear, "Does that feel sweet?"

"Am I pushing you away?" she countered, gliding her slick skin across his and rolling on top of him. Rodin's sculpture *Paolo and Francesca* came to mind. Now she knew why that erotic piece had always held her fascination: The position put her in control. Tate planted her hands next to his face on the floor. "Harder, faster, more. I want it all, and I want it right now."

Then all thoughts zoomed from her head as Nathan sat up, and hooked her ankles at the small of his back. He kept her on his lap, wrapped around him as he impaled her with each deepening stroke of his cock. Shudders of absolute ecstasy racked her body.

The earth stopped but for the points where their bodies connected and pulsed as one. A lifetime passed before he joined his mouth to hers in a heartfelt kiss that showed her the sharing of hopes and dreams was as intimate as the sharing of bodies.

In that instant, Tate knew she hadn't found nirvana. She'd found love.

𐆞 𐆞 𐆞

Although the night air was balmy, Nathan shivered as he climbed into his truck. Tate had sent him packing again. He'd wanted to spend the night— the whole night—with her. Waking up together. Indulging in passion when she curled her lissome body into him in the early morning hours. But she'd given him some lame excuse and shooed him out the door. It confused the hell out of him.

He'd given her space she seemed to need after they'd lost control in the Bobcat. He should've been the one embarrassed, coming in his pants like an overanxious teen. To that end, he'd given up on any pretense of romance. Instead of acknowledging that their relationship had changed, she blithely continued on as before, spreading sunshine over every avenue of his life. He'd be content basking in the glow if it weren't for the fact he'd nearly completed her landscaping project.

And if it weren't for the other fact he was hopelessly in love with her.

Telling her proved the major problem, although he had spilled his guts pretty good tonight about the kind of life he wished he had. The kind of life he now envisioned only with her.

Damn. He knew she'd be gone the minute the ink dried on the realty contract marking her house sold. Tate was a city girl. Even when she feigned nonchalance about her career and the strained relationship with her mother, an undercurrent of anxiety colored her every action. With good reason, given her past history. He had nightmares about her reaction when she discovered his deception. Mostly, he was mired in guilt on why he hadn't confessed when he'd had ample opportunity. Then again, whenever he brought up the future—hers or theirs—that blasted woman changed the subject.

They'd have to address these issues soon, because her time in Spearfish was running out and his luck was wearing mighty thin.

𐆞 𐆞 𐆞

The next afternoon as Nathan and Tate took a breather from planting trees, the phone rang. "Hello? Paul? No, no, that's fine you weren't interrupting anything." Tate raked a dirty hand through her hair and started to pace, ignoring Nathan's quizzical stare.

Her heart pounded. A trickle of dread replaced the sweat running down her back. This couldn't be good news. She could count on one hand the number of times her supervisor had called her.

After listening to Paul's ubiquitous small talk, she forced a dry chuckle. "Okay, I'm stumped on why I'm getting your personal attention on a Sunday." She grabbed a pen and paper and wrote furiously. "How soon do you need it?... No, that's fine... Six *full* pages?... Sure. No problem. I'll expect it tomorrow then... Of course FedEx delivers here." She laughed. It sounded fake. "I'll call the minute it arrives. Bye." Tate hit the off button and scratched her chin with the phone's antennae.

"What's up?"

"I don't know." She stared at the portable phone as if it might disappear. "That was the head of my department. He's sending me some big rush project. Top priority layout for one of the firm's biggest clients."

Nathan guzzled the glass of water and wiped his mouth. "I wouldn't think suspended employees got those kinds of projects."

Tate sniffed. "They don't and I certainly haven't before today."

"So what does that mean?"

"They're giving me a chance to redeem myself?"

He went cross-eyed staring at a dirt smudge on the end of his nose. "Think it's a good sign?"

"Either that," she crossed to him and wiped off the spot he missed, "or Paul will deem whatever I create as lousy and use it as an excuse to can me."

"Would he really do that?"

"With glee."

When Nathan's cell phone rang, Tate stared out the kitchen window, relieved for the disruption.

This whole spur-of-the-moment assignment felt hugely wrong. It wasn't luck that'd landed this in her lap. Projects of this size were lined up months in advance. Was this a test?

Another problem niggled. Of all the partners in the firm, Paul had wanted to fire *her* immediately—not golden boy Malcolm. Not only had he questioned the legality of her proposed extended leave, he'd never believed in her ability to handle the designs of their prominent clients in the first place. So why was Paul dangling this plum assignment in front of her now? To see if she'd blow it? Then he'd have concrete proof to convince the other partners to cancel her contract at the reinstatement hearing.

It galled her. After years of questioning the sacrifices she'd made in her life for the career she'd never really wanted, everything ultimately boiled down to one man's decision.

Tate steeled her resolve. So, she just wouldn't fail. No matter if she had to spend the next week working nonstop, she'd blow everyone's socks—and Paul's argyles particularly—right out of Arapahoe County.

Nathan's strong arms wrapped around her. "You really need this to project to dazzle them, don't you?"

"Yeah." Her reply sounded lackluster even to her own ears. She snuggled into him, wondering when he'd sensed she needed to be held. "Sounds like I'll be surgically attached to my drafting table."

"Then come to Val's with me tonight. My mom is making her famous pot roast with all the trimmings. I know Val, Richard and the brats would love to see you."

A family dinner. God, it'd been months since she'd passed pleasantries along with the potatoes. She missed her parents, but not that irritating feeling of their restrained tolerance. A wave of homesickness enveloped her. But where was home? Tate wasn't sure she knew anymore.

Her dinner that night with the LeBeau/Westfield clan only added to her confused state. What would it be like to be part of such an accepting, loving family on a permanent basis?

Nathan had been aware of her melancholy upon returning to her house. He teased, tickled, and taunted her until she chased him outside and they rolled around in her backyard like a couple of frisky puppies. Sex between them had been intense and spontaneous but never silly and fun. She giggled, imagining the odd places on her body she'd discover grass stains.

Afterwards, they stargazed on a blanket, wrapped in the secret world of lovers; hushed whispers, stolen caresses. The simplicity of this intimacy filled her soul with joy and sadness. Leaving Nathan would be the hardest thing she'd ever done. But she had no choice. And he hadn't mentioned he wanted more.

For the next few days, Tate scarcely moved from her dining room table. She'd reluctantly called Grace and cancelled her art classes. She'd miss her students, their enthusiasm, pride, and yes, even the pencil shavings, and spilled paint. Teaching had taught her far more about herself than the little she'd been able to impart to them.

Grace had been strangely brusque but understanding of her dilemma. All was not right with her friend but Tate didn't have the time to push for answers Grace wasn't inclined to give.

Elated with her project design and the fact she'd slipped under Paul's deadline by a full day, Tate returned the package express mail. Any decision regarding her career was out of her hands now. She'd delivered her best work and if it wasn't good enough, she could stop running from her past mistakes and start her future with no regrets.

   

Later that week, through the torrential downpour, Nathan checked to see that the new retaining walls had held. The tiny new patches of buffalo berry soaked up the moisture. Even the bushes and trees had sprouted in the past week. Good. When the committee inspected the work tomorrow, everything would be green and lush.

Thunder rumbled; lightning cracked. The hair on the back of Nathan's neck prickled and he ran for the shelter of Tate's porch.

Inside the pitch black house he called, "Tate?"

No answer.

As his eyes adjusted he crossed through the living room and dining area into the kitchen. He half-expected to see Tate standing at the back door, a filmy white gown frothing at her ankles, a tiny nymph mesmerized by the powerful beauty of the storm.

Nope. Where was she? He moved through the main floor in silence.

A damp breeze blew through the opened windows at the far end of the hall. Her erotic scent beckoned him up the staircase. He paused at door leading to Tate's bedroom.

He watched the curtains billow and curl against the wind, sending humid air swirling into the room. Small puddles glistened on the wood floor as raindrops pelted the screen.

His fingers fumbled against the wall searching for the light switch.

"Don't," she warned in a hoarse voice. "Leave it dark."

"Tate?" he said, striding toward a muffled sniff beneath the rumpled covers. "What's wrong? Honey, are you sick?"

He eased onto the bed. Only the top of her scalp was visible beneath the down comforter. His fingers swept the blonde spikes from her forehead. "If you're cold I can shut the window."

"Leave them open. I'm not cold. I like the smell of rain."

The soft sounds of falling water mixed with the quiet hitches in her breathing. Gently, he peeled the covers back. When he glimpsed her tearstained face, her sadness sliced straight through him.

"What is it?" he asked, holding her chin in his palms, letting his cool fingers brush her damp cheeks. He ignored the rapid beat of his own pulse. "You afraid of the storm?"

"No. The storm will blow over." Tate's head nestled further into the pillow but her lips trembled. "I'm afraid this won't."

The room stayed silent except for the beat of rain on the windowsill. It felt like Chinese water torture, the steady drips of rain against the agonizing wait for Tate to speak.

She exhaled. "I heard from the agency today."

Nathan's stomach turned at her flat tone. He didn't have to ask to know it had been bad news. Kicking off his clothes, he slid in beside her, ready to offer any kind of comfort she needed.

She moved into him arms automatically, clung to his neck and sobbed. Great gasping breaths followed a torrent of tears that soaked his chest and broke his heart. He held her, murmuring calming words, stroking her, kissing her until finally she settled down.

Tate's moist breath floated over his chest in a hesitant stutter. "Nathan. Please. Don't go."

"Ssh. I'll stay right here."

"Promise?"

"I promise. Just rest." A few hiccups later, her breathing slowed. When had Tate ever allowed herself to need him? To need anyone? Nathan's hold on her tightened. With Tate snuggled against him, he drifted, content in ways he'd ever dreamed possible. Wishing for things he'd long forgotten he had ever wanted.

A crack of thunder jolted him awake. Disoriented by the tickle of silky hair under his chin, Nathan glanced down and saw Tate trying to sit up. She couldn't move with his arms banded around her stomach. "Relax."

"What time is it?" she said groggily.

"I don't know." He lazily stroked the soft bare skin above her abdomen. "I think the power went out. You okay?"

"Yeah."

"Want to talk about it?"

Tate shuddered. "I'd rather not relive my blubbering idiot routine, thank you very much."

"Don't apologize," he said, drawing in her sweet, warm fragrance mixed with the clean scent of rain. "Although I had fantasized that the first time I was invited into your bed your cries would have been from pleasure."

After a second of silence she placed a small kiss on his biceps. "It could be pleasure. But as you can see my bed is not exactly seduction central. Flannel sheets instead of satin. A goose-down comforter instead of a silk duvet. And I don't look the part of a temptress in this ratty old T-shirt. Maybe if I wore a slinky scarlet negligee I'd appeal to your romantic nature?"

Nathan rolled on top of her, silencing her protests with a scorching kiss. "Look at me. It's never been about that and you damn well know it."

Her eyes widened. "That coming from Mr. Romance? I thought you'd be appalled at my utter lack of frills and imagination for the boudoir."

"No." He seized her gaze. "The appalling reason you haven't invited me into your boudoir, my sweet Tate, is because you knew once I'd been in your bed, I'd never leave it. And then you couldn't deny what is between us." He kissed her thoroughly, with a measure of harshness, melding their mouths until their very breathing became one. Until she shifted restlessly beneath him.

"Fine. Now that you're here, make yourself useful and touch me," she said, provocatively arching her hips.

Nathan pinned her hands above her head to ensure he held her undivided attention. "Make myself useful? My, aren't we flip. Why are you so scared?"

Tate squirmed, but not from arousal. "I'm not scared."

"Uh-huh." He kissed the frown lines between her eyes before relocking his dark gaze on hers. "Physically no, you're very confident. We've made love in every conceivable place, in every conceivable way in the last few weeks, and it's been phenomenal. But emotionally, it's a different story."

"What more do you want?"

"This." His voice dropped to a low whisper. "I've fantasized about this, Tate. You, under me."

She tried pushing him away. He held firm.

"Let me get this straight," she said crossly. "After all the Kama Sutra stuff we tried and the damn near contortionist ways we've done it, *this* is what you fantasize about? Sex in missionary position?"

"No." He nipped the corner of her pouty mouth, nuzzling the pulse beating erratically near temple that gave away her panic. "I've fantasized about making love to you while looking in your eyes. Face-to-face, heart-to-heart. Since you can't escape from me in this position, you can't help but see the way I feel about you." Every emotion, fear especially, clenched his gut hard at his admittance, but for once he didn't try to hide it from her.

Her frank, startled gaze didn't waver. But neither did she ask him for an explanation.

Nathan ignored the ripping sensation near his heart from her silence. He swallowed her gasp of distress with a determined kiss, using his body to convey the love and tenderness he didn't dare put into words. She went from warm to hot. From tensed to yielding. His sex hardened at her sweet surrender even as he fought to be gentle. "Let me show you this is more than some Faustian agreement," he murmured. "Let me make love to you in the most romantic way I know. With my heart."

He removed her tattered T-shirt and the tiny pair of blue bikini panties. Nathan shucked off his socks, shuddering at the thrill of her small hands sliding down his boxers. His pants and underwear hit the floor in record time.

He moaned when she slowly rolled on a condom. His mouth took hers in a ravenous kiss as his knee spread her thighs apart.

Tate bowed, circling her arms around his shoulders, letting their bodies connect chest-to-chest, belly-to-belly, thigh-to-thigh. He immersed himself in her tight wet heat slowly, to draw out the moment. He stopped moving to hold himself stiff-armed above her.

"What?" she breathed, teasing frantic kisses over his chin, his jaw, his neck, any place her eager mouth could reach.

"Do you feel that?" he growled. "How perfectly we line up? How I fit you like I was made to love you?"

Tate clamped down on her internal muscles. "I don't need the words, Nathan. I need the action." Her fingers dug into his backside, not-so-subtly urging him to get moving. "Now."

He went completely still, ground his teeth and slowly pulled out.

Nathan sat back on his heels. He'd never believed he'd have the fortitude to back off when heaven summoned, but Tate had wrested control of the situation with harder-faster-now demands. This was not the special communing of bodies and souls he'd envisioned.

Damn. She was tricky.

Then again, so was he. This night he wanted to show her the other side of sex. The magic. The beauty. The romance. The rarity of what they shared. To make her understand the depth of his feelings before it was too late.

"What's wrong?" she asked with a hint of annoyance.

He absentmindedly ran his hand up her quivering thighs. "It's too dark in here. Got any candles lying around?"

Chapter Nineteen

"Candles?" she repeated, alarmed by Nathan's abrupt departure from her body. Had she done something wrong?

"Indulge me," he said, brushing his knuckles across her cheek. "I want to make love to you by candlelight. Is that so terrible?"

"No." She chose to ignore the *make love* comment. She watched his muscles ripple as he strode naked across her bedroom to the dressing table. "There's a candle on the right," she directed him. "Should be a light there someplace too."

"Ah. Here we go." A match flared, releasing a whiff of sulfur. The wick spit blue fire and began to glow. The sultry scent of vanilla drifted to her when Nathan placed the candle on the nightstand. He slipped back into her bed and the flame flickered wildly, but not nearly as wildly as her pulse.

Twin flames of desire burned in his eyes, along with something else. Determination. She sensed his restraint, his control, but mostly the maleness that gave her a forbidden thrill.

Propped up on his elbow, he said, "Much better. Now," he leaned over to drag his mouth over the tops of her breasts, "where were we?"

"Umm…" Tate tried to slide beneath him, to feel every bit of his warm hard flesh enveloping hers again. "Actually, we were already—"

"I don't remember exactly." The very tip of his tongue swirled maddening little circles over her nipple. "Guess that means we'll have to start over."

"Nathan," she protested. Tiny puffs of air puckered the nub into a hot, tight point and she gasped.

"Tate," he teased right back, offering sweet torture on the other breast. "Relax. No hurry." His warm breath flowed over her skin, sweeter than honey, thicker than syrup. His hands, usually eager and rough, caressed her like gentle waves. Yet he made no move to bridge the distance to her straining nakedness.

Need lashed through her. Images of his sweaty body plastered to hers, blood burning, sweat dripping, skin slapping. Cries. Moans. Screams. Tate wanted that blinding rush. Craved it. Dammit, she deserved it because his tender side was far more alarming than his sexual hunger. That she could handle. This type of...*reverence* scared the bejeezus out of her.

"You are so soft," he murmured, tasting the curve of her shoulder, sweeping his fingertips from the crest of a peaked breast to shaking knee. "In the rush to be inside you, I forget just how perfect the outside is. How perfect every part of you is to me."

She crashed. Burned. Utterly melted.

Tate closed her eyes and knew she'd lost the battle for control as she'd lost herself in Nathan's potent words. She hadn't allowed this unhurried meeting of bodies. For good reason. The glorious journey would undo her, especially when the route he'd mapped out was torturously slow. He meant to imprint his soul to hers so she'd never forget him. Her body ached for this surrender. Could her heart remain firmly out of his reach or was it already too late?

"I love your hands," he said, nibbling the knuckles. "Small, yet strong." He sucked her pinky into his mouth, swirling his tongue around only to release it with a perceptible pop. Nathan suckled and licked every digit. Good God. Even her *hands* were putty in his hands. She went limp. Only then did he move on.

And there was no rushing him, no matter what signals her body screamed. If she arched closer, he retreated. If she touched him, his languorous touches stopped entirely. Her only action was inaction. Regardless if she felt her flesh was unraveling from her bones with every lingering sweep of his tongue, every provoking nip of his teeth, every calculated touch, he controlled the pace.

Candlelight flickered, deepening the mysterious planes and hollows of his masculine face. No cocky smile. No smug gleam in his eye. Just Nathan engrossed in providing her pleasure. Tate was spellbound. Helpless. Completely lost in the way he made her feel. The tight rein she held on her heart slipped a notch.

Where Nathan's mouth touched, paths of fire exploded over her skin. He didn't dally over one particular spot, preferring to nibble, lick, and stroke before leveling her with wonderful exploratory kisses. Tate cherished those endless moments. The slide of soft lips and wet mouths. Hearts slowed, raced. Blood, body, breathing became one.

Still, he seduced her with unhurried bliss.

Drugged by his heated touches, she floated in a myriad of sensations. His hot mouth suctioned to her neck while he used all ten fingers to massage her scalp. Thumbs teased her lower abdomen into a rolling quiver as his teeth playfully tugged at her earlobe. His gentle tongue tangled with hers. His callused fingertips stroked the sensitive underside of her arm, from the erratic pulse thumping in her wrist to the ticklish bend in her waist. He used the tremendous strength in his hand to tame her, to gentle her to his pace.

His scent, her scent, mingled with the vanilla candle and the cool aroma of rain. He'd steeped her in an erotic pool; she was drowning. A husky groan rumbled from her throat. "Please, Nathan. Enough. I want you."

"I know," he breathed in her ear. Fiery shudders turned chaotic inside her, extracting another whip of desire. "We'll get there. But I'm not done. Other side."

Tate was long past arguing. He rolled her over on her stomach and stretched her arms high above her head. Briefly, his heavy erection dipped between her thighs. She instinctively bowed back to reach his cock to show him how much she burned to have that thickness buried deep inside her.

"Naughty, naughty," he growled near her temple. Nathan rocked his pelvis forward, brushing the stiff length firmly in the shadowy cleft of her rear. "I am not giving in to you this time."

"Please," her voice wobbled as she glanced over her shoulder, believing he'd reconsider when he glimpsed her wild eyes.

"No." Abruptly he pulled away, using his strong thighs to urge her legs wide open as he knelt down between them.

First, he curved his large fingers through her smaller ones, his rough-skinned hands clasped to the softer backs of hers. Simultaneously he drew those work-roughened palms down the outside of each arm. Moisture dripped from her sex at the unexpectedness of his simple caress. He'd trapped her in a veil of sexual awareness, blinding her to anything but the knowledge that every loving stroke, every tender touch, bound her to him. Body, soul and heart.

The erstwhile caresses tapered off. The bed shifted and butterfly touches danced down her back to the dimples above her buttocks. Tate gasped the second his tongue replaced his fingers. He flicked, teased until she trembled violently. "Lift your shoulders," he commanded.

Her compliance was immediate. Nathan's large hands slipped beneath her to knead the plump breasts hard, like she liked it. He twirled, plucked, pulled the nipples into tight points that begged for his tongue to ease the sharp sting.

Several agonizing seconds ticked by when he didn't touch her at all. Finally, a silken stream of hair meandered down her spine. Once. Twice. Followed by a slow, warm tongue gliding up from tailbone to the base of her skull. When his teeth sank into her nape, Tate nearly came off the bed.

His sweet, hot breath at her shoulder echoed as a shudder in her soul. "I love touching you. Tasting you. Making you want more."

"No more teasing," she gasped when his hands massaged her butt.

"Just a little," he said, drawing one long finger down the cleft, delving that finger into the wetness between her thighs. He groaned. "You are so unbelievably responsive. So hot. So wet. You make me want to forget to go slow."

"Not slow. Fast. Hard. Right now."

"Fast has its place, but slow and steady wins the race." He pushed firmly against her hot core. "Am I winning, Tate?"

A, "Yes," wrenched from her lips as he added another finger. Nathan's bristly beard rubbing back and forth on shoulder blade increasing her longing to fever pitch. The more she writhed, the stiffer her nipples became, scraping against the flannel sheets. Tate contracted her internal muscles, attempting to pull both fingers higher, deeper.

"Good." He removed his hand with acute gentleness and then eased her onto her back.

Tate's lungs were devoid of air. She couldn't breathe for wanting him.

"*Now* I'm done teasing." Rising above her, he created space between her legs. The intense fire burning in his eyes softened. A ragged sigh ripped from his mouth and he paused, looking completely forlorn.

"What?" she said, finally able to frame his rugged face in her hands. He was so sweet. So perfect. So damn romantic she wanted to cry with the beauty of it. "What's wrong?"

"Nothing. I just...looking at you startles me sometimes. You are beautiful." Nathan lightly touched his lips to her trembling mouth. "You steal my breath, Tate. The way you make me feel." He broke eye contact, turning his head into her small hand, still cradling his face. He placed a delicate kiss in the center of her palm.

For the first time, Tate realized Nathan felt it too and he was equally unprepared. Whatever he'd set out to prove to her tonight had gotten lost in the pure emotion they brought to each other. At that moment, whether she liked it or not, or even understood it, she knew she belonged only to him.

"Show me," she whispered. "Make love to me with your heart, Nathan, like you promised."

Without another word, he lowered to her until they met body-to-body, skin-to-skin, heart-to-heart. Her belly quivered when his fingertips breached the thatch of wet curls. "Let me in," he said, brushing his lips to her forehead. "I need you, Tate. I need to feel everything that is you surrounding me."

His welcome weight pressed her to the mattress. For a moment they merely stared into each other's eyes.

When Nathan slid inside, Tate knew she'd finally found home.

❦ ❦ ❦

The next morning, Tate leaned against the doorframe of the back porch, letting her coffee cool as she inhaled the fresh summer breeze. She loved days like these, sun on her face, birdsong ringing in her ears. The stench of smog and the constant hum of traffic seemed light years away.

Was that was her reality, back to the city? The layout she'd created had been a smashing success. The company president had been ecstatic enough to reinstate her and put aside the ugly business with Malcolm. Everything she'd worked to achieve in the unpredictable business was finally within her grasp.

So why wasn't she reaching out with both hands for that brass ring and her second chance? Why wasn't she celebrating? Instead she'd curled up in bed and cried as if her life was coming to an end. Why?

Because she suspected it was.

To achieve her professional dream, she'd have to leave the personal fantasy behind. And it had been fanciful, thinking she could maintain physical intimacy without involving her heart. The deal she'd made with Nathan now seemed selfish. A childish whim.

Nathan. Why had he waited until the most vulnerable time of her life to show her lovemaking at its deepest, its finest, its sweetest? Oh Mr. Romance had impeccable timing. Waltzing in, stealing her will, marking her soul his. The electricity of the storm had only heightened the sensuality...and the burden of her decision. She'd woken up this morning, wedged against his body. Lying there in her bed, feeling his deep exhalations against her crown, his arms banding them together in the ultimate lover's embrace had felt right beyond imagining.

Tate loved him. She wanted more than sex. She wanted the whole messy side of love. Dogs, kids, in-laws, fighting and making up.

So, she'd made her decision. If he asked her to stay, she would. But he had to ask. Nathan had to tell her with words, not with his body, how *he* felt. No way would she throw her heart out there without a clear sign from him that it wouldn't bear the mark of his work boots as he strolled out the door.

His heavy step squeaked the floorboard the grip on her cup increased. This was it.

Mint scented breath drifted over her nape, drawing gooseflesh. "Morning, gorgeous," he said, pressing his warm lips to the back of her head. "You smell good. You're up early."

"It's past eight-thirty," she said dryly.

"You are a bad influence on me." The waistband of his jeans brushed the tiny patch of bare skin in the small of her back. "Usually I would have already put in a solid two hours."

"You work too hard." Tate reluctantly moved away from his roving lips. "Sorry. That was uncalled for. Not your fault I couldn't sleep."

"Did I snore?"

"I don't remember." She sipped her coffee calmly as if her heart and throat weren't being crushed by the weight of her unspoken words. "When will the inspectors be here?"

"Any minute. I'm gonna be stuck in Deadwood until midnight finishing up that septic system as it is. Why?"

"Just curious. Will they let me know right away if the improvements pass inspection?"

"I assume so. Are you worried?"

Tate nodded.

"Don't be. We've followed their guidelines." He hesitated. "If you want, I'm used to dealing with this type of thing. You can hang out in here and I'll let you know how it goes."

Something about his tone wasn't right. And he looked…guilty. "What else is going on? You seem anxious. You okay?"

"I'm fine. Just ready for this to be over."

It took a second for Tate to realize the series of loud knocks wasn't her heart thumping, but someone hammering at the front door. "The inspectors must be here." She tried to sidestep him.

But Nathan clamped onto her arm. "We need to talk. Later?"

Without answering, she scooted to the door, cursing her thin veneer of calm. Then again, telling a man you loved him and planned on changing your whole life to include him *should* make a woman skittish.

Tate exchanged polite, perfunctory greetings with the two inspectors. Once they'd begun wandering around the property, she left Nathan in charge to detail the required changes he'd made. She followed along, half-listening to their words of praise. But the unyielding line of Nathan's back captured her attention. The tight smile flattened his usual full grin and the curt, professional way he dealt with them showed a side of him she hadn't seen. Didn't he deal with inspectors all the time? So why the bout of nerves? Another thought jarred her. Unless… He had regrets about opening up to her last night? She shivered in her silk tank top. Talk about being paranoid.

When the ordeal ended, the elderly woman beamed and put-forth a glove-encased hand. "Well, Ms. Cross, you've done a fine job here. Needless to say you passed with flying colors."

"Thank you," Tate said, ignoring Nathan's quizzical stare. "But Mr. LeBeau deserves the credit. He did all the work."

"You provided the inspiration," Nathan added with false modesty. "Ms. Cross didn't balk at some of my…bolder suggestions."

Tate colored scarlet upon recalling some of his suggestions.

Neither the woman nor her rotund male companion noticed her discomfort. Sunlight gleamed off the man's balding head. "I must agree with Florence. I am impressed. Marvelous things can happen when vision is mixed with a little imagination. I'll admit that design for the new fire station was even more of a knock-out than the plans for here."

"Yes. You are quite the artist, Mr. LeBeau. And it was a shrewd business decision to use it to sway our opinion. We only want what's best for our city."

Nathan drew in a quick, harsh breath. "Actually the final proposed sketch in your office is Ms. Cross' design."

Her design? On a fire station? What fire station? Tate's head snapped his direction.

"Regardless," the woman waved dismissively. "I'm so pleased we accepted this property as your entry into the Maxwell Memorial Landscaping Award competition. We killed two birds with one stone, so to speak."

Contest? What contest? Tate frowned at Nathan, who all of a sudden was avoiding her probing gaze.

"I was under the impression that entry in that competition remained confidential," Nathan said cautiously.

"Of course it is. But I'm sure that's not something you'd keep from Ms. Cross," the woman chided. "That would be highly unethical. Besides, I've done some checking on you and I've heard nothing but praise." The powdered wrinkles on her forehead drew into a frown. "I must say, after denying your entry request last year, this surprised me. Especially when I checked your accreditations—seems you've been busy learning the trade. Now I can see why you'd want to branch out into landscape design." She gestured to the renovated property. "You have quite the knack for it."

Tate watched color flood Nathan's face.

The woman's birdlike gaze turned sharp. "Would you feel vindicated if I said I've chosen this project as the grand prize winner?"

Nathan's smile was slow in coming. "I guess."

"Good." She leaned on her cane. "Once word gets out that you've won, I imagine the demand for your landscaping services will skyrocket. Your business should double."

Tate stared at the ground until it seemed to shift beneath her feet. Time stopped. The dizzy sensation moved from her stomach to her head in record time as the truth hit her like a ton of paving bricks.

Nathan's motive in taking on her landscaping project hadn't been because of the promise of art lessons or unencumbered sex, but the possibility of winning a contest. A contest which she knew nothing about. A contest in which he'd submitted her draft as his own.

She had been played for a fool. Again.

The familiar, bitter betrayal arose. No wonder he'd insisted on romance. From the very beginning he'd needed to save his energy for making retaining walls instead of making love to her.

To think she'd fallen for him. Last night had been the real clincher. She'd even foolishly contemplated giving up...everything if he'd asked her to stay. But he hadn't asked. It was obvious his work, his damn job, would always come first.

No doubt she'd cause serious problems for him and his business reputation if she insisted he hadn't disclosed the contest entry. But in this case revenge felt wrong. Suddenly everything felt wrong. And there was no reason for her to remain in sleepy Spearfish, South Dakota. She'd passed the inspection and the only thing left was to sign the realtor contract and hire a cleaning service to ready the house for potential buyers. Once the house sold she'd come back with a U-haul for the few decent pieces of her aunt's furniture and never return.

That thought punched a hole straight in her heart, effectively breaking it in two.

"Ms. Cross?" The elderly woman set a shaking hand on her arm, prompting her from her nightmare. "Are you all right?"

"I'm fine." Tate smiled awkwardly. "Just confused as to what I do now. My attorney insists I get the final details documented."

"Naturally. If you'd like, you can sign everything at our office. When would it be convenient for you to drop by?"

"It'd be great if we could get this out of the way this morning. Could I catch a ride to your office? I'd love to hear more about this award. Mr. LeBeau was pretty mum on the details."

Before Nathan could object, the woman trilled, "What a lovely idea. That'd be fine."

Tate smiled even when she felt like part of her had died. "I'll grab my purse. While you're waiting, why don't you tell Mr. LeBeau about the award ceremony? I'm sure he's anxious to know when and where," she flashed her teeth at him, "so he can pass out flyers." Dirty pool, but he deserved it. She blindly passed the stone birdbath, tripped over a clump of buffalo grass on her escape to the house.

She'd barely stumbled past the couch when the screen door slammed. She didn't need turn around to gauge Nathan's mood; his anger pulsed across the room like a sonic wave.

His voice was hard as steel. "What's the deal?"

Physically coming face-to-face with him would have to wait until she regained control. She sorted through junk mail on the table, grabbing her half-full coffee cup. "The *deal* is completed. You fulfilled your end of the agreement. I fulfilled mine. Time to move on."

"Move on?" he repeated dully.

"I called a real estate agent. She'll be here at two o'clock."

A minute of stunned silence followed. "You called a realtor? When?"

She glanced up. "Yesterday."

"Right after you got the news."

Tate nodded, but didn't tell him yesterday she hadn't made any firm plans. She'd foolishly hoped they'd make future plans together. "That's why I wondered what time the inspectors would be finished. The realtor needs written documentation that I've met the Beautification Committee's requirements before she can list the house."

"Is there a reason why didn't you tell me this last night?"

The ceramic cup between her palms held firm under her increasing grip. "It didn't exactly come up while we were having sex, did it?"

"Making love," he corrected with an edge to his voice. "We were making love last night, Tate." His eyes searched hers. "And you didn't think to tell me about this sudden development?"

"That's because it wasn't sudden." Tate drained her cold coffee. "It's simple. We've both known all along what happens now. I'm returning to Colorado."

Silence stretched between them, heavy, thick, oppressive.

"Why?" he said finally. "If you lost your job in Denver why are you leaving here?" His eyes turned shrewd. "If this is about money—"

"It's not about money," she snapped.

"Then what?" he snapped back.

It took every ounce of Tate's resolve to keep her gaze firmly locked to the distress growing in his. "Because I didn't lose my job, Nathan. They held the hearing early. I was cleared and promoted. I can start Monday."

Blood drained from his face, turning his robust complexion pasty white. She fought the guilt that swamped her and maintained an aloofness she didn't feel.

"Whoa." He stepped away, wrapping his big hands on the top rung of the ladder back chair in a death grip. "Wait a minute. You didn't get fired? If you were reinstated," he repeated slowly, "then why were you crying last night?" He waited for her response.

The sound of his ragged breathing resonated in the silent room. Tate didn't dare glance up to confirm that the anger in his voice was reflected in his eyes. She knew.

"Fine. We'll do it the hard way," he said. "Why were you crying? And don't feed me some bullshit about those tears being tears of joy. I'm not stupid. I know the difference."

As usual he was dead-on. She couldn't lie to him, but the truth of her pathetic hopes seemed worse.

"Tate? Answer me."

She shook her head.

"Goddammit. At least look at me." He loomed above her, filling every inch of available space until she couldn't breathe. "Look me in the eyes and tell me that last night and everything that happened between us the past few weeks were nothing more than a business arrangement. Tell me you're not that blind."

A thread of anger rose to the surface, supplanting her misery. She grabbed it with both hands. "Blind?" she spit, pleased when he retreated. "Yes, I'll admit after what I've seen and heard this morning I might've been blind. Blind to the real reason that you agreed to this 'deal'. Winning the award was the new direction for your business, wasn't it? Seems you neglected to tell me that fact. Why?"

His gaze zoomed to the china hutch. Then to the crystal teardrop chandelier and the arrangement of yellow, white and purple daisies in the center of the table, but never once landed on her. "Because you were selling the house anyway and I didn't think it would matter."

"Look me in the eye, Nathan LeBeau. Look me in the eye and tell me that you didn't mislead me in *any* way about *any* thing."

He turned and studied her without comment.

Tate's heart dropped to her Tevas. It was true. She'd been nothing but a means to an end. And the end was here. She yanked her backpack off the teacart, knocking the phone book to the floor. "I've gotta go. They're waiting—"

"They're gone," he said crossly. "I told them I'd give you a ride downtown."

Her grip on the thick straps tightened as she fought the urge to whirl around and smack him with it. "You had no right."

"I have every right. You're not going anywhere until we talk about this. You are avoiding the main issue here, Tate."

"Which is what? That you lied to me?" She gave him a scornful once over. "You never wanted the intimacy—"

"Yeah? Then how did we get to be so very intimate?"

"At my urging," she argued against his pseudo-seductive tone. "From day one you tried to avoid the physical aspect of the deal." The truth made another sharp stab at her soul. "God. I've been so stupid. That romance angle was completely bogus, wasn't it? No way did any woman tell you that you were a bad lover. You would have done anything, *said* anything to me to feed the lie because you only wanted to win that stupid contest. I'm not stupid either, Nathan. Entering that contest meant everything to you if you'd been planning it for a year."

Guilt flared in his eyes. "You're right."

His admission floored her. "I am?"

"Yes. I didn't tell you about the damn contest. Honestly, I could care less about it now." He shuffled his feet and seemed equally at a loss as to where to place his hands. "But that's not the worst part, okay?"

Tate managed to keep cool even as her stomach roiled. "What else?"

"I never wanted—" Nathan scrubbed his hands roughly over his face. "Hell, it's complicated." His laugh was bitter. "Jesus. This is gonna sound so wimpy. The truth is, for the first time in my life I didn't want just a sexual relationship."

"Why?"

"Because that's the only kind of relationships I've ever had."

Tate didn't block her disbelief. "I find that hard to swallow."

"Look at me." He threw his arms wide open. "I'm not some high-powered suit and tie-wearing businessman that regularly sweeps women off their feet. I build sewers, Tate. I get dirty and I like it. I've never felt the need to apologize for it or change my ways until…"

"Kathy?" she prompted with a sneer.

"Partly." He lifted a shoulder in a half-shrug. "She was a catalyst of sorts. She never said I was lousy in bed, but she did tell me I wasn't relationship material. Guess I'm the kind of guy who's only good for a tumble in the hay as long as I'm cleaned up. I wanted to prove her wrong."

"And you used me to do that." Another realization dawned as that sick feeling invaded her stomach again. "Did you decide on the romance angle before or after we'd met?"

Nathan frowned. "Why does that matter now?"

Tate clenched her teeth to keep her chin from trembling. "Because if you made that decision *after* we met, then you saw me as the pitiable friend of Val's who would gladly accept whatever crumbs you offered. A good girl like me would agree to a romantic relationship instead of a sexual one. Then you'd be off the hook and wouldn't have to feel guilty about using me to further your business plans, right? Now it makes perfect sense as to why we didn't continue the art lessons after you submitted *my* drawings for both this place and the fire station."

He didn't refute her claim. "We're getting off track here. The main issue—"

"The only issue is that you lied to me and used me."

"No. I never used you." His mouth turned hard. "As long as my embarrassing truths are laid on the table, yours had better be too."

"What are you talking about?"

"You. Instead of staying here and figuring out what *you* want to do with your future, you're running back to Denver to live out the life your mother has mapped out for you."

Tate shrunk back. Was his accusation was true? "How dare you. You can't possibly stand there and judge me when you're guilty of the same thing."

"Yeah?" Nathan rocked back on his heels, crossing his beefy arms over his puffed-out chest, acting every inch the macho male. "How so?"

She straightened her own spine against his defensive posture. "Maybe you don't run, but you sure as hell hide, claiming your business eats up every minute of your time."

"You know it does."

"It doesn't have to, and you know it." His reaction was surprisingly cool to this touchy subject. In fact, he looked calm and rested. For the first time in weeks his brown eyes were clear and free of shadows. Why? Because she hadn't kicked him out of her bed last night? Oh no. She was not taking the blame for his faults. Nathan worked too much. One night rolling around in her flannel sheets wasn't the cure-all. It never would be.

"Come on, quit stalling." he urged. "This, I'm dying to hear."

"No, you don't want to hear that you live in a perpetual state of exhaustion. Of loneliness. Of complete isolation that doesn't have a damn thing to do with the color of your skin."

The muscle in his temple jumped. "Pretty broad judgment, don't you think? Let's cut to the chase and save the lecture. I'm self-employed. I have no one to rely on but myself. I'm tired. So? A little hard work never killed anyone."

"You have *no* life outside of work. You're so busy killing yourself trying to prove you're not another lazy Indian and to prove to your father you're not screwing up his business, that you use it as an excuse to avoid everything. Even your dog—"

"—don't you drag Duke into this," he warned. "You don't even like him."

"Because I don't know him. Neither do you. There's no room in your life for anything but work." She pushed her final point, regardless of the stark expression in his eyes. "The truth hurts, doesn't it? Nancy, Tina and Vickie's husbands are in the construction business. Even they mentioned how hard it was to convince you to take time to join a simple pool league."

Nathan did a double take. "You talked about me to them? Where do they get off poking their noses into my business? Did you tell them about the landscaping?"

"No. But why does that matter?"

"Because it's something I've kept quiet on purpose. The online courses, the weeks I spent down South in the off-season learning the basics of how xeriscaping works." He inhaled. "No one knows I've been going to school."

"Why did you keep that to yourself? I'd think you'd be proud—"

"I am proud. But the guys I work with will give me a rash of shit for changing the focus of my business to 'planting posies'. I didn't want anyone to know until I had a contract. Even then they'll harp on the fact that I think I'm too good to dig utilities."

"Nathan, they are your friends. I doubt they'd believe that." Tate softened her tone. "Besides, it seemed they were hoping that I'd show you there's more to life than work."

"Don't you think I know that?" he exploded. "Everything has changed in the last few weeks since I met you. How can I prove—"

As if on cue, his cell phone trilled.

Heartsick, she closed her eyes, willing him to ignore it. *Please just this one time let it go. I'll stay here and talk to you, just don't answer it. Prove it to me now. Show me I mean more to you than a business call. Ask me to stay. Please.*

After five rings, he cursed, flipped it open and snarled, "What?"

Tate bolted while she still had the chance.

Chapter Twenty

After packing her car in record time Tate drove to Val's. Sneaking out of town like a guest who'd outstayed their welcome was a poor way to repay her friend. Although she promised herself the announcement of the end of her "deal" with Nathan and her departure from Spearfish would be as cheerily civilized as their first conversation about her lackluster love life. Quips only, no hysterical sobbing. During the last few weeks she'd definitely experienced that awesome sex she'd craved. Too bad she'd lost her heart in the process.

Val answered the door, sleeping baby nestled in the crook of her arm. While Maddie's sweet pink mouth was slack with sleep, Val's perpetual smile seemed slow in coming.

She motioned her inside, kicking a path through Legos, headless Barbies and stacks of board games.

Wow. The hallway used to be spotless. Tate tried not to gawk but the living room looked worse. Puzzles, videos, naked baby dolls, towering erector sets competed with clothes piled higher than the Big Wheels parked in front of the floor-to-ceiling windows.

With Maddie settled in the wicker bassinet, Val flopped on the leather couch. She tossed aside a package of graham crackers she'd inadvertently crushed between the seat cushions.

"Where are the kids?" Tate whispered, staggered as much by the god-awful mess as the absolute quiet.

"You don't have to whisper." Val shoved a hand through her already tousled hair. "They're at the fish hatchery and park with my mom, *all afternoon*, thank God."

"You okay?"

"Exhausted beyond belief. C-sections are awful. Strange, how you block out the amount of work there is taking care of a baby. Seems I just get Maddie quieted down and she's howling again. Or the kids need food, attention or a referee all at the exact same time."

Tate noticed Val's shirt was on inside out. Best not to mention it. "Doesn't Richard help?"

"When he's home." Val's attempted smile was wan at best as she gestured to the cluttered space. "Welcome to chaos central. You want something to drink?"

Eyeing the dozen or so sticky glasses on the slate fireplace, Tate shook her head. "If I've come at a bad time—"

"No. I'm glad you're here. I didn't mean to unload on you the minute you tripped through the door."

"That's okay, I've unloaded on you plenty of times."

"Friends do that." She yawned and stretched. "So what's up?"

Don't stall, just spit it out. "I stopped by to tell you I'm leaving tonight."

The blurry, sleep-deprived look left Val's eyes pronto. "What do you mean you're leaving?"

Tate fiddled with the hem unraveling on her sundress. The same one she'd worn in the Bobcat with Nathan. Her imagination or had she caught a whiff of diesel fuel? "Let me explain before you completely freak out."

"Too late," Val snapped.

"Oh no you don't." She wagged her finger. "You knew I never intended to stay in Spearfish permanently." After she offered the abbreviated version of her reinstatement, she added, "The Beautification Committee approved the landscaping this morning, so I'm good to go."

"Was Nathan there?"

"Yes. *I* might not have bothered being there for the way the committee members fawned over him." She snorted. "I couldn't very well let on that he hadn't informed me that he'd even *entered* the Maxwell Memorial Award contest, especially after he'd won the damn thing."

"He won?" Val faltered, clearly torn between excitement for Nathan's accomplishment and commiserating Tate's misery. "You didn't know that he'd entered your project in the competition?"

"No. Did he tell you?"

"I'd suspected."

Tate's broken heart constricted. She couldn't stand it if Val had been part of the deception. "Was that the reason you suggested it?"

"No." She scowled, scrubbing at what looked like a mustard stain on her shorts. "Actually, he'd been so busy that I thought *he'd* forgotten until I convinced him to meet with you and talk about your landscaping problem."

"Convinced," Tate repeated slowly. "How hard did you have to beg your brother to have sex with me?" They'd headed into dangerous territory— not only could their friendship suffer, but Val's relationship with Nathan might be strained as a result of this deal gone wrong.

Val went still. "What are you talking about?"

"Nathan never wanted to sleep with me." Hot, erotic images danced through her mind making a mockery of the statement. Okay, she could admit Nathan may have been reluctant in the beginning, but at the end he'd been an equal participant.

"Well, he certainly fooled me," Val continued sarcastically, "with the way he couldn't keep his hands off you."

When Tate neither confirmed nor denied her statement, Val said, "Maybe you'd better start at the beginning because I think I missed something."

"That day you asked me whether we'd done the deed? I lied about me being the one who backed off on wanting wild sex." Tate grabbed a lilac unicorn with a tattered leg. "Nathan wanted to go slow and, somehow, Mr. Charming convinced me to go along with it. So initially, our 'lessons' were all about his need for romance." She squeezed the animal so hard stuffing popped from the mangled horn. "How could I have been so stupid? He didn't want romance. All he'd really wanted was to buy time to win that damn contest."

"Whoa…back up. He said he wanted romance? Instead of sex? We are talking about *my* brother, aren't we?"

"Wild flowers, a moonlit boat ride, candles…" Oh God. *Don't cry, don't cry, don't cry.* She crushed the unicorn to her chest and rocked, wishing it really had magical powers to spirit her away.

"Nathan did all that? Wow. I'm impressed."

"I was too." Tears leaked from the corners of her eyes and slid down her cheeks anyway. "Why does he have to be so damn s-sweet and n-nice…and why am I such an idiot to f-fall for him?" Great hitching sobs ripped from her soul.

Val pulled the spit up rag from her shoulder and handed it over. When that didn't quell the torrent of tears, she wrapped her arms around Tate and the unicorn and let her cry. After what seemed like hours, Val brushed away the last of Tate's tears and smoothed her damp hair from her forehead. "Better?"

Another howl broke free. "N-no! I've never felt like this. God. I don't know what to do."

"I do," Val muttered. She rooted for something on the end table and knocked an apple juice box to the carpet.

Horrified, Tate yanked the portable phone from Val's grasp. "You can't call him."

"Why not?"

"Because I got the no-strings-attached sex and he won the contest. We both ended up with what we wanted."

Val's sympathetic expression turned skeptical. "No matter that you ended up falling in love with him?"

"I didn't mean to."

"Does Nathan love you?"

Tate shrugged, wishing the toy-strewn floor would open up and swallow her.

"Oh my God." Val slapped her own forehead. "*Please* don't tell me that instead of asking him how he feels, or talking about this, or even fighting about it, you're just gonna take off like nothing happened?"

"No," Tate corrected quietly, feeling decidedly calmer. "I'm going back to Denver like I'd originally planned. My job and my family are there, Val, not here. I can't change everything because I've rather stupidly fallen in love with a man who was supposed to be nothing more than a summer fling."

"But—"

Tate scooted forward and ignored the squeaky ball she'd dislodged with her heel. "But nothing. Honestly, even if Nathan does have feelings for me, can you see him moving? He isn't willing to sacrifice his work time *here* to be with me. I wouldn't ask him to give up something he loves despite the crazy schedule he keeps. And we both know he'd never offer."

"You aren't giving him the choice." Val argued. "If your career was as important to you as you've claimed, you wouldn't have run back here in the first place. Think about that."

Tate didn't want to consider Val's point. Maybe later, during the long drive, she'd dissect it. "I have. That's why I'm going back to Colorado. How can I not give my career another fair shot? What if I change my life, move here to be with Nathan and realize that's not what I want either? I've been so busy trying to please other people—my parents, my bosses—that I lost sight of the fact *I* need to make my own choices. Never again will I make a rash decision based on emotions and tears."

"Aren't you doing that now by leaving?"

"No. Leaving was in my original plan, staying wasn't."

Val stared through her for several agonizing moments. "As long as we're baring our souls, I'll tell you—" Maddie wailed from the bassinet but Val only spared her a cursory glance. "I planned on setting you up with Nathan from day one. Except you were both damn resistant, so when opportunity presented itself, almost like karma…" Her brief smile was unexpectedly sad. "Do I feel guilty? No. Maybe it is selfish to want you and my brother to find the same kind of happiness that I share with Rich."

"Not everyone is destined to have that happiness, Val. Look at Grace and Luke. They are both counselors, for godsake. It didn't matter that they were wildly in love, or that they still are. It wasn't enough. And if they can't figure out a way to make a relationship work then what hope is there for the rest of us?"

"There's always hope. Make no mistake, Tate, being with you makes Nathan happy. I see it every time he looks at you. It's mirrored in your eyes when you look at him. You fit him. And that's not easy, because he's not an easy man."

"I know." Tate shook her head. "I don't see—"

"You wouldn't. For years I've watched him dig himself deeper into his business. Nathan works too hard. You do too, I suspect." Val paused, eyes bright. "You are both missing out on the best thing in life. And contrary to what you might believe, it's not mind-blowing orgasms." Her voice softened. "It's love."

Tate passed the damp spit up rag back to Val, lost for response. But she held tight to the stuffed animal.

"I think you and Nathan could strike a happy balance. I wish you'd try. If you put half the effort into a relationship that you've invested in your careers it couldn't fail. I wish I could tell Grace and Luke the same damn thing because it's true for them, too."

Silence stretched between them with no clear resolution.

"I have to go." Tate stood, gently placing the well-loved unicorn in the baby doll cradle next to a one-armed monkey. "I didn't want to leave without saying good-bye."

"Will you at least think about what I've said?"

Choking back another wave of tears, Tate nodded. She doubted she'd think of anything else. "I'll call you next week. Thanks for everything." She rushed from the cluttered room as quickly as possible without looking back.

And she didn't stop crying until she'd hit Cheyenne.

ಒ ಒ ಒ

That night Nathan cranked up the Dwight Yoakam CD and got rip-roaring drunk. Even Duke cowered in the corner, far away from his foul mood.

Alone again. Yippee. He tipped the Maker's Mark whiskey bottle to his mouth, splashing a good portion on his grungy work coveralls. He hadn't changed clothes. Why bother? He'd just get dirty again tomorrow, and the next day, and the day after that... Hell, everything seemed endless. Pointless.

His life was seriously fucked. Tate was gone. She'd sneaked out while he'd been on the phone earlier this morning and he'd been dumbfounded to find she'd blown town. He'd sure heard it from his little sister, who'd seen fit to leave a snotty message on his answering machine. And his cell phone. And his pager. Seemed Val was pissed off at him now, too. She suggested that he get his shit together before he made a bigger ass of himself than he already had. For Val to utter such crude words *and* ban him from her home indefinitely, well, her being pissed was putting it mildly.

Women, he thought. Who needs them? His life had been great before Tate had waltzed into it with her sweetness, her sunshine smile, her surprisingly wicked ways.

He took another determined swig, embracing the alcohol's burning sting. He was free. Free to get wild, free to romance the hell out of any woman that crossed his path. Why, he could go out and... He rubbed his forehead. And do what?

Nothing. Wasn't that Tate's entire point? Part of the reason she'd left? That he never did a damn thing besides work?

He scowled. When had that become a bad thing?

When it had become the only thing?

His life had revolved around jobsites, machinery and deadlines for as long as he could remember. He loved the freedom...even when he admitted he didn't take advantage of it.

Not once? Not ever?

That thought brought a fleeting moment of clarity.

Hey? What *was* the point of being his own boss if he adhered to a schedule that'd chased even the toughest young bucks from his employ?

Why hadn't he made more time for life?

More importantly, why hadn't he made more time for *her*?

Tate had made time for him. The million sweet ways she showed him she cared about him spun round in his brain until he felt dizzy from the implications, not the booze. How could such a little slip of a thing have wreaked so much havoc on his life?

Nathan slammed the whiskey bottle on the table. Goddamn it, he was a gutless bastard. With all his pathetic attempts at romance he hadn't learned enough to tell Tate how he'd felt.

Why hadn't he told her he loved her?

Tate had given him a priceless gift; she'd shown him the side of himself filled with passion. With fun. A man with the capacity to love to the point of pain. He'd felt safe with her. Happy. She'd wrapped love and acceptance around his heart like a cocoon.

And what had he given her in return? Besides orgasms that made her scream and award winning landscaping that insured she'd leave?

His bleary-eyed gaze took in his meager furnishings and the cold impersonality of his home. Damned lonely place he lived in. No wonder he couldn't stand being here.

Yep. He'd finally proven himself landscaping god to his peers and the world at large. He had the city contract, he had the qualifications, hell, he even had a big fat check. Seemed he had everything he'd ever wanted.

Except he didn't have Tate.

Why did he feel like he had nothing?

Nathan chugged another hit of liquid fire. The churning in his gut and the pain in his head were the only signs he hadn't gone completely numb.

Maybe he should go after her. Demand she come back. He could change. He *wanted* to change. Wasn't that what he'd tried to get across to her this morning? He needed to think of a plan. Luckily the whiskey seemed to clear things up a whole bunch.

The phone rang. He ignored it. His cell phone rang. Quit. Rang again. He stumbled out the back door and threw the ringing object against the concrete patio, crushing the plastic chunks that hadn't exploded upon impact under his boot heel. Feeling decidedly calmer, he staggered back inside and knocked back another drink.

Male pride reared its ugly head with each additional shot.

Nathan's thought processes began to blur. Pride, not love was what got him into this mess. He'd damn well use it to get himself back out.

Even muddled by alcohol, he knew he deserved every second of his misery. And miserable didn't begin to describe the horrors lurking in his soul and the paralyzing fear that he'd never see her again.

He itched to throw things, so he wouldn't be haunted by the memory of her touch. Bellow his rage, so he could forget her infectious smile. Finish the bottle of whiskey until he passed out, so he wouldn't feel like part of him had died.

Well, the bottle was already empty. So was his life.

For the first time in his adult life, Nathan LeBeau laid his head on the table and wept.

Chapter Twenty-One

One month later...

Nathan hadn't even stepped foot off the welcome mat in Val's grand hallway when he demanded, "Where is she?"

"Sleeping." Val plunked herself directly in front of him. She used her free hand like a school crossing guard to ward him off. "And don't think you're gonna go charging in there like some renegade bear and wake Tate up. She's exhausted."

"Running will do that to you," he said through clenched teeth. He could not believe that Tate was here, less than a hundred feet away and he still couldn't get to her. Couldn't see her. Couldn't talk to her. Couldn't touch her.

Val poked him in the chest. "Back off. How did you find out she was in town?"

Nathan's jaw tightened further and glanced away.

"Oh no you don't, buster. I know that look. You're hiding something. Either spill it right now or I'll shove your sorry butt right back out the door."

"Yeah?" He knew his belligerent tone wasn't helping matters any but he didn't care. "You and what army?"

"Have it your way." She shrugged. "My house, my rules. If you don't follow my rules you don't get to see her."

He threatened, and then pleaded—all to no avail. Val wouldn't budge. She tormented him with that cocky half-smile that had driven him nuts his whole life. She had the upper hand and she knew *he* knew it. Time to change tactics.

"You think you're so clever," he sneered. "I'll bet even *you* don't know why she's back in town."

That comment offended know-everything Val, which he'd expected. "I certainly do. There's some problem with a potential buyer—" She clapped a hand over her mouth before she used it to whap him on the arm. "That was sneaky."

Val had no idea of the sneaky lengths he'd gone to get Tate back in his life. He inhaled, willing himself to remain calm, hoping his whole world wasn't about to crumble around him like a cave-in at the jobsite. "Here's the truth. *I* contacted the realtor. Fed her a bogus story about meeting the owner in person before I put a bid on the house."

"Nathan Francis LeBeau!" Val gasped, clutching the baby in her arms to her heart. "Why would you do such a rotten thing?"

"Because I'm desperate! I'll buy the damn house if it means that much to her. I've been trying to get a hold of her for three weeks." Angrily, he thrust his hand through his hair. "She won't talk to me, you won't talk to me. This is a fucking nightmare."

She scowled at his language. "How did you find her?"

"Some new secretary in her office let it slip that Tate had quit last week without giving notice. Evidently that caused quite a cluster fu—" Val cleared her throat and Nathan amended, "an uproar. They wouldn't give me any more information. I kept calling her parent's house and getting no answer, no machine, no nothing. Then I realized I'd written down the wrong damn number."

He kneaded the back of his neck to stave off the impending headache. "When I finally got the right phone number, they forwarded the call to her brother Ryan. He acted like I was some psycho stalker. I had to give him my name, address, social security number, phone number and military history so he could run a check *before* he'd even talk to me. I just got off the phone with him and he informed me she'd come back to Spearfish. Then about ten minutes later, the realtor called and left *your* phone number as Tate's contact number." He glared at his sister. "Jesus, Val. I can't believe you didn't call me."

"She asked me not to."

"For godsake, I'm your brother!"

"Yeah? And that's the reason I didn't track you down and kill you last month." Val gave him a disdainful once over. "At this point I don't know who I'm angrier with. You or myself."

"Not at her, though?"

"No. It is not her fault that you are such a flaming idiot." Val smoothed the fuzz on Maddie's tiny head. "I never would've introduced you to her if I would've known you weren't being up front with me. Romance? Instead of no-strings attached sex? Gee, Nathan, I didn't know whether to laugh or cry."

"See?" He resisted his usual urge to cuff her lightly on the arm, since she was holding the baby. "If I would've told you from the start I wanted ah…a romance you would've made fun of me until my dying day."

Val had the grace to look abashed. "But you lied to me."

"Lied? No. Stretched the painful truth maybe." He stared at the dust covering his work boots. "When you told me about Tate and her lack of sexual experience I figured it was a perfect opportunity to try to become the kind of romantic man all women want. Maybe if I could be that, I could have a real relationship not based on sex."

"I am sorry." Val peered at him intently. "You do realize that there is no cut and dried formula for romance?"

"Yeah." Nathan kicked at a Cheerio imbedded in the rug. "Even if I had found one, *I* sure couldn't make it work."

"And it doesn't change anything with Tate."

He met her sympathetic gaze. "It changes everything, Val. I want to spend the rest of my life with her."

The weight of his confession hung in the air-conditioned room. Val measured him coolly. "Why would she want to spend her life with you?"

That startled him. "What?"

"You heard me. Take a long, hard look at yourself."

"Even *you* don't think I'm good enough for her?" Another idea clicked and his anger rose up. "That's why you suggested me as her temporary stud—"

"Knock off the wounded male act." She rocked the baby with that innate, fluid mother's grace but her eyes remained heavy. "Dang it, Nathan, you work too hard. If you love Tate don't doom her to a life of waiting for you to come home. Before you tell her you want to spend the rest of your life with her, you'd better decide how much of that life you're willing to give her."

Nathan bristled at Val's pull-no-punches tone. "What is up with you? Like I'm the only man on the planet with a job. Richard works hard."

"True. But work isn't what matters most to him. *I* matter. Our family matters. If he has to give up a big case so he can come home early and have a family dinner, he will. Without me begging or nagging him. He does it because he wants to. Trust me, Richard could be a partner right now, his name could be on the letterhead." Val's chin wobbled. "If Tate is willing to make changes, you should too."

"Changes? What changes?"

"Let me finish." She repositioned the baby, angling forward so he got the full impact of her whispered words. "She spent the last five years trying to get ahead in the rat race and only in the last few weeks has she been convinced to leave it." Val's gaze turned sharp. "On the other hand, if you're unwilling to meet her halfway, I'd sign off on you too. Been tempted to do the same a time or two myself."

Nathan was stunned. He *had* changed in the last month. More than Val realized since she'd kept him out of her life. He'd enrolled Duke in obedience class. Cut his hours and interviewed potential employees and hired a supervisor for his utility business. He'd even made it to Jim's weekly support group and discovered he wasn't alone in dealing with racism and prejudice.

Yeah, he still had a helluva lot to learn about balance, but he was willing to try. However his sister wasn't the one he had to convince that he'd changed.

"Well," he ventured quietly, "I'll admit you know us both better than you should. You may think you understand her, but I guarantee I know Tate in ways you don't. If she wants to tell me to go to hell then she can damn well say it to my face."

He tried to step around Val but she blocked him. "What part of 'go away' don't you understand? Tate is sleeping."

"Val," he implored. "I'm dying here. I need to see her."

Her voice softened to a croon as she tickled the baby's tiny chin. "I know. If Tate wants to contact you then she will."

"Can I just come in? Spend some time with the kids? I miss them." He saw a flash of pink chiffon as Chelsea zipped into the family room. "I swear I won't bother Tate," he lied.

Curls like mean little corkscrews escaped Val's tight bun as she shook her head. "I think it'd be best if you left."

Nathan's shoulders slumped against the wall, even when he wanted to punch his fist through the Sheetrock from sheer frustration. "Will you at least tell her I was here?"

She nodded, striding nonchalantly toward the sound of a crash followed by a blood-curdling shriek.

He considered making a break for the stairs. He could easily outrun her, even without Val holding a baby in her arms. While he debated, Val stuck her head back around the corner.

"Don't even think about it," she warned, giving him the evil mom eye as an added threat.

Damn her instincts. Dejected, depressed and doubtful, Nathan walked out the door, without a clue as to where to go.

ა ა ა

A sharp finger poked Tate, jolting her awake from a deep sleep. Disoriented, she rolled over and faced the culprit.

Chelsea Westfield stood by the nightstand, face somber, expression grim.

"Hey, Chels," she said groggily, "what's up?"

"How come you're being so mean to Uncle Nathan?"

Out of the mouth of babes. Tate eased back against the headboard, choosing her words carefully. "What makes you think I'm being mean to him?"

Chelsea's elfin chin jutted out, causing her plastic crown to slide off the back of her head. "Because he was here. And Mommy wouldn't even let him in. He wanted to see *you*, not us. How come?"

Tate's heart skipped a beat. Nathan had been here? When? Why? Before she could pump Chelsea for more information, the young girl added, "And then he left because Mommy made him. That's mean."

"Do you know where he went?"

"Like I'd tell you." Chelsea clutched the unicorn and flounced from the room in her princess costume, leaving Tate with an acute sense of unease.

She dressed quickly. Val's house had returned to its normal pristine state in the last three weeks, but chaos still reigned. The loud argument in the family room was only marginally less annoying than the cartoons blaring from the television in the living room. Maddie screamed from the nursery. She sought the one place at the Westfield residence that offered solitude.

Twilight had fallen while she'd slept. Tate pushed back the heavy pine branches surrounding the stone bench and stopped.

Nathan sat on her bench. Close enough to touch. Close enough that she saw the dirt stains on his shirt and the pain in his eyes. Her heart rate tripled and it took every ounce of restraint not to leap into his arms.

Not that his muscular arms were outstretched in anticipation. In fact, he looked a little wary.

Tate swallowed, but her voice still cracked from her too-dry throat. "Nathan?"

Several long seconds passed. "So. You aren't an apparition.

"You accused me of being a wood sprite the first time we met."

He didn't return her smile.

"What are you doing here?"

"Waiting." He lifted the beer bottle dangling from his fingers up to his lips and drank. "Thinking mostly."

She searched his face, noting the shadows under his eyes and the hard set of his unshaven jaw. Her stomach roiled. "About?"

He sighed, staring down at his well-worn boots.

"It's too nice a night for such a profound sigh."

Nathan glanced at her sharply. "You remember that?"

"I remember everything," she said softly. "Mind if I sit down? Or is this particular hiding spot taken?"

"Suit yourself."

Tate perched on the bench corner, careful not to touch him, though she wanted to. Lord, did she ache to feel his sweet breath against her mouth as she tasted his lips. She just wanted to hold him close and never let him go. "Thinking about anything in particular?"

"Lots of things."

"Sometimes it helps to talk them out with a perfect stranger."

He smirked. "Interesting that you'd think you're perfect."

"A perfect idiot," she mumbled.

"What?"

"Nothing." She scooted next to him, brushing her bare knee against his. "Would you rather be alone?"

"Hell no. I finally figured out in the last month I'm sick of spending my life alone. And just for the record, I'm not hiding from anything or anyone. Not anymore."

"Tell me what's going on." She took his hand and brought his rough knuckles against her mouth. "Come on, come on, come on, you know you want to."

"Sweetheart, no wonder you and Duke don't get along. You are a damn bulldog." Nathan squeezed her hand. "I don't know where to start."

"Then I'll start," she said. "I am sorry."

"No, I'm the one who's sorry. You were right, going after me the day of the inspection. I should've told you about the Maxwell competition and my reasons for entering it. I felt guilty, especially after you told me what happened with Malcolm. From the beginning I'd convinced myself by the time I finished the landscaping you'd be long gone and it wouldn't matter."

Tate refrained from comment and let him talk.

"The last month has sucked big time. Course, I worked eighteen hours a day the first week so I wouldn't have to think about you." He drained the last swig of beer and set the bottle beside the bench. "For the first time in my life work didn't help. So I stopped working entirely."

"What?"

"Hard to believe. But I did it." A small grin curled up the corners of his mouth. "However I did spend a disproportionate amount of time just sitting in the Bobcat thinking."

"Nathan. I didn't mean to hurt you."

"I know. Still, you made me question everything. Trust me. I didn't like the answers I found. I expected any woman who came along had to accept me for what I am." His laugh was harsh. "Arrogant, huh? When I found that *winyan* and had your acceptance, I let you go. I did nothing to stop you."

Tate held tightly to his hand.

"When I stormed in here today, Val was having none of it. Told me unless I took a good hard look at myself, my pathetic one-track life and made some changes, that I wasn't good enough for you. Which is what I feared all along." A spark of hurt dimmed his eyes.

"You are good enough for me—"

"No," he dropped a gentle kiss on her palm, "I'm not. Or at least I wasn't until I made up my mind to try." He paused. "Guess spending all my time working shows that I had little time to work on how to be a good man, huh? But I think I can learn."

She caressed the frown marring his cheek, biting back the hot rush of tears before placing her finger over his lips. "Hush. You are a good man. You're the best man I've ever known."

His back remained stiff even as his voice lowered to a whisper. "And yet you left."

Tate winced at his pain filled tone. "And yet you didn't ask me to stay."

"I would have if you'd given me the chance." He faced her. "Let me get this out, okay? After you'd gone back to Colorado I was furious. Not at you, at myself. You'd gotten exactly what you wanted, sex without strings. Not your fault that I had fallen for you. But I was afraid to tell you. I couldn't figure out why you'd want a hick Indian who knew nothing about relationships. I'm an idiot when it comes to this romance stuff."

"I always thought you were a romantic idiot. I still do."

He kissed her. "God, I've missed you. If being with you means moving to Denver, then I'll go. Right now." His hand caressed her shoulder but an expectant pause hovered in the air.

Tate inhaled. Exhaled. "There's something you should know."

"What?"

"Nothing you could have said or done that day after the inspection would have changed my mind. Val tried. Grace tried. But I had to go back to Colorado."

"Why?"

"Because I didn't trust the changes I'd been through. I didn't want to give up everything I'd worked for. Regardless if my mother was the one who initially pushed me, it was my own drive that forged my career. And I couldn't trust myself on why I'd fallen for you. Was it sex? Was it love? I wasn't sure whether I was rebelling against my mother by latching onto the one thing guaranteed to prove she had no control over my life or my decisions—a serious relationship.

"That excruciating drive to Denver gave me lots of time to think." Nathan's thumb feathered gentle caresses over her knuckles. Tate felt the heat and the need between them expand. "I spent three miserable weeks at my job, I realized that no matter how high I climbed that ladder, I wouldn't be happy."

"Why not?"

"Because I was on the wrong ladder. I don't want to be a graphic artist. I create art because I love it. Somehow I'd lost the thrill of creating. I'm still going back to Denver."

His hand dropped like a rock. "But—"

"Only to collect my stuff," she assured him, clasping his big, rough hand in hers, loving the way they fit together. "Aunt Beatrice left me some cool things." She frowned. "Along with some bizarre things, but I want my own furniture, dishes, all the stuff I'll need when I go back to school for a teacher's certificate. I'm finally going to do what *I* want to do. Teach kids to love art."

He hauled her onto his lap, holding her so tight to his chest that she almost couldn't breathe. "And your mother?"

"I told her if she wanted a career in graphic design, she should apply for the recently vacated senior artist's job in my old firm. I'm done trying to please her. Guess I realized I'm happier living away from my parents. They'll come and visit." She scowled. "Probably way too often."

Nathan tipped her chin up. She shivered at the raw emotion etched on his face. "Of course they'll be welcome in our home anytime. I want our children to know their grandparents."

She swore her heart stopped beating. "What?"

"That's my clumsy, highly unromantic way of telling you I love you, Tate. Marry me." He rested their brows together and whispered, "I've been dying inside a little each day without you."

Her mouth trembled. "Nathan—"

"Ssh. You changed me. Besides pointing out my workaholic tendencies, you showed me unconditional love. Every second I'm without you is time wasted."

Tate was happily stunned into silence.

He pulled her closer. "Say something. Say you love me or I swear I'll do something drastic."

The rumble of his deep voice against her ear sent shock waves rippling through her body. "Hmm. Like what?"

"Like something...romantic. I'll show up on bended knee with a gigantic diamond, a bottle of champagne and a box of chocolates. Hell, I'll even buy you one of those puffy white kittens you've always wanted if it'll help my cause."

"You don't have to—"

"Yes. I do. Before you waltzed in here tonight, I'd made up my mind that selling my business would be the ultimate romantic gesture." He held her face in his hands with the utmost tenderness. "Tate. I can't live without you. I need you so damn much its scary."

Every doubt fled in the face of his love. "I don't need romantic gestures, Nathan. Surely you realize that?" Circling her arms around his neck, she whispered, "You're all I need. Wherever you are is home." She pressed her lips to his softly. Once. Twice. Three times. "I love you."

"Thank God," he muttered, diving into her mouth for a complete taste of her. She shivered when she realized he needed her as much as she needed him. "Say it again," he urged, peppering kisses over every inch of her face. "Say it so I'll believe you're really here giving me, giving us, another chance."

"I love you." She wrapped her body around his. Mmm. Mmm. The man surely could set her on fire with just his sweet words.

He broke away by slow degrees, seeming reluctant to let her go. "So you *are* going to marry me?"

"But don't you want to woo me? Take things slow? Discover whether or not our relationship is based on more than sex?"

"Not on your life. I think I loved you before we ever officially sealed the deal that night in the bathroom."

"Then my answer is yes." Tate ran her tongue down the column of his throat until he groaned. "But part of me is thinking the big diamond and the kitten are pretty good ideas. Will you keep me in cat food now that I'm unemployed? At least until I sell the house?"

His hands slid down to squeeze her butt and a familiar, wicked gleam lit his eyes. "I have a better idea."

"Out here on the bench? I'm game."

"I love that completely sexy look. We are going to make love until neither of us can walk. Later." He kissed her, giving her a hot sample of what was to come. "Here's the deal: how about if I pay your tuition in exchange for you teaching me everything about computer graphic arts so I can create my own landscape designs? We'll sell my house and keep yours. It's nearly a done deal anyway."

"What?"

A splash of red dotted his cheeks. "I was the potential buyer you're here to meet. I hope you're not mad but I was going crazy without you."

Another wave of love flowed through her. "Really? You'd want to keep the money pit? Why?"

"You love it and I love you."

Smart, sweet man. He understood her strange affection for the old Victorian. She had a feeling Aunt Beatrice would be pleased the house would again be filled with love and laughter.

"Besides," he continued, "the award winning xeriscaping is awesome. Plus it's big. Tons of room for Duke." He grinned, nipping her chin when it dropped.

"Duke?" she repeated. Visions of doggy holes the size of craters danced through her mind. "Won't he destroy all your beautiful landscaping?"

"Nah. Our kids will keep him in line."

She shivered as another dream thrilled through her. "How many kids?"

"Twice as many as Val and Richard. She and I have always been pretty competitive."

Tate gasped until she felt his smile against her skin.

"Kidding. We'll see. It'll probably take lots of practice." He grinned. "Tons of practice. Two, three times a day. For fifty or sixty years at least."

"Sounds like a plan." As Nathan captured her mouth in a lusty kiss she felt their bonds strengthen with every touch, every breath.

He framed her face in his big, callused hands. "You are so beautiful, so sweet, inside and out. I never believed I'd find someone like you. I never thought I could be this happy."

"Me either," she whispered.

"You really want me just as I am, jungle girl? Red skin, long hair and all? Not gonna be an easy road for either of us."

Sadly, she thought of Grace and Luke and how they seemed to have hit a dead-end. She hoped it was temporary. Maybe since Grace had taken the first step and was spending time in Rosebud with Luke to straighten out their problems, they would have a happy ending too.

Tate knew happily-ever-after wasn't just for fairy tales. Nathan's parents had forged their own path for almost forty years.

She gave him an indulgent smile.

Which he returned with a frown. "You sure it doesn't bother you that I'm dirty most of my working hours?"

"The only dirty thing about you is your mind, Nathan LeBeau," she said haughtily. "And I happen to love that."

"Want me to show you dirty?" In one quick movement he'd moved them off the bench and down to the ground.

Sprawled across his chest, Tate felt their hearts beating as one. And the emotions crackling between them owed only the barest debt to their original trade. It went deeper than simple lust, more fulfilling than even the promise of wild squirrel sex. It was love. Pure, strong and true. They stared at each other without speaking for the longest time.

The happiness shining in Nathan's eyes mirrored her own. They'd found their own nirvana.

A slow, sexy smile lit up his face. "So you want to get down and dirty? Right now?"

Tate grinned back at him. "I thought you'd never ask."

About the Author

Lorelei James pens sexy, fun contemporary romances set in the modern day Wild West. When she's not squirreled away behind her laptop creating tales of sex, lies and murder, she can be found reading, practicing yoga, running a kid's taxi service, glued to the TV watching the Professional Bullriders Tour, and shootin' her .22 ~ all in the guise of avoiding housework, rustling up vittles and paying bills. She lives in the beautiful Black Hills of western South Dakota with her husband of 20+ years and their three beautiful daughters.

Look for these titles

Now Available
Beginnings Anthology: Babe in the Woods

Coming Soon:
Running with the Devil

Fly Away

Discover the Talons Series

5 STEAMY NEW PARANORMAL ROMANCES
TO HOOK YOU IN

Kiss Me Deadly, by Shannon Stacey
King of Prey, by Mandy M. Roth
Firebird, by Jaycee Clark
Caged Desire, by Sydney Somers
Seize the Hunter, by Michelle M. Pillow

AVAILABLE IN EBOOK—COMING SOON IN PRINT!

Samhain
Publishing, ltd

WWW.SAMHAINPUBLISHING.COM

hot
stuff

Discover Samhain!
THE HOTTEST NEW PUBLISHER ON THE PLANET

Romance, fantasy, mystery, thriller, mainstream and
more—Samhain has more selection, hotter authors, and
everything's available in both ebook and print.

Pick your favorite, sit back, and enjoy the ride!
Hot stuff indeed.